CLAIRE DeWITT
AND THE
BOHEMIAN HIGHWAY

CLAIRE DeWITT

AND THE

BOHEMIAN HIGHWAY

—▪—▮—▪—

Sara Gran

Houghton Mifflin Harcourt

BOSTON   NEW YORK

2013

Copyright © 2013 by Sara Gran

For information about permission to reproduce selections from this book,
write to Permissions, Houghton Mifflin Harcourt Publishing Company,
215 Park Avenue South, New York, New York 10003.

www.hmhbooks.com

Library of Congress Cataloging-in-Publication Data is available.
ISBN 978-0-547-42933-5

Book design by Brian Moore

Printed in the United States of America
DOC 10 9 8 7 6 5 4 3 2 1

The detective thinks he is investigating a murder or a missing girl but truly he is investigating something else all together, something he cannot grasp hold of directly. Satisfaction will be rare. Uncertainty will be your natural state. Much of your life will be spent in the dark woods, no path visible, with fear and loneliness your only companions.

But answers exist. Solutions wait for you, trembling, pulling you to them, calling your name, even if you cannot hear. And when you are sure that you have been forgotten, and that every step has been wrong, and that the woods are swallowing you whole, remember this: I too was once in those woods, and I have emerged to give you, if not a map or a path, hopefully at least a few clues. Remember that I, if no one else, know you are there, and will never give up hope for you, not in this lifetime or the next. And the day I came out of the woods I saw the sun as I had never seen it before, which is the only consolation I can offer as of now.

I believe that someday, perhaps many lifetimes from now, all will be explained, and all mysteries will be solved. All knowledge will be free for the taking, including the biggest mystery of all —who we really are. But for now, each detective, alone in the woods, must take her clues, and solve her mysteries for herself.

— JACQUES SILETTE, *Détection*

I

San Francisco

I MET PAUL WHEN a friend of my friend Tabitha played at the Hotel Utah late one Thursday night. About twenty people were there to see the friend's friend's band. One of the about-twenty was Paul. I was at a table in the corner with Tabitha and her friend. Tabitha was tall and pole-thin with orange hair, and arms and legs covered with tattoos. Tabitha's friend was one of those guys who was too sweet to be real. Or desirable. He was a little younger than me and smiled like he meant it.

I saw Paul at the bar looking at me, and when he caught me looking he looked away. It happened a few more times, enough times that I was sure it wasn't my imagination. Things like that happened to me often enough, and it was not exactly noteworthy for a man to make eyes at me across a dark and dirty bar in San Francisco.

Except something about Paul, about his big dark eyes and his quick, shy, smile, a smile he tried to hide, made me take note.

At the end of the night I felt his eyes on me when Tabitha and I left the bar, and I wondered why he hadn't talked to me and I wondered if he'd planned that, too, to make me think about him, because with men you never can tell. At least I can't.

Two weeks later we went to the Hotel Utah again to see the

same band and Paul was there again. I wouldn't have admitted that that was why I went, but it was. Paul was friends with the guitar player. Tabitha's friend played drums. Paul and I avoided each other, although I didn't notice it at the time. He went over to sit with the band while they were hanging out drinking before the show and I left to go to the bathroom. I came back and Paul left to get a drink. I'd been thinking he was a kind of cute, kind of smart-looking guy who maybe I would meet and maybe I would sleep with.

But that night I felt something in the pit of my stomach, more bats than butterflies, and right before I finally shook his hand I felt a wave of dread come over me, like we were being pulled into a black undertow we couldn't fight our way out of. Or didn't want to.

Jacques Silette, the great detective, would have said we knew. That we knew what was coming and made the choice to pursue it. "Karma," he said once, "is not a sentence already printed. It is a series of words the author can arrange as she chooses."

Love. Murder. A broken heart. The professor in the drawing room with the candlestick. The detective in the bar with the gun. The guitar player backstage with the pick.

Maybe it was true: Life was a series of words we'd been given to arrange as we pleased, only no one seemed to know how. A word game with no right solution, a crossword puzzle where we couldn't quite remember the name of that song. 1962, "I Wish That We Were _____."

Finally we met.

"I'm Paul," he said, extending a cool rough hand, callused from years of guitar. He had dark eyes and his smile was a little wry, as if we were both in on a private joke.

"I'm Claire," I said, taking his hand.

"Are you also a musician?" he asked.

"No," I said. "I'm a private eye."

"Wow," he said. "That's so cool."

"I know," I said. "It is."

We talked for a while. We'd both been traveling, had been traveling for years, and we traded war stories. Holiday Inns in Savannah, missed flights in Orlando, grazed by a bullet in Detroit —maybe being a musician and a PI weren't so different. Except at least some people liked musicians. Paul was smart. You could jump up a few levels in conversation right away, without warming up. He wore a brown suit with white chalk stripes, frayed at the collar and cuffs, and he held but didn't wear a dark brown, almost black hat that was close to a fedora but not exactly. In San Francisco men knew how to dress. No cargo shorts and white sneakers, no pastel polo shirts and misplaced socks hiding an otherwise good man.

Tabitha spent half the night in the bathroom doing some awful coke—it was cut with horse dewormer or cat tranquilizer or dog stimulant, depending on who you believed. It was going around town. I did a little and tasted the chemicals thick in my throat and passed on the rest.

Later Tabitha's friend went home with a different girl and I found out he wasn't really a friend. He was a guy she'd been sleeping with. The girl he went home with was younger than us and her eyes were bright and her hair was long and blond and unbleached and she smiled with white, unbroken teeth.

Tabitha was too drunk and had had too much of the horse-deworming cocaine and started to cry. I gave Paul my number for another day and took her home.

"I was so stupid," she cried bitterly, stumbling down the street. "Someone that nice would never like me."

I didn't know what to say because it was true. Tabitha was a lot of things, many of them good, but nice wasn't one of them. I took her home, helped her get upstairs, and left her on the sofa watching *Spellbound,* her favorite movie. "Liverwurst," she muttered along with Ingrid Bergman.

When I got home Paul had already called. I called him back. It was two fifteen. We talked until the sun came up. He was one of those men who are shy in a crowd but not alone. He'd just come back from six months in Haiti, studying with *bokos* and their drummers. I didn't know much about music, not the technical parts, but we both understood what it was like to devote yourself to one thing above all else. Something you gave your life to, and

3

never knew if you were right to do it or not. It wasn't something you could talk to many people about.

We all want to be someone else. And sometimes we succeed in convincing ourselves we can be.

But it doesn't last, and our own true selves, broken and scarred, always win out in the end.

2

PAUL AND I DATED for a few months after that. Maybe closer to a half a year. Then I went to Peru for a week on the Case of the Silver Pearl and stayed for another six weeks studying coca leaves with a man I met in a bar in Lima. I could have called Paul, or written him, or emailed, or sent smoke signals, but I didn't. When I got back to San Francisco he was dating someone else and soon enough I was too. Or at least sleeping with someone, which was almost the same thing.

And one night a year or so after our thing, whatever our thing was, had ended, I ran into him at the Shanghai Low, a bar near my place in Chinatown. Paul had on an old leather jacket and brand-new blue jeans, dark blue and stiff with folded-up cuffs. We were both there to see a band play. We were, if not technically *nursing*, slowly drinking cocktails and talking about a trip he'd just taken to eastern Europe when my friend Lydia walked in the door. I saw the look on Paul's face before I turned around to see what he was looking at and saw Lydia.

I knew that look.

"Claire!"

"Lydia."

She sat with us and got a drink. Lydia was barely a friend. More like a woman I knew. An acquaintance. She was a friend of my friend Eli, Eli who had long ago moved to Los Angeles with his lawyer husband, betraying us all by marrying well. But I liked Lydia okay. She was a tough girl from Hayward who'd worked hard to make herself into something she wanted to be. She played guitar in a fairly successful band called the Flying Fish. She had fancy, expensive tattoos up and down her arms. Her hair was long with short bangs and dyed black, and she wore a tight black T-shirt and cropped jeans and patent leather high heels that revealed more tattoos on her legs and ankles. Even without the high heels, she was a looker. With them, she was something else. Paul wasn't the only one staring when she walked into the bar.

Nice work if you can get it. You always get a little extra at the deli counter and you get fewer speeding tickets and no one tries to steal your place on line, ever. On the other hand, a pretty girl is always the object, never the subject. People think you're dumb and treat you accordingly, which is sometimes helpful but always annoying. I figure once you hit thirty it's diminishing returns on your investment anyway. Might as well move on and put your money into more useful skills.

That was me. Lydia was a different kind of girl; the kind who milked her symmetrical features and flat belly for all they were worth. I figured Lydia hadn't paid for a drink since she was four-teen. Fine with me if it made her happy. It was making Paul happy too. They started talking about bands and music and Cuban claves and Mexican *guitarras* and people they knew. Maybe they'd met before and just didn't remember. They knew plenty of the same people, not just me. But wouldn't they have remembered?

Maybe they'd met before but the other time wasn't the time. Maybe only this was the time that mattered.

Watching people fall in love is like watching two trains rush toward each other at top speed, with no way to stop them. I pretended to see someone I knew at the bar and wandered away. Then I really did see someone I knew, a PI named Oliver. He was a solid, mediocre PI who specialized in things like credit card fraud and embezzlement, the dull and damp shores of greed.

"Look," he said. "Lydia Nunez."

I'd forgotten Lydia was kind of famous. There weren't too many pretty girls out there playing guitar; the few who did got a lot of coverage. San Francisco was, like New Orleans or Brooklyn, smugly proud of its local celebrities.

And besides, Lydia was a hell of a guitar player.

"Yeah," I said. "She's a friend of mine. You know her?"

"I wish," he said. Oliver got that achingly sad look men sometimes get when they want a woman they can't have. Like he was losing a limb.

Oliver bought me a drink. Paul and Lydia came to get me when the band started, but I pretended I really wanted to talk to Oliver and told them to go without me. When I introduced Oliver to Lydia, he spilled half his drink on his lap. Later, I went downstairs looking for Lydia and Paul to say good night. But they were already gone.

That night I dreamed about Lydia for the first time. I was standing on the roof of my apartment building, surrounded by black, inky water. White stars glittered in the black sky above.

I watched Lydia drown.

"Help!" she screamed. Black muck was streaked on her face and matted her hair. "Help me!"

But I didn't help. Instead I lit a cigarette and watched her drown. Then I put on a pair of thick black-rimmed glasses and watched her drown more closely.

"The client already knows the solution to his mystery," Jacques Silette wrote. "But he doesn't want to know. He doesn't hire a detective to solve his mystery. He hires a detective to prove that his mystery can't be solved.

"This applies equally, of course, to the detective herself."

Two or three days later Lydia got my number from Eli and called me. We talked for a while about Eli and other people we knew in common and then got around to the real reason she'd called.

"So, are you sure you don't mind?" she asked. "About me and Paul? Because we both really like you and—"

"No," I said. "Of course I don't mind. Me and Paul weren't—"

"Oh, I know," Lydia said. "I would never—I mean, if you'd still been—"

"No," I said. "Really. So are you guys still—"

"Oh my God," Lydia said. "I've seen him like every day. It's been great."

"That's wonderful," I said.

"Do you really think so?" Lydia said. "Do you really think it's wonderful?"

Did I really think it was wonderful? *Wonderful* was probably an exaggeration. I thought it was fine. Maybe even good. I couldn't say the last time I thought anything was exactly *wonderful*. That implied more joy than I may ever have felt. But that was what she wanted to hear.

"Yes," I told her. "Of course. I think it's *wonderful*."

Lydia and Paul started a new band together, Bluebird. After a year or so Bluebird broke up and they each started their own bands again; Paul started a Rom-ish, Klezmer-ish outfit called Philemon and Lydia started a bluesy, roots-y, Harry Smith–inspired punk band called the Anthologies. I saw each band once or twice. They were good. Better than good. I saw Paul and Lydia together at an Anthologies show and they seemed happy, smiling and supportive and generally kind of joyous. And when they got married, one year later, they sent me a sterling silver magnifying glass from Tiffany's, a kind of bridesmaid's gift even though I wasn't a bridesmaid. *Thank you*, the card with the glass said. I wasn't sure if they were thanking me for introducing them or for stepping aside so gracefully.

I was invited to the wedding but I was in L.A. on the Case of the Omens of No Tomorrow. It was a good magnifying glass and I used it often until two years later when, stuck in Mexico City with no passport and no ID and little cash, I pawned it to pay a coyote named Francisco to smuggle me across the border.

Nothing lasts forever. Everything changes.

Maybe Lydia and Paul's story wasn't a series of words that had already been printed in ink. Maybe it was a novel they would write themselves. Maybe it could even have a happy ending.

Or maybe it would be just another crime story where someone kills somebody else and nobody pays and it's never really over.

"Mysteries never end," Constance Darling, Silette's student, told me once. "And I always thought maybe none of them really get solved, either. We only pretend we understand when we can't bear it anymore. We close the file and close the case, but that doesn't mean we've found the truth, Claire. It only means that we've given up on this mystery and decided to look for the truth someplace else."

3

January 18, 2011

I'D SPENT THE NIGHT in Oakland, in the redwood forests in the hills high above the city, talking with the Red Detective. He said he smelled change coming. For him, for me, for all of us. He pulled tarot cards, and no matter how many times we shuffled we got Death.

"I'm not sayin' it's anything more than a change," the Red Detective said. "I'm just sayin' it's gonna be one hell of a shakeup."

At two or three I drove back to my place in San Francisco and took off my clothes and crawled into bed in a T-shirt and underwear, twigs and leaves still in my hair.

At five o'clock the phone rang. I didn't plan on answering it, but my hands picked it up all the same.

"Claire?"

The voice on the other end was brusque and female and I didn't recognize it.

"Yeah," I said.

"Hey. It's Detective Huong from the SFPD."

I knew Madeline Huong. She was all right, as far as cops went. At least she tried. That was more than you could say about most people these days.

"What's up?" I asked. My mind was blank, still not quite awake.

"I've got bad news," she said. "I'm sorry to have to tell you. There's been a murder."

"Who?" I said. But then suddenly black flashed before my eyes and I knew.

"Paul Casablancas," we said at the same time.

"What?" she said. "What did you say?"

"Nothing," I said.

"Well, anyway, I'm sorry," Huong said again "I saw your number in the wife's phone and I figured you'd. You know. Not everyone . . ."

She meant that I was accustomed to death, that I would know what to do and who to call and I wouldn't faint or cry.

She was right.

"Claire? Claire?"

"Yeah," I said. "I'm here."

"If you could come down to the scene. We're at his house. The wife, she could use someone."

"Lydia," I said. "Her name is Lydia. And yeah, I'll be there soon."

I hung up with Huong and called Claude. He'd been my assistant since I came back from the Case of the Green Parrot in New Orleans. I didn't need an assistant because my workload was so big. I needed an assistant because so much of it was boring. Looking up credit card statements, making phone calls, going to city hall to check the bill of sale on a house, following up on miniature horse feed distributors — I was tired of it.

Claude was the latest in a string of assistants I'd hired and then fired over the years. Or would have fired, if they hadn't quit first. Claude was a good worker, smart, loyal, and with an encyclopedic knowledge of Medieval economics, which came in handier than you might think.

On the night Paul died Claude picked up his phone on the fifth ring. He'd been sleeping.

"There's been a murder," I said.

"Okay," he said, unsure. "Is this how we do this now?" Usually we didn't get involved in a case until a bunch of other people had already had their hand in it and screwed up. No one called a private detective, especially not me, until every rational option had been explored and dismissed. Like an exorcist or a feng shui consultant. I'd never called Claude in the middle of the night to start a new case before.

"I don't know," I said. "I think I just wanted to say that."

I didn't tell him the person who'd been murdered was Paul. That it was someone I knew.

"Do you want me to go somewhere?" Claude said. "Wait, I think I'm supposed to say, 'Meet you at the scene,' or 'I'll be there in five,' and then hang up. I don't think I can be there in five. But I could be there in like an hour."

I didn't say anything.

Paul was dead. Words didn't seem strong enough to hold that fact. Paul, who'd once made me an origami swan. Paul, who knew every Burmese restaurant in the Bay Area, who spent every Sunday at flea markets, buying speakers and tube testers and ohm meters.

I imagined the big flea market in Alameda, the tube testers sitting there, untouched, unbought, alone.

"No suspects," I said. "No known motive."

"Okay," Claude said. "So, uh. Can I do something to help? Or?"

"I don't think so," I said.

"Claire," Claude said. "Are you okay?"

"Of course," I said. "Listen, can you start a new file?"

"Sure," he said. "What are we calling it?"

"The Case of . . ."

I closed my eyes and saw something against my eyelids—a bird fluttering, fireworks exploding, a ghost. According to one school of thought we were in the Kali Yuga, a long stretch of time that might be as short as a hundred thousand years or as long as a million, depending on who you asked. In other yugas we have been, and will be, better-looking and kinder and taller and we won't kill each other all the time. The sky will be clear and the sun will shine. But in the Kali Yuga every virtue is engulfed in sin. All the good books are gone. Everyone marries the wrong person and no one is content with what they've got. The wise sell secrets and sadhus live in palaces. There's a demon named Kali; he loves slaughterhouses and gold. He likes to gamble and he likes to fuck things up.

In this yuga, we never know anything until it's too late, and the people we love are the last people to tell us the truth. We're blind, stumbling toward what's real without eyes to see or ears to hear. Someday, in another yuga, we'll wake up and see what we have done and we'll cry a river of tears for our own stupid selves.

"Claire?" Claude said. "Claire, are you okay?"

"Of course," I said. "I'm fine. And it's the Case of the Kali Yuga."

When Claude walked into my apartment for the first time he looked like he had never had a good day in his life. He wore a jacket and shirt and clean blue jeans and real shoes, not sneakers. That told you something positive right there. He was thin and handsome—my guess was one parent with ancestors in Japan and another with history in Africa, with a few different coasts of Europe thrown in, and later I found out I was right.

I interviewed him.

"You're a student, right?"

"I'm getting my PhD," Claude said. "Medieval history."

"So let's say we're on a case," I said. "I call at five in the morning to bounce some ideas around. Is that going to pose a problem for you?"

"Absolutely not," Claude said, still not smiling. "I am an idea guy. Anytime. Always happy to bounce ideas around. Or, you know, do stuff. That's also good. I can do stuff."

He didn't sound so sure about doing stuff.

"Why are you getting a PhD?" I asked him. "And why do you want this job?"

He sighed.

"I thought that was what I wanted," he said. "I mean the PhD. Berkeley. I thought that was what I wanted since I was, like, fifteen. This is exactly it. And now I'm here, and—" He looked around the room and furrowed his brow. "I don't think it's what I want," he said. "I mean, I'm not giving it up. Not yet. I've put too much work into it. And I'm in a really, really good place right now professionally. Academically. But I don't think it's what I want." Claude threw his hands up in the air as if he were talking about someone else, someone crazy, a man he could not understand. "I think I want to be a detective," he said.

"A detective," I said. "Why?"

"I have no idea," Claude said. "Sometimes I think it's what I always wanted. It just seemed too . . . too—"

"Unprofitable?" I suggested.

"Yes," he said. "But also—"

"Dangerous?" I said.

"Maybe," he said. "But also just—"

He held out a hand to stop me when I opened my mouth.

"Just," he went on, "unrealistic. I mean, everyone wants to do it, right? I figured the competition must be just, you know, astronomical. And me with no experience, not even insurance investigations or anything. But when I heard you were looking for someone, I figured I might as well try. I knew the odds were slim. And I know you're probably interviewing people much more qualified than me. But, life is short. I figured—I mean—"

Claude frowned.

"In 2001," he said, and all of a sudden I knew he was telling the truth, and he had never said it out loud before. "I was doing research in the library at Stanford. And somehow I ended up in the criminology department—I think I was looking for penal codes in fifteenth-century Russia. And this book, this little paperback. It was like—I know this sounds stupid. But it was like it fell off the shelf right by my feet. And I picked it up and opened it and I read this line: 'Above all, the inner knowing of the detective trumps every piece of evidence, every clue, every rational assumption. If we do not put it first and foremost, always, there is no point in carrying on, in detection or in life.'"

The room was quiet. We were in my apartment in Chinatown. I had the top floor of a building on Ross Alley. Beneath me were three stories of light industry and immigrant housing, nearly all of it illegal. My place was big, close to fifteen hundred square feet, and served as both a home and an office. Or neither.

My best friend, Tracy, had found the same book in my parents' house when we were younger than seemed possible now. The book that would save our lives and ruin them.

Even the noise of the street outside was hushed as Claude talked about the moment he became Claude. Only he didn't know it then, and I could see he still didn't know it now.

"I don't know," he said. He sounded sad and maybe a little angry. "I don't even know what it means. It was like—like what everyone's always told me? Like the things they tell you to do, you know? All of that. I don't know how to say it. I mean, it's like coming down here, to Chinatown, and you see the signs but they're all in a different language, and it's just like your life but it's—like it's out of register, or in another time. Another yuga. Like, all my life, you know, you walk out of the house every day and turn right. And then one day you realize, left was always there too, only you never saw it, and instead of ending up in Berkeley, you're in Chinatown. Or China. Like that dream when you're in the house you grew up in and there's a secret room no one told you about, you know? And it was like everyone knew about it and no one told you. Like that. And all around you, still, no one sees it. It's like they don't even know it's there. Or they know, but they'd just rather not know at all. Like they just, you know, like insects. Like a hive. Does that make sense? Does that make any sense at all?"

"Yes," I said. "It does."

"So I checked the book out of the library," Claude continued, upset. "To be honest, I never gave it back. Which I guess is technically stealing, but. I mean, it hadn't been checked out since 1974. And ever since then—I know this sounds crazy—I wanted to be a detective."

I didn't say anything. Claude started to fidget and cough. Then he started to cry, little trickles of tears squeezing their way out of his eyes at first, stingy and cheap, then big sobs as something died inside him. Maybe it was his hope of being someone else. His hope of being a normal person with a nice life and a pretty girl and a good job. All that was over now, or would be soon. Good riddance to it.

We sat in my office for an hour or so and Claude cried and he was hired.

I never saw him cry again.

Jacques Silette's *Détection,* the book that found Claude in the sterile Stanford library, was a book that had ruined many lives, as it had ruined Claude's. And mine. For three years I'd lived in New

Orleans and studied with Silette's student, Constance Darling. Constance spent the better part of the fifties and sixties in France with Silette, learning everything he had to teach as they became friends and then lovers. He'd been a renowned detective, the best in Europe. But after he published *Détection,* he was written off as a crackpot. Almost no one understood the book, or admitted they did. Instead they pretended that he, Silette, was the crazy one while they, the other detectives of midcentury Europe and America, with their abysmal solve rates and idiotic pseudoscientific methods, were the clever ones. Silette had anticipated this, and from what I'd heard wasn't especially hurt by the reaction. I can't believe it didn't sting at least a little, though, when even his closest friends in the world of detectives stopped taking his calls. But over the years he developed a new set of friends and fans—few and far between, but devoted.

Jacques Silette was the best detective the world had ever seen. So I thought. His methods were unusual, but I and a few others were loyal to them. I'd never met Silette—he'd died in 1980, when I was still a child, heartbroken after his daughter, Belle, was kidnapped and never seen again. A few years later his wife, Marie, died from heartbreak. His genius was no defense against pain. It never is. His role as the best detective in the world did not protect him from also playing the role of the heartbroken, beaten-down sap left behind.

Constance was Silette's favorite and best student—also his lover, friend, and companion. Constance was one branch of the Silettian tree, and I was her fruit, but there were other branches too—other detectives who had studied with Silette and imagined a claim on his legacy. There was Hans Jacobson, who gave up detection for finance. Hans made fortune after fortune, and joyfully threw it all away on women, boats, art, and drugs. Now he lived under a bridge in Amsterdam. I'd met him and I was pretty sure he was the happiest man I'd ever met. Jeanette Foster became a good, if dull, detective specializing in corporate espionage. She'd died just last year in Perth. And there was Jay Gleason, who went on to develop a scam correspondence school in Las Vegas that advertised in the back of *Soldier of Fortune* and *Men's World* and *True Detective:* BE A DETECTIVE OR JUST LOOK LIKE ONE or something like that.

Jay was one of Silette's last students. He moved to France in 1975, just fifteen years old, to study with Silette. It was two years after Silette's daughter Belle had disappeared, since everything good had drained from his life. Supposedly, Jay showed up on Silette's doorstep one day. Without even a hello, messy blond hair in his pretty face, in dirty bell bottoms and a rock-and-roll T-shirt, Jay launched into his solution to the one-hundred-year-old Case of the Murdered Madam, a famous unsolved case in Paris that had done in better detectives than Jay. He was sure he was right and sure he would impress the old man. It was the ex-husband, Jay was certain. When he was done, Silette laughed, the first time he'd laughed since the last time he'd seen his daughter. Something in Jay—his earnestness, his intelligence, his faith in Silette—amused the older man.

"You're wrong," Silette said to the young American, having of course solved the case many years ago himself. "You did some good work. But you missed the most important clue of all."

"What was it?" Jay asked.

"Close your eyes," Silette said.

Jay did as he was told.

"What do you see?" Silette said.

Jay hesitated. He didn't know what the right answer was. More than anything, he had wanted to impress the old man.

"Blackness," Jay said. "I mean, nothing. I—"

"Shhh," Silette said. He put a hand on Jay's back to calm him. "Keep your eyes closed. What do you see? Not what do you want to see. Not what do you think I want you to see. Me or anyone else. Not that. Use your eyes. What do you see?"

No one knows what Jay saw. But, so the story goes, Jay saw something—something that made him shake and cry and, finally, eyes still closed, collapse on Silette's doorstep, ruined. Ruined and saved, the two sides of the Silettian coin.

"It was the son," Jay finally choked out. "It was the son. Oh, God. He killed his own mother. It was the son."

Silette smiled. That was the answer. Silette invited Jay in and let him stay.

Jay was from a wealthy northeastern family with branches in Newport and Long Island's gold coast, along the groves of the

Hudson River and in rich wooded corners of the Mid-Atlantic. He could have been anything he wanted, or, like most of his family, nothing. There's no shame in being idly rich — not among the other idle rich, at least. But Jay wanted to be a detective. And now he was peddling official PI certificates suitable for framing.

Some took this, these mixed outcomes, as proof that Silettian detection was a sham. There were only a few of us Silettians and we did get more than our share of negative attention. Our enemies said it was because we were strange and unreliable, theatrical in our methods, dramatic in our solutions.

I said it was because we solved so many fucking cases. And usually by the time a Silettian got his hands on a case, ten other detectives had already failed. Most cases never even got to a Silettian unless the client was desperate enough, the way a person with cancer goes to an herbal clinic in Tijuana when the doctors tell her she's got no chance.

"The detective's only responsibility," Jacques Silette said in an interview for *Le trimestrielle des détectives* in 1960, "is not to his client or to the public, but only to the awful, monstrous truth."

I knew someone who went to one of those clinics in Tijuana. Brain cancer. Stage four. Before she crossed the border the doctors told her she had six months, maybe nine. Maybe less.

When she came back they put her in one of those full-body scanners and took lots of blood and ran test after test after test.

Not one cell of cancer remained.

4

LYDIA WAS SITTING on the steps of their house—Paul's house—on Florida Street in the Mission. She wasn't crying. She was still in shock. Police cars surrounded her in a half-circle, sending their long white lights into the shadows. Before Lydia saw me I noticed Officer Lou Ramirez and Detective Huong drinking coffee by one of the cars. I went over to them.

"What happened?" I asked.

"B and E," Huong said, unmoved. "As far as we can tell. Probably thought no one was home, panicked when there was."

"How'd they get through the door?" I asked.

"Either picked the lock or found a key. Or maybe they forgot to lock it. Wife says a bunch of stuff's missing—TV, VCR, musical instruments. Had a lot of valuable things, sounds like."

"They were both musicians," I said.

"That where she was?" Ramirez asked. "The wife? Playing music?"

"I can find out," I said. A thousand cops had probably already asked Lydia that question tonight. But they didn't talk to each other. That wasn't how they worked. "What happened?"

Huong answered, "Neighbor heard a shot. Waited a minute, went out to look, didn't see anything, called the police anyway. Ramirez got here first. Rang the doorbell, no one answered, broke through the lock, went in and found . . . the deceased."

"What else?" I asked Ramirez.

"What else *what*?" Ramirez asked.

Ramirez didn't like me much, but he owed me. The Murder at the Kabuki. That and a whole lot more, but that was the one where we agreed on the debt. But I knew Ramirez and Huong hadn't called me to do me any favors. They wanted a buffer between them and Lydia's raw pain. I didn't blame them. When the ugliest parts were over they'd want me gone and out of the case. We weren't friends.

"*Anything* what," I said. "What'd you notice?"

He wrinkled his brow. He didn't know what to say.

"Anything," I said. "What was the first thing that came to mind when you saw—"

I felt dizzy, and put my hand on the squad car to steady myself.

I am a detective, I told myself. *I am a detective on a very important case. Just like I always wanted.*

Ramirez wrinkled his already wrinkled brow again. "I thought, *Someone sure hated this guy,*" he said. He rushed to add, "I mean, I don't know if that's true. But that was what I thought."

"Thanks," I said. He shrugged and turned away, as if I'd insulted him. Huong met his eyes and they each made a little face.

I didn't care if they thought I was crazy. I would solve the case. I would find out who killed Paul. And they would still think I was crazy and I still wouldn't care.

I looked up at the police and the lights and Lydia and for a minute I wondered if this was real.

Huong and Ramirez started to walk away.

"Wait," I said. "Wait."

They turned around.

"He had a gun," I said. "If he was surprised Paul was home, why would he have a gun?"

"Or she," Huong said.

I nodded. Girls didn't pull a whole lot of B&Es, but it was possible.

"All that equipment," I said. "Guitars, amplifiers. Some of it's worth a lot. Hundreds, maybe thousands."

Huong shrugged and walked away. She knew what I was thinking: a robbery, but not random; a robbery by someone who knew what their gear was worth and knew one or the other of them might be home. But that should make it an easy crime to solve:

Paul and Lydia had probably never jotted down their serial numbers, but it didn't matter—vintage musical instruments like the ones they played had a lot of quirks and dings and stains and were easy to identify. Lydia would know one of her or Paul's guitars anywhere. Plus, Lydia and Paul were both fairly successful and were photographed often enough that their gear was well documented, at least the most-used items. As long as we kept on top of the pawnshops and music stores and websites where people sold guitars, we should find out who killed Paul within a month or two.

Not that it would matter much to Lydia.

I went over and sat by her. She'd finally started to cry, quietly, tears pouring out of her eyes and a steady choking noise coming from her throat. After a while Ramirez came over. I looked up. Lydia didn't. She was gone, sailing the oceans of grief. Drowning, more likely.

"Think she can give a statement now?" he asked.

"Can it wait?" I asked. "Tomorrow afternoon?"

He nodded. We made a date for four o'clock tomorrow at the Mission station on Valencia Street.

I left Lydia and took my car and found a twenty-four-hour coffee shop and came back with two big trays of coffee and a plate of snacks for the cops and the crime scene guys. Cops and their ilk work hard, if futilely, and anything you can do to make your case more attractive helps.

Of course, some of them knew me already. A little coffee and a buttermilk muffin wouldn't solve that.

It didn't matter anyway. I wasn't counting on the cops to solve the case. I was counting on solving the case myself. If they would help me by sharing whatever information they had, that would be good, but it wasn't necessary. I would solve it just fine alone. I would find out who killed Paul and then—

Before I could stop myself my mind said, *And then Paul can come back.*

As the sun rose the police and investigators started packing up and going home. When the last few were nearly done and I was sure they wouldn't need us anymore, I put my arm around Lydia and helped her stand and led her to my car. I put her in the passenger seat and buckled her in and shut the door. I took us to my place, where I got her out of the car and up the stairs and into bed. In bed I gave her an Ativan I'd been saving for a special occasion. Soon the choking sound subsided and she fell asleep. I watched her. In her sleep her hands clenched and unclenched, grabbing at the sheets. Her face was stuck in the shape of crying even though no sounds came out. She'd never be the same. She was already a different girl, a girl with a different face.

I lay on the sofa and didn't sleep. In Lydia's jacket I found a pack of cigarettes and smoked a few. I thought about nothing. There was a big white hole where normal thoughts usually were. Soon enough my mind hooked onto the missing guitars and the locked door and the hole filled up with clues and suspects and all the detective stuff and I could pretend it was just another case.

The guitars. The lock. The keys. The gun. The musician in the drawing room with the gun. The duchess in the kitchen with the guitar. I let my mind fill with the case. It was only a case. Only another case. Another sentence of words to rearrange.

Maybe that was all there was to life. One long case, only you kept switching roles. Detective, witness, client, suspect. Then one day I'd be the victim instead of the detective or the client and it would all be over. Then I'd finally have a fucking day off.

5

A T NOON I GOT UP and called the cops; they didn't
know anything new. I got out a phone book and
started calling music stores and pawnshops. I didn't
know exactly what had been stolen, but I gave a general description to each store—vintage, high-end, unusual gear, heavily used
—and let them knew there was a reward much bigger than what
they could make on a few guitars or amps. Next I posted some
messages on Internet forums and blogs for collectors, dealers, and
repair people. A lot of these people knew Paul and Lydia, or knew
who they were and knew what gear they played; they would be on
our side. Some people were already talking about it.

While Lydia slept I made her a big shake with protein pow-
der and espresso and chocolate and maca root and astragalus and
ground wolfberries. Death and solid food don't mix. At two I
woke her up for our appointment at the police station at four. She
didn't say anything. She drank a little of her shake and started to
cry again.

I got her to the police station by four thirty. It was like moving
a corpse that could walk a little.

It would help the police to know everything she remembered
about that night. I waited outside—the cops don't let PIs sit in on
things like this. I took Lydia's phone while she talked to them and
called the most dialed number in it. It was her friend Carolyn. I'd
met her once or twice. I explained everything to her and she said

she would come to the station. I asked her to start telling people about Paul. I also asked if she knew how to arrange a funeral.

"Yeah," she said bitterly. "I sure do."

When Carolyn got there the police were still in with Lydia. Carolyn had big curly blond hair and wore a thick layer of makeup and a black dress and a black vintage coat with a white fur collar. She looked angry. I gave her the short version of what had happened.

"Fucking scum," she said. "They should hang them up by their fucking balls and let them rot."

That wasn't exactly how I saw it. But I couldn't say her view had no validity. I waited until the interview was over and I saw Lydia leave the interview room. Carolyn seemed competent enough and ready to take charge, so I let her.

I drove back home and parked my car in the garage on Stockton where I rented a space by the year. When I shut the door behind me I remembered—Paul's car. The *victim's* car, I corrected myself. Where was it? I made a list on the back of an envelope from a parking ticket: *car, house keys, guitars, neighbor.*

The gun, the neighbor. Keys, amplifiers. A murderer. A victim.

And the rest of us poor suckers they left behind.

Back at home it was dark and raining. Everything seemed sharp and the lighting in my apartment seemed wrong. It was a big loft with ill-defined areas serving as bedroom, bathroom, kitchen, closet. Mostly it was a big space with lots of vintage furniture and too many books and clothes and papers scattered around and a collection of strange things on the walls, like thrift store paintings and old mug shots and a vision chart in Hindustani. Things I thought were beautiful. It was all arranged to do something to me, soothe some kind of raw edges, but it wasn't working today. In the medicine cabinet I found half a bottle of very soporific cough syrup I'd brought back from Mexico a few years ago: I swallowed a quarter of it and went to bed and slept like a dead woman, without dreams, and I didn't wake up until almost noon the next day.

Later I pieced together the whole story. Earlier that evening, at approximately six p.m., the victim had packed his car, a 1972

24

Ford Bronco, with two guitars, an amp, and a small suitcase, and headed toward Los Angeles. He had a small show booked at USC the next night. He'd planned to leave earlier and didn't; the victim was often late. Lydia hung around the house and went out at about ten p.m. to the Make-Out Room, a club on Twenty-Fourth Street, to see a band called Silent Film. At about midnight a neighbor heard what he thought was a shot and called the police. The police came. The body was found. Lydia came home and saw the scene. Everyone figured Paul's car had broken down somewhere and somehow he'd gotten a ride back home, but no one knew the exact sequence of events yet. But it made the most sense and I figured it was true. The police figured he'd surprised the thief, who had shot Paul to avoid getting caught.

That part I wasn't so sure about.

6

A T TWENTY-THREE I WAS LIVING in Los Angeles, if you can call it living. I had nothing else to do. A detective I knew named Sean Risling had me working on an encyclopedia of poisonous orchids he was putting together. I sampled and researched and wrote. At night I bought little twenty-dollar bindles of cocaine and sometimes cheaper bags of heroin wrapped in pages of *Cat Fancy* magazine on Sunset Boulevard. I slept in a series of hotel rooms in Hollywood. When Constance Darling, the famous detective from New Orleans, came to town on the HappyBurger Murder Case and needed an assistant, Sean introduced us. Risling said little and knew much.

Constance was famous—famous to other detectives, at least. Years ago, when we were finished being children, my friend Tracy found a copy of Jacques Silette's little yellow book *Détection* in my parent's musty, bitter house in Brooklyn. After that we were ruined: being detectives was all that mattered to us. Especially Tracy, who became the best detective of us all—and when she vanished a few years later became a mystery herself, leaving only a Tracy-shaped hole behind, a paper doll cut out from the page.

To me, Silette and his students were rock stars, celebrities. I was always surprised when no one else seemed to have heard of them.

Wasn't solving mysteries important? Didn't the truth matter? Of course, Silette had foreseen this. He knew the truth always was, and always would be, the most unpopular point of view. "If there is anything that can unify us," he wrote to Constance during the

Paris uprising, already old and bitter, "it is our love of deceit and lies, and our abhorrence of the truth."

Constance was pleased enough with me when the HappyBurger case was done, but I hardly let myself hope she would take me on as a permanent assistant. Or as close to permanent as we get; she died three years later, shot in New Orleans for the few hundred bucks she had in her Chanel bag, a bag that was now mine.

Constance had set me up in a room at the Chateau Marmont down the hall from her own. I didn't know what she was doing now that we were done with the case. I figured I'd hang around the Marmont until she kicked me out. I had no place to go, anyway. I'd let my cheap Hollywood Boulevard hotel room go when she hired me, and when we were done I'd sleep in the bus station or maybe in Griffin Park, up by the observatory. When Sean paid me I'd get another hotel room or a room in a share.

But the next morning Constance called me to her room.

"DeWitt," she said. She was sitting at a table drinking a cup of coffee with chicory, a woody smell I didn't recognize at the time but would later. She peered at me, head tilted like a little bird. Constance was already old. She was born old, with her Chanel suits and spectator pumps and white hair in a topknot.

"DeWitt, are you free for another job tomorrow?"

"Sure," I said, heart thumping.

"Do you drive?" she asked.

"Legally?"

Constance flicked her hand in the air. The law was for people who needed instructions, she would later tell me. The same people who needed to be told not to put a baby in the dryer or a dog in the microwave.

"We're going to Las Vegas," she said. "Or close to it. Do you know the way?"

"I'll get a map," I said. "Give me the address and I'll plan it tonight."

She nodded and tossed me the keys to her car. For the trip she'd rented a Jaguar identical to the one she drove in New Orleans, as she would in every city we visited.

That night I plotted out our trip on a few maps. I asked the concierge at the hotel for recommended stops along the way, and

I marked the least filthy gas stations and the best date shakes. When I was done I took the Jaguar and drove around Los Angeles, up Sunset Boulevard into the hills and out toward the ocean.

It had been eight years since Tracy had disappeared from a subway platform in New York City. We were going to grow up to be great detectives together, Tracy and Kelly and I. We were detectives already, just not great ones. But we were pretty good for kids.

Now Tracy was gone and Kelly was becoming someone ugly. She was so devastated by our inability to find Tracy that I was pretty sure she'd never left New York City at all, scared of overlooking a single clue, missing the phone call that would explain everything. She hated me for leaving. She hated me for being here while Tracy, so much wiser and kinder and prettier, was gone. I agreed. But there was nothing I could do about it.

On the end of the Sunset Strip I pulled over to a pay phone and put in a handful of change. First I called Tracy. She'd disappeared in 1987. No one knew if she was alive or dead. Kelly had fixed her old phone number so it was never given away, never changed. I called it. No one answered.

I'm here, I said aloud, or maybe thought. I'd spent so much time alone, I couldn't tell the difference sometimes. *I'm here, just where we were supposed to be.*

But Tracy didn't answer, because Tracy wasn't there.

Next I called Kelly. She picked up the phone and didn't say anything. I didn't say anything either. I knew she knew it was me and I knew she knew exactly where I was and who I was working for, the great Constance Darling. How could she not know? Wouldn't the angels be singing? Wouldn't Silette's hand come down from heaven and mark us, all over again, with the mark of Cain, the stain of the detective, the scar of initiation, as he had when we'd read his book? Wasn't it the most obvious thing in the world that something had actually happened, that my course, finally, was changed?

Genius, we were learning, was only skin deep. Brilliance is as brilliance does. Our ability to solve mysteries was not particularly helpful in actual living.

We didn't say anything. The silence on the phone sounded like Brooklyn. After a minute Kelly hung up and I had a sour taste in my mouth and I remembered that even the best things would never be good again.

I drove back to the hotel and used a sewing needle and the ink from a ballpoint pen to give myself a tattoo of a four-leaf clover on the top of my left foot, where it hurt the most. Maybe someday someone would ask me about it, and I would get to tell them about today. This day when everything changed. And then everything would change again, because someone cared enough to ask.

The next day we started late. Constance was always a night person and liked her morning routine of coffee and poached eggs and meditation. She was quiet on the drive and almost seemed anxious, the tiniest cracks showing in her cool veneer. I asked a few times if she wanted to stop and she didn't, my carefully plotted breaks just spots on the map.

We didn't go into the city proper but circled around it, starting at the cheaper suburbs and moving up to streets with mansions and gates.

"Here it is," she said. "This is the house."

A curved driveway led to a high fence surrounding a property lush with palms and hedges and desert flowers. Behind the plants I saw glimpses of a white mansion that looked like it'd been spun out of cardboard and cotton candy, brand new, and dropped in Las Vegas. I heard rustling in the plants—animals or maybe other humans were moving around, hiding.

"Wait here," she said. "I may be a while."

I waited outside the gate and watched Constance ring the buzzer, say a few words, and get buzzed in. She disappeared into the hedges. I waited. Even with the air full blast, the sun was hot and I felt a little queasy.

Nine minutes later I saw a man in blue jeans and a black shirt and cowboy boots pulling her away from the house.

I tried to catch Constance's eye but she didn't see me. Constance looked like she always did—too intelligent and a little bit bored.

But when she tried to take her arm back from the man in the black shirt, he twisted, hard, and didn't let go.

I watched for another minute. They argued. Constance didn't look scared. They exchanged a few more words and it didn't look too heated, but when she tried to pull away again the man in the black shirt held on tight.

I got out of the car and left the motor running and the door open. No one saw me. I went up to the gate and pulled a cheap little Saturday night special from the back of my waistband and pointed it at the man's heart.

Constance and the man were about fifteen feet away. I'd bought the gun when I'd first come to L.A. I liked to travel armed back then. It was the only way I knew to speed up time, to bend reality to my will. Constance taught me more effective and less painful ways to make thoughts real.

I knocked on the gate with the gun.

"Hey," I said.

Constance and the man turned to look at me.

"Who are you?" the man said.

"Let her go," I said.

He looked at me and didn't let her go. Constance looked bored. She let out a big sigh, like it was all too stupid for words. Which of course it was. It always is.

"Get your fucking hands off her," I said.

He looked at me and did not take his fucking hands off her.

"You think I'm kidding?" I cocked the gun.

"You'll be three," I said. "Three dead."

He didn't let go.

"It gets easier every time," I said. It wasn't true. "I think I'm starting to like it."

Another man came from the direction of the house. Maybe he was young or maybe he was just one of those men whose face never grows up. He was thin and had blond hair to his shoulders. He looked like a gigolo.

I kept my gun on the man in the black shirt.

"I'll never think of you again," I said. "Either of you." I thought about the two men I'd killed all the time. I dreamed about them. I felt like since I'd killed them they'd crawled under my skin and moved in with me. At night I got high to try to escape them, but it never entirely worked. Some days were like a nightmare I couldn't wake up from. I didn't understand at the time that by killing them I'd bound myself to them for life. This life and more to come.

I met eyes with the blond man. "I'll kill you and forget about you and so will everyone else. No one will remember you. It'll be like you were never here at all."

I figured if I killed him I'd have to kill myself, too, because I couldn't live with another one. Behind the blond man a llama raised his head to eat from a high hedge. Maybe it was an alpaca.

"Go away, Allie," the blond man said softly to the animal. "Go away now, come on."

I figured I'd try not to hit the llama but I wouldn't make myself any promises. I kept my gun on the man in the black shirt. Constance rolled her eyes like she was watching a bad movie. For the first time I noticed that pecking out from the hedges behind the blond man was a white Rolls Royce, empty.

I shot one bullet through the windshield of the Rolls and fixed my gun back on the man in the black shirt. Everyone except me jumped a little when the gun popped and the windshield shattered. The animal galloped away. The shards of the window sparkled in the sun, hard to look at.

"There won't even be a funeral," I said. "Because no one will find your bodies. And in a few years no one will remember you. Except us. You'll be our big joke. The thing we laugh about when we drink too much. The time we shot the two assholes in Vegas."

The blond man looked at the man in the black shirt.

"Let her go," he said.

The blond man stepped toward the fence and pushed something I couldn't see, and the gate opened. The man in the black shirt let Constance go, shoving her toward me. She stepped briskly through the gate and toward the car. When she got to the car I saw that her hands were shaking and her face was damp, and for the first time I realized she'd been scared for her life.

I already knew I'd kill for Constance. I'd burn down the world for her if she asked.

I raised an eyebrow at her and she gave me a quick nod. I aimed my gun and shot the man in the black shirt in his arm. He let out a scream and fell to his knees. Blood poured from his bicep.

He screamed again. He'd be okay.

I pointed my gun at the blond man.

"Don't," Constance said quickly and softly. "We need him."

Constance got into the Jaguar and shut the door behind her. Gun still on the blond man, I got into the car and handed the gun to her. She pointed it at him through the windshield and kept it on him as we backed away.

I backed up until we were on the street and then drove away hitting but not exceeding the speed limit and got on to the closest freeway. Once we were on I-15 out in the desert I pulled over and parked the car on the shoulder and threw up in the hot sun. I thought of the blood pouring out of the man's arm, about how I had caused that, and I threw up again and knew I would never forgive myself. Never forgive myself for anything. But I would have killed him if I'd had to. If Constance had asked. I got back in the car and drove us back to Los Angeles.

The next day Constance hired me as her assistant and asked me to move to New Orleans with her. I said yes. The first person I met in New Orleans was Mick Pendell, Constance's other assistant and already a detective of ill repute. We were stuck with each other, siblings born into the same strange family.

Three years later, Constance was murdered.

Those of us who Constance brought together never let each other go, not entirely. Every time we tried to walk away we remembered our promises, and the debt that we could never repay.

Later I found out that the blond man had been Jay Gleason, Jacques Silette's last student, he of the messy hair and bell bottoms, face still pretty.

Those of us Silette brought together would, as the Kali Yuga went on, have a more complicated relationship.

7

AFTER LEAVING LYDIA at the police station I didn't hear from her for a few days. First I heard from Paul's sister, Emily. While Lydia was talking to the police and I was talking to Carolyn, she called and left a message. I didn't call her back. The next day she called again. She said she was coming into town and wanted to talk to me.

Everyone thinks their grief is the first grief. Everyone thinks their grief is primary and everyone else's is secondary. But I wasn't ready to be the Supportive Friend yet. I wasn't ready to be the fucking selfless person who helps arrange the funeral. I wasn't in the mood to be the person who says, *Oh, of course you were so much closer,* and *Of course this is so much harder for you.* Let her find someone else.

But then I left my apartment, five days after Paul died, and a woman was standing on my doorstep waiting for me. She was white and tall and thin and didn't look like she was from here. She wore brown leather ankle boots and blue jeans and a gray sweater.

"Claire?" she said. "Claire DeWitt?"

I didn't say anything. Her face was pretty, or would have been if it wasn't haunted. She had dark circles under her eyes, and her clothes sagged on her frame—she'd lost some weight recently.

"I'm Paul's sister," she said. "Paul Casablancas. I'm Emily."

"I'm sorry about Paul," I said. "I really am."

"Can I talk to you?" she said.

"Sure," I said. "Go ahead."

"No," she said, looking like she might cry. "I mean, I think I want to hire you. I think someone murdered Paul."

"Someone did murder Paul," I said. "I don't know what the police told you, but—"

"No," she said again. "I mean, I think someone I know murdered Paul." She dropped her voice to a whisper. "I think it was his wife. Lydia. I think Lydia murdered Paul."

We went to a restaurant near my house. The restaurant is run by a cult. They love, honor, and obey a lady named the Enlightened Mistress who lives in Shanghai. She advocates kindness, veganism, and meditation. Other than calling herself the Enlightened Mistress she seems okay. They run a chain of vegan restaurants in Asia and in Chinatowns across the United States, and they teach free meditation classes once or twice a week.

We got a table by the window looking out to Stockton Street. Paul's sister, Emily, stared blankly out the window, rigid and tense. The waitress came. I ordered chicken stew, which would be fake chicken. Emily seemed startled, as if she'd forgotten where we were. I suggested she order the beef with broccoli. She did.

"There's something you probably don't know about us," Emily said when we were done. "Paul usually didn't tell people—I don't know, maybe he told you."

I shook my head, although I knew what she was going to say.

"We're rich," she said. "You know Casablanca Candy?"

I nodded. Casablanca's was one of the big candy companies, up there with Russell Stover and Mars. I knew Paul was rich. He never told me. But he never looked at prices when he ordered in a restaurant. When his car went in the shop it came out the very next day, because he went to the very best shop. He always had new shoes. And most of all, he never complained about money. Only a rich person never complains about money. Even then it's not a sure bet.

And, of course, as soon as we'd started dating I'd learned everything about him, from his bank account balances to his hat size. I had a file on Paul as thick as my thumb was long. I knew nearly everything about Emily: her husband's income, her daughter's traffic tickets, her million-dollar home in Connecticut, her overused account at Neiman Marcus.

"That's us," she said. "We're rich. When Paul got married, the lawyers told him—you know, do a background check. Sign a pre-nup. But Paul was never into any of that. He wanted to live like a regular person. He never told people about the money, hardly spent any of it. And when it came to getting married, he wanted to do it just like everyone else. No lawyers, no prenup. Nothing."

The food came. Emily stared at it like she'd forgotten what food was.

"Try it," I said. "It's better than it looks."

She took a bite hesitantly, like a cat tasting something new, and then ate a little more. When her cheeks looked a little pinker I asked, "Why do you think it was Lydia?"

"For the money," Emily said. "I knew from the beginning—I mean, she's from *nothing*." A quick look of liberal guilt passed her face. "Not that I—I mean, I didn't—"

"No, of course," I said. "I didn't think that you did. And that's reasonable. It's a really natural assumption." I had no idea if that was reasonable or natural, but I wanted to keep her talking. "But did anything happen?" I asked. "Anything specific or concrete to make you think Lydia . . . ?"

Emily frowned. "No, nothing," she said. It sounded like that wasn't the question she'd wanted me to ask. "Just I can't imagine why . . ."

Her voice trailed off. Of course she couldn't imagine why. All Emily's life she'd imagined no one would like her if she didn't have money. Lydia had been born with nothing or less, but she had her music and her brains and her looks to get what she needed. She didn't need to kill Paul for his money. She could have gotten money from a hundred men without asking. She'd just have to not say no to what they offered. Besides, she and Paul didn't live so high on the hog. Other than their house in the Mission, which had cost about a billion dollars, they lived like everyone else, except they didn't worry about money while they did it.

Of course, I'd considered it myself. The wife was always the first suspect, and for good reason. But it didn't make any sense. There was no logic to it. Lydia had nothing to gain. If she'd wanted to leave Paul—and I didn't think she did—he would have given her a divorce and plenty of dough.

Paul hadn't said nice things about his sister to me. Her name had come up a few times: She lived in "that fucking house in Connecticut." She was married to "some fucking guy who works for Goldman Sachs." Paul could be a little bitchy if you touched the right nerve. Like most people he wasn't especially proud of where he'd come from. Lots of investment bankers and charity fundraisers, lots of women with highlighted hair and perfect teeth. Private schools and fancy colleges. The ghetto of the rich, insular and narrow-minded.

I told Emily I'd think about it. And I didn't say outright, but I implied that things always seem awful after the death of a loved one, and it's natural to look for easy answers, but those answers are usually wrong. I also told her I'd be working on the case anyway. She didn't have to pay me or try to persuade me. Paul had been a friend, a friend I was very fond of, and I was going to find out who killed him.

I also told her I didn't think Lydia did it. Above the counter at the back of the restaurant something called Enlightened Mistress TV played a loop of the Enlightened Mistress speaking to crowds around the world. She had bleached hair and wore a suit that looked like it was from Macy's. The sound was turned off and subtitles in a dozen languages streamed across the bottom of the screen: *The truth is yours for the taking. Life is happiness and happiness is service.*

"You know how when a kid dies?" I said. "Maybe he fell in a swimming pool or whatever? And then the next day they pass all this legislation banning swimming pools or requiring gates or lifeguards or whatever? And no one's really safer after all? You see what I'm saying?"

Emily looked at me, her eyes swollen from holding back tears.

"I think Lydia killed Paul," she said. "I think Lydia killed my brother for his money, and I—"

She started to cry, and couldn't talk anymore. I went back to eating and didn't think about Paul and didn't think about why Emily was crying. My mind shut its doors and wouldn't let it in.

Finally Emily left, still crying. I watched her through the window, crying on Stockton Street, confused and broken, no one stopping to help. San Francisco wasn't so big, but people liked to pretend they were in a big city here, with no time for sympathy. Both of Emily and Paul's parents were long gone. Paul was the only family she'd had left.

I looked back at my fake chicken and ate it with a good imitation of appetite.

After lunch I ate my fortune cookie and read my fortune.

You are at the start of a great adventure, the fortune said. *The road will be hard, but the world is on your side.*

Never give up.

8

THAT EVENING I WENT by Nick Chang's office for a checkup. He'd been nagging me, like when the dentist sends you those little cards reminding you of a visit. Except I lived around the corner from Nick, so every time I walked by his office a random young apprentice or assistant or whatever the next pay grade was would come out and say in broken English, "Dr. Chang want to see you now! Today!" Like a human version of the dentist's cards.

Old Man Chang had been Constance's doctor since they met in Los Angeles years before I was born. He taught Nick and now Nick treated me. The Chang family practiced traditional Chinese acupuncture and herbalism, among other things—some of which they told me about and some of which they didn't.

The Changs owned a tenement building like the one I lived in. Theirs was on Waverly Place, a kind of alley/street hybrid that ran for one block, sunny and bright on a good day. They lived upstairs, each generation in their own apartment, and practiced on the bottom floor. Their shop looked like any other in Chinatown: big wooden chest of herbs; dusty shelves of patent medicines; always at least a few people waiting around for prescriptions or to see the doctor or just hanging out smelling the good smell of Chinese medicine.

I went in and one of the apprentices was at the counter. I knew this one. Mei. She'd been with Nick a long time and I figured they'd get married someday. She was a good girl, smart and kind and capable. Nick was close to fifty now, just about ten years older than I was. He was reaching that age even men like Nick seem to reach eventually—men who love women and love sex and don't want to stop falling in love—when settling down with one woman started to look good. There'd been one woman who was different. Carrie. I'd met her a few times. She was Chinese American but her family had been in San Francisco since forever. They wouldn't set foot in Chinatown. Carrie thought North Beach was slumming it. They had a kid together but it had never worked out, and soon Carrie married a rich businessman from her neck of the woods. I suspected Nick still loved her. The kid was ten now and whenever his mom wasn't looking he hopped on the bus from Nob Hill to Chinatown. I was rooting for him.

Mei wore a pretty black dress and a little too much makeup and black clog-ish shoes like waitresses wear. She stood behind the counter with her chin in her hand. She never seemed like she was working but I'd heard she was a genius.

"Hey, Claire," she said. She was born here and spoke English better than Chinese. "Nick wants to see you."

"So I heard," I said.

"Sorry to hear about your friend," she said. "Anything we can do?"

"Nah," I said. "Thanks. How you been?"

"Good," she said. "Slow day."

"Nick gonna be a while?" I asked.

"A bit," she said. "He's in with Henry."

That was the kid.

"Do me a favor," I said.

"Yeah?" she said.

"Gimme that can of oil under the register."

Mei smiled and found the can of oil and gave it to me. The door squeaked like hell, and I bet so did the big paper cutter they used to wrap up their packets of herbs. I tested it and I was right. God forbid a Chang get his hands dirty. I was like their Schneider. I oiled the paper cutter and then got up on a chair to get the door hinges. They needed a whole new entryway with better security, but that wouldn't happen unless I did it for them. I figured some Saturday I could re-hang the door, at least.

Mei went to the back and called out to the senior Chang in Chinese, "Claire's here, she fixed your door. Come say thank you."

The old man came out smiling. He shuffled his feet and walked about one step per hour. He was older than old. I'd never seen anyone smile as much as him.

"Claire DeWitt," he said in Chinese. "Always a pleasure. I had a dream about Constance last night."

"What'd she say?" I asked. My heart strained a little: I was hoping for a secret message, a little affection, maybe the solution to the Case of the Kali Yuga.

"Poppies!" he said. "I'm helping Mei treat a woman with tuberculosis. Constance said to try poppies."

He laughed some more, but then he stopped and looked at me. Really looked, the way only a Chinese doctor does.

"What happened?" he said. He wasn't smiling now.

I looked away. "Someone died," I said. "But I'm fine."

He shook his head and gave me that look you get from people who feel sorry for you.

Nick came out with his little boy next to him.

"Hey," I said to Nick. "Hey, kid."

Nick smiled. "Say hi to Claire," he said to the boy. But the boy was shy and squirmed, turning his head toward his dad. Everyone laughed.

Mei volunteered to drive the kid home and Nick took me into his exam room. I sat up on an exam table and he started taking my pulses.

"Who died?" he asked.

"This guy," I said. I didn't want to talk about it anymore. Nick got it and dropped the topic.

"Your liver is still overheated," he said. "Are you taking your herbs?"

"No," I said. "They taste bad. And they make me feel weird."

"Right," he said. "Because you hate feeling weird. Look up."

I rolled my eyes up and he looked at them. When he was done he looked at my tongue.

"What's up?" he said. "Your lungs are overheated and toxic. Your liver is bad as always. And your heart is weak."

"Nothing's up," I said. "I'll start taking the herbs."

He looked at me again. "You really don't want to talk about it?" he said.

"There's nothing to talk about," I said. "This guy died. It's a new case."

Nick raised an eyebrow.

"When you want to talk about it," he said, "I'm around."

He wrote me a new prescription for herbs, which a different intern filled at the counter, leaves and twigs and seashells I was supposed to boil in a tea. If I were smart I would have married Nick. We had a little thing after Carrie. Would have given up detective work and been an herbalist. But if I were smart I would have done a lot differently.

The world didn't hire me to be smart and happy. It hired me to be a detective, and solve mysteries.

9

P AUL NEVER SAT STILL; he was always drumming his fingers or nodding his head or standing up or sitting down. But it wasn't anxiety, just a little too much energy for the boundaries of his own skin. Paul seemed to be at peace with himself, to have reached some type of truce with his demons, in a way that I figured was rare and hard-earned. He'd put down roots here and now; made a commitment to inhabit this body, this life, demons and all.

The third or fourth time we went out we met for coffee in this place on Valencia.

"They take their coffee way too seriously here," Paul said, and it was true. You had to read a lot before you could order a coffee. He took our too-serious coffee from the counter and grabbed us a table. I went out to take a call—always a call, always a case—and when I came back in I felt his eyes on me as I walked through the crowded coffee place to our table, felt them in a way that made me feel like someone else. Someone better.

"I could watch that all day," he said when I sat down, and he said it like he meant it. And then he said "Hey," and he leaned over and kissed me—not for the first time, but it still felt like something. Like something I didn't remember having felt before, or at least for a long time. Like a door had been opened that had been shut so long ago that I forgot it was there, and whatever was behind that door was brighter and less burdened than what I'd become.

It was just one kiss and a minute later we were back to our cof-fee.

"You're smiling," he said. He said it a little shyly, and I looked at my coffee and wondered if we were both blushing a little. And I thought but didn't say *Because you make me smile*.

But then I felt tense, and the moment turned yellow and eerie, like the moment when the clouds have gathered and the light turns before it starts to storm. Like in a movie when you see a cou-ple looking so happy and alive, but you knew when you bought your ticket: This wasn't a story about love. This was a story about murder.

10

LYDIA HAD PAUL BURIED in a private ceremony, for family only. She said she couldn't handle a big crowd, which made sense. She had the funeral at a cemetery up in Sonoma County, near the Bohemian Highway where Paul owned a house and spent much of his childhood. He'd been gone a week. At the same time as the private funeral there was a public memorial service in Delores Park. His murder had been big news in the neighborhood. He'd been well liked. Since his death secrets had come out: he'd given a substantial piece of money to the local arts group that put on the Day of the Dead parade; he'd given more cash to an outreach program for kids to bring them into the strong Mexican American culture of the Mission. Paul was very public with his appreciation of the Mexican/Missionion/San Franciscan culture of the neighborhood. He never wanted to change it, never wanted a Starbucks or a Pinkberries to replace the taquerias and botanicas.

I don't know who organized it. Maybe no one did; maybe it just happened. Later I couldn't remember how I'd heard of it, or how I knew to go to Delores Park that day.

A hundred people were already there, milling about. More people were building a kind of ersatz altar around a big old live oak, hanging pictures, CDs, records, and even instruments from the tree. Someone hung a bunch of small Mexican sugar skulls, someone else hung up ticket stubs from dozens of his shows. A lot of musicians were there, of course, and soon enough people started playing. Everyone knew "Danny Boy" and "Auld Lang Syne" and "When the Saints Go Marching In" and "Will the Circle Be Unbroken."

People started crying and a few broke down completely. I saw Paul's bass player, Phil, sobbing. Maryanne, his drummer, stood alone in the crowd near the altar with her hands on her hips, shaking her head and looking furious. Someone tried to hug her and she shrugged him off.

Anthony Gides, a music critic who had been a big fan of Paul's, brought the music to a close and stood near the tree and started to talk. He talked about Paul's music; about his mentorship of other bands, his study of Roma guitar, his passion for Haitian drums and Cuban claves. About how empty the music world would be without him. About—

But then the band started playing again, suddenly doing "Brother, Can You Can Spare a Dime." The crowd, now several hundred, cheered. Nancy O'Brien, a keyboardist who played with Paul sometimes, came over and hugged me. She looked exhausted and we didn't say anything. Josh Rule, another guitar player Paul was friends with, also came over and hugged me.

"You know he was fucking crazy about you," Josh said.

I shrugged. Now that he was gone I guessed it seemed like he'd been crazy about everyone. Death erased complications.

"I want to go," Josh said. "This feels weird."

"Me too," I said. We left the park and started walking down the hill. The crowd was hundreds strong by now. Soon someone would do something stupid and someone else would call the cops and it would all be in the papers tomorrow.

"This is completely fucked up," Josh said. "I can't believe neither of us were invited to the funeral."

I told him it didn't bother me. Family was family.

"*Family?*" he said. "*We* were his fucking family. *We* were."

I didn't argue. I drove Josh back to his place in Albany, north of Berkeley. When we got to his house he asked if I wanted to come in for a drink and I said yes. Everyone wants to have sex after a funeral. The sex was okay and we ordered pretty good Nepalese

45

food afterward and then fell asleep watching *Naked City* on TV. I left as quickly as I could the next day, leaving Josh naked and asleep and alone.

Josh was a sweet, quiet sleeper, a man who would make someone a good husband one day. But as I got dressed and hooked my bra behind me in the hushed bedroom I felt the cold winter sun in my eyes and a shiver up my spine and a thick spill of shame in my solar plexus and I knew: This case was going to be complicated.

II

"HEY. IT'S CLAIRE."
When I left Josh I swallowed two Valium I'd stolen from his bathroom and drove around the city. But
even with the gentle numbing of the diazepam I felt something
sick and painful where my chest met my belly. Back at home I
took a Percocet out from my stash of painkillers I had squirreled
away for actual pain and crushed it with the handle of a knife on a
cutting board in the kitchen. I snorted half the Percocet and felt a
little better, or at least like there might be a cure for the sickness.
I called Andray.

"Just wondering if you were okay. If you were busy or working
or, I don't know. If you need anything. You know."

I'd met Andray in New Orleans on the Case of the Green Parrot. Andray was a born detective, like Tracy and Constance. Un-
like them he was alive, although just barely. He could be working
for any detective in the world. Even the very best. Instead he was
drowning in New Orleans, selling drugs and guns and getting
high. He'd been shot at least once since I'd seen him last.

I'd had Constance, sober, wise, and in her own way loving and
pure, to guide me to dry land. Andray had me, Claire DeWitt,
who despite being the very best detective in the world was at this
moment snorting a crushed painkiller off her kitchen counter.

I hung up. Andray didn't call me back. The sickness, which had abated for a minute, came back. It didn't feel like it was leaving anytime soon.

"All these fucking missing girls," Silette, bitter and old, wrote to Constance, "and the one I can't find is my own. If it were a detective novel it would be too utterly stupid to read."

"As a wise man once told me," Constance wrote back, "solutions are always possible, and the limits of the truth far exceed the limits of human understanding."

"Enough with my fucking platitudes," he wrote back. "Consider everything I said a lie, a mistake. I was wrong, and I regret every word of it. The only true thing is pain."

I fell asleep watching *Murder, She Wrote*. No one knew about Jessica Fletcher's past in England as George Cukor's ne'er-do-well maid.

When I woke up Tracy was sitting on the edge of my bed. She was young again, fifteen, but had a knowing look on her face you don't get before thirty or forty. She sat on the bed with ease, like a woman, not a child.

"The things you don't know," she said, "could fill the ocean."

I looked over the side of the bed. My apartment had flooded sometime during the night. Black water trickled around the floor, the trickles connecting into an ocean.

The ocean rose.

"The things you don't see," she said, her Brooklyn accent sharp, "could light up the whole damn sky."

I looked up. The sky above me was filled with stars, glittering gold and white. They swirled around to form new constellations: the Parrot, the Key, the Gun, the Ring. Then the stars rearranged themselves into a solid white wall.

We were on the subway, steel ceiling above us. The constellations were now graffiti: a knife, a can of spray paint, a pigeon.

On the walls of the subway were words. Thousands of them; *ocean* and *storm* and *boot* and *dagger* and *mission* and *Nevada*.

Tracy sat across from me. We were on a double R subway from the mideighties. Next stop, Atlantic Avenue, transfer to the —

"And with the words you forgot," she said, "you coulda solved the whole damn mystery already."

From the pocket of her jacket she pulled out a paint pen and wrote more words on the wall. *Truth. Key. Bird. Ring.*

"Which mystery?" I asked.

"All of 'em," she said. "Remember. The Case of the End of the World."

She snapped her fingers and I sat upright in my bed, awake.

12

Brooklyn
January 3, 1986

DID SHE TAKE HER KEYS?"
It was 1986. Chloe and Reena were Tracy's friends. They were a few years older than us—Chloe was eighteen and Reena, nineteen. Reena worked at a vintage clothing store on Seventh Street. Chloe worked for a filmmaker named Ace Apocalypse. He paid her almost nothing, but she loved the job. She wanted to make movies herself someday, or so she said.

Chloe and Reena lived together on Fifth Street near Avenue A. Tracy had met them one night about a year before in Sophie's, a bar down the block from their apartment—the bar where we now sat with warm beer in front of us. Chloe and Reena liked Tracy and treated her like a kid sister: Reena gave Tracy a discount in the store where she worked; Chloe invited her to clubs and gallery openings and performance art nights around Alphabet City and Brooklyn.

Tracy, Kelly, and I were detectives. According to Silette, we'd always been detectives, of course, but we'd recognized that fact a few years ago and we'd been solving cases ever since. We'd started off in our neighborhood in Brooklyn and, as our reputation spread, started taking on cases around the city. Who'd planted the answers to Tuesday's quiz in Dori's locker? Who'd stolen Jamal's weed? Who was Janelle's real father? Being girl detectives in

Brooklyn made cases easy to come by, but solutions were rare and troubling.

It was Chloe who disappeared. With her keys.

Tracy got the call late one Monday night. It was January, after the holidays but before school had started again. The next afternoon Tracy, Kelly, and I met Reena and Alex, her boyfriend, in Sophie's. Reena and Alex looked exhausted and hungover, with dirty hair and circles under their eyes. Their hands shook and they chain-smoked. The time for heavy drinking had passed; instead, they each nursed a big mug of draft beer. Reena wore a fake leopard coat with a wide collar, coat wrapped tightly around her. Blinking white Christmas lights were still strung over the bar.

The last time Alex and Reena had seen Chloe was Thursday night. Reena and Alex stayed home and watched TV. "We're like an old married couple," Reena said, a little embarrassed. Chloe came home at about midnight. Ace Apocalypse, the filmmaker she worked for, was making a documentary about a band called Vanishing Center. The movie was called *The End of the World*. Chloe and Reena exchanged a few words and Chloe went to bed. A few minutes later Alex walked home. He had to get up early the next day—he worked in construction—and it was Reena's day off and she wanted to sleep in. At eleven the next morning the ringing phone woke her up.

It was Ace Apocalypse. He was wondering where Chloe was. She hadn't shown up to work. Reena went to Chloe's bedroom, planning to wake her up. But Chloe wasn't there.

Reena was a little worried but not excessively so, she told us.

"I mean, shit happens, right?" she said through a cloud of Camel smoke. "I mean, maybe she decided to call in sick or whatever and go have a fun day. And Ace, he's *cra*-zy. Crazy mad fucked-up guy. So I'm thinking maybe he's got the wrong day or time or whatever, and Chloe's out waiting for him in Queens somewhere or wherever, right? And when I saw her, she didn't actually say she was going to work the next day. I just assumed. So, you know. It wasn't a really big deal."

"And then we didn't see her Friday night," Alex said. He looked as concerned as Reena. I made a note in my notebook (*Alex: good boyfriend*). "Obviously. So that was when it first started to seem, you know, a little weird. We called Ben—"

"That's this guy she used to date," Reena interjected. "Do you guys know him? He's a bartender at the Horseshoe Bar over on Seventh and B?"

I nodded.

"A little," Kelly said. "Go on."

Ben, Horseshoe, I wrote down. *Ex-boyfriend.*

"Right," Reena said. "They used to date, but as far as I know, they hadn't seen each other for a while. But I figured, you know, it was worth a try?"

We three detectives nodded encouragingly; yes, it had certainly been worth a try.

"He hadn't talked to her in, like, forever." Reena went on. "But, well, we were worried, but we didn't want to be ridiculous. I mean, we're all grownups, right? It's not like she has a curfew or anything. It's not like we're her parents. But then on Sunday, her friend Rain calls and leaves this long, pissed-off message on the answering machine. I guess Chloe was supposed to see her that night, they had this big night planned, to have dinner and see a movie at Theatre Eighty."

"What movie?" I asked.

Reena looked at me. "What movie? Why would that matter?"

"Everything matters," Tracy assured her.

Theatre 80, I wrote in my book. *Sunday, evening show.*

Reena shrugged. "I don't know. But they hadn't seen each other in a while, and neither of them had a boyfriend, so they decided to make a thing of it. I called Rain and asked her. They were supposed to meet at Dojo's for dinner at six thirty and then see the movie at eight and then probably go out afterward. But Chloe never showed up, never called, nothing."

"When did they make the plans?" I asked.

"I don't know," Reena said. "I didn't ask."

"That's not like her," Alex said. "That's *totally* not like her."

"That's pretty much it," Reena said. "We didn't find out anything at all. We don't want to call the cops—"

"But we will," Alex said. "If you think we should."

"Yeah, we will," Reena said. "But we'd rather not." The police

52

were not to be counted on for help, and besides, at any given moment we were each engaged in at least a few illegal acts—at the moment, underage drinking and smoking. "After we talked to Rain we decided we'd give it one more day before we freaked out. So then on Monday, well, we freaked out," she said, laughing a little. "And we know you guys have this whole detective thing, with your book or whatever. So we figured . . ."

"We can do it," Tracy said, the little professional in her Dr. Martens boots, vintage orange minidress, and black leather coat two sizes too big. "We can find her. And since she's a friend, there'll be no fee. Except"—she looked at me and then back to Reena—"I think Claire and Kelly should get the staff discount on clothes at the store. They've been totally cool about paying full price while the rest of us pay, like, nothing. And they have like *no* money. It's only fair."

"I can't do staff discount," Reena said. "Not for anyone anymore. They put the kibosh on that. But I can do twenty percent. Plus my eternal gratitude."

Tracy looked at me. I nodded. We looked over at Kelly. She agreed. We looked back at Reena.

We had a deal.

We would find Chloe.

"The last time you saw her, that Thursday night," Tracy said. "Let's go over that again."

Reena bit her lip. "Well," she began, "me and Alex were watching TV. And—"

"What were you watching?" Kelly asked.

Reena looked at Alex.

"*Simon and Simon,*" Alex said.

"So we were watching TV and smoking a J and I think I was eating cereal—"

"Lucky Charms." Alex broke in. He was getting the hang of this.

"And Chloe walks in and we said hi, hello, normal stuff. She looked a little, well, like maybe she'd been drinking a little. Her eyes were kind of red and . . . what's the word? Bleary. She was bleary-eyed."

Bleary-eyed, I wrote in my book. *Lucky Charms.*

53

"So she got a bowl of cereal and watched TV with us for a few minutes. And then she stands up and says . . . What did she say?"

Reena looked at Alex.

"'Enough of this shit,'" Alex quoted. "She said, 'Enough of this shit. I can't take any more.' And then she went to bed. Or so we thought."

"I thought she was talking about the TV show," Reena said. "Now . . ." She closed her eyes and frowned. "I don't know. Now I just want to find her. I just really, really want to find her."

A quivering, shaking look, like crying, passed over her face. She swallowed it away.

"Did she take her keys?" Tracy asked.

Keys, I wrote in my book. It was a good question.

"Uh, I, yeah," Reena said. "She did. I noticed that when I was looking through her stuff. Her keys weren't there."

Next to keys I wrote, *Took them.* Tracy looked in the notebook. She took the pen out of my hand and wrote, *Left, not taken.* It wasn't until later that I realized she meant Chloe.

I looked through my notes and went back to *Lucky Charms* and wrote down what I remembered from the commercial: *Pink clovers. Green horseshoes. Yellow diamonds. Blue stars. Orange Moons. Purple hearts.*

We made plans to come over later — Reena had a staff meeting at the clothing store. Alex went wherever he went. Kelly and Tracy and I stayed in the bar and got another round of dollar glasses of beer.

Kelly and I looked at Tracy. Tracy knew Chloe best.

"Do you think she would . . ." I asked.

"I don't know," Tracy said. "I mean."

She frowned.

"We'll assume she didn't," Tracy said firmly. "We'll assume she's alive, and out there somewhere, until proven otherwise. Okay?"

Kelly and I nodded; we agreed.

Kelly stood up.

"I gotta go," she said. "Jonah's got a show tonight."

Jonah. Tracy and I must have rolled our eyes because Kelly said, "You bitches just wish you had boyfriends."

Tracy and I each made a face. Maybe we did wish we had boyfriends. Or maybe we just didn't want anyone else to have them. Jonah didn't seem like such a prize to me. He was in a band that played at parties and all-ages punk shows. Kid stuff. He almost never talked to me and I'd stopped trying to get along with him. He didn't seem to be especially nice to Kelly, either. He was a boyfriend; he was an accessory like a new bag or a new pair of shoes but the best one of all, the one who kept you company when you were bored, the one who made you more interesting to other girls, more desirable to other boys. But I wouldn't want to actually be alone with him. Sex was more interesting in theory than practice to me and Tracy.

Kelly left. Tracy and I didn't say anything. Jonah had been occupying more and more of Kelly's time since they'd been going out, nearly six months now. But this was the first time she'd walked out on a case.

Ever.

"Well," Tracy said, answering the unasked question. "I guess we'll begin with their apartment."

I agreed. I didn't know Chloe well. Her fondness for Tracy only extended halfway to me and Kelly. She was nice to me, but we'd never spent time alone. I was a little in awe of her. She had short hair that she dyed black and wore long in front of her eyes. She knew all the after-hours spots and every doorman at every club. She knew the bartenders at all the bars and probably hadn't paid for a drink in years. Everything about her seemed effortless and natural. She was the first girl I knew to get a tattoo, a little bluebird on her back. She'd been an extra in a bunch of Ace's movies. She wasn't the prettiest girl—she had an overbite and a wide mouth and she was too skinny, with a nearly flat chest and bones sticking out through her vintage clothes—but boys always liked her. She had a quick smile and a fast tongue, and I'd seen her slap a girl in a club who'd pushed her away and refused to apologize.

I looked at Tracy and I figured she was thinking the same thing I was. That if *Chloe* could slip away, if *Chloe* could disappear . . .

Chloe, who seemed so solid, so real.

The Case of the End of the World had begun.

13

TRACY AND I MET REENA back at her and Chloe's apartment. It was a one-bedroom with a big living room, which Alex the carpenter/boyfriend had split into a living room and a separate, illegal bedroom. In the living room was a futon and a coffee table and a TV on a stand and a bookshelf overflowing with books: Henry Miller, William S. Burroughs, Philip K. Dick, *The Stranger.*

"Those are all Chloe's," Reena said. "Mine are in my room."

"Does she read them?" Tracy asked. She crouched down to see the titles.

"Sometimes," Reena said. "To be honest, she seems to like start one, get halfway through, and then give up." She shrugged. "I don't know. She likes real books but has, like, no attention span. Sometimes she's holding a book but then when I look at her she's just staring at the wall. I read, like, V. C. Andrews and Judith Krantz. Sometimes I read romances."

There was nothing remarkable about the apartment: wood floors, white walls, views to fire escapes and air vents. Everything in it was from thrift shops or street corners. Reena opened the door to Chloe's room, the real bedroom.

"There you go," Reena said nervously, as if Chloe might come in at any second and catch us going through her stuff. "Knock yourselves out."

We shut the door behind us.

It was less than a hundred square feet. A bed, a closet, a desk, an armchair. Messy but not unusually so. On one wall was a Joe Strummer poster, Strummer's face positioned to watch over Chloe as she slept. On another wall was a Vanishing Center poster. The singer, CC, was bleeding from where he'd cut an *X* into the skin of his chest with a razorblade. On another wall was a group of five or six postcards.

We stood near the door and looked around the room, both thinking the same thing: *What if I were Chloe?*

Tracy pointed toward a desk near the door. On the desk was a little bowl of change, a small pile of mail. That's where she would stop first. Tracy went over and flipped through the mail. I watched over her shoulder. Bank statement, credit card offer, junk mail. You could feel that this was where her keys would go.

Tracy took the letters and put them in her bag, a cheap version of a Dutch schoolbag. Then she went and flopped on the bed. She looked at Joe Strummer.

I looked at the postcards on the far wall. Sid Vicious, scowling at the camera. Iggy Pop, blood dripping from his chest.

"Sid Vicious," I said. "Iggy Pop. CC."

Tracy looked at me. I held up my right hand and used it to cut my left wrist.

"They all cut themselves," she said.

Tracy sat up and looked around. She slipped her hand in the narrow space between the bed and the wall. I came over to help her look. We pulled and pushed the futon to look in its cracks and crevices.

"Got it," Tracy said after a minute.

"Got it?" I said. I was holding the mattress up and couldn't see what she was looking at.

"Got it." She took whatever she was holding and I let the corner of the mattress go.

We looked at what Tracy found. Just what we expected: a razorblade wrapped in a dirty paper towel.

Cutter, I wrote in my notebook. Girls like that weren't rare —when the pressure mounted, they took little nips at themselves to let it out. Neither me or Tracy did it, but we understood it well enough.

Still, though. Chloe? A cutter?

"The truth holds no prisoners," Silette wrote. "It takes no hostages. And if you don't want to meet with the same terrible fate, better not to approach at all. Stay on the other side of town, outside of the woods, and do not enter, not at any cost."

I looked at the floor and shivered. A feeling came over me, a black feeling like I'd fallen into a pool of dirty water. Like I'd stepped into the woods and didn't know my way back.

Tracy lay back on the bed and looked at Joe Strummer. I lay next to her. The sun came in at its sideways December angle.

"It's like he was watching her," Tracy said.

"But was he helping?" I asked. "Or was he, I don't know, judging? Like, looking down on her?"

"Good question," Tracy said.

We looked at Joe.

"Helping," Tracy said, gazing at the poster, falling under Strummer's spell. "I think he would definitely help."

On our way out we saw a photo-booth picture of Chloe and Reena that Chloe had stuck in her mirror. There were four pictures on the strip: two of both of them, one of Reena alone, and one of Chloe.

Tracy took the strip and ripped the picture of Chloe off and stuck the rest back in the mirror.

"Let's go," she said.

That night I had a dream about Chloe. We were near the edge of a woods, on the border of a dark clearing lit by thin moonlight. I'd never seen a woods before, not bigger than Central or Prospect Parks', but in my mind it was clear and vivid. Enormous trees rose up hundreds of feet into the air, thick dark red bark wrapped around them. Green piney needles covered the forest floor, and new shoots clustered around the base of the trees. In the clearing, little yellow flowers shot up around giant clovers.

Chloe and I sat next to each other on big mossy rocks at the edge of the clearing. We were dressed as we would be for a typical day in the city: boots, vintage dresses, leather jackets. We were talking softly, trading secrets and whispers.

Then, suddenly, Chloe was naked. Her ribs and hips stuck out painfully through her skin. Her face was turned to the ground. When she looked up, her face started to turn black—or rather, little holes of blackness appeared where her face fell apart. One bit at a time her face collapsed into itself, leaving a black emptiness in its place.

I woke up talking, twisting and turning in bed, not sure if I was trying to get closer to Chloe or run away.

14

NINETEEN DAYS AFTER Paul died, I got a phone call from an EMT in New Orleans. When you answer the phone at three in the morning and someone says "Is this Miss Clara DeMitt?" you know it isn't good news.

"Yes," I said. "This is, I mean, I am. Claire. Clara. Clara De-Mitt."

"I have some bad news, Miss DeMitt. Bad news, but he's going to be okay."

Andray, I thought. *Andray's been shot.*

Instead the EMT guy said: "Clara, Mick Pendell has had an incident."

"Incident?" I said. "Did someone shoot him?"

"Overdose," the EMT said. "We think it was intentional. He's in Touro."

I felt a strange lump in my throat when I realized that sometime, no matter how long ago, Mick—or anyone—had put me down as his emergency contact.

I hadn't seen Mick since the Case of the Green Parrot in New Orleans. Mick had worked for Constance, like I did. Before he met her Mick was on his way to a life of domestic terrorism, prison, and bad tattoos. He started riots in the Pacific Northwest and chained himself to redwoods in California. He helped people escape from jail and firebombed politicians' houses. But there's a series of fine lines between fighting for a cause and just fighting. He stole from the rich and gave to the poor—first among them himself—until he tried to rob Constance. Constance was one of the rich—the Darlings had reserves to keep them flush for generations.

Constance helped Mick see that there are never any sides. Only things we understand and things we have chosen to pretend we don't understand. Only those we admit we love and those we pretend we don't recognize.

Mick was a detective. He knew it while Constance was around to tell him, and forgot after she died.

After I hung up with the EMT, I called the hospital. I was transferred around a few times until I reached a nurse on Mick's floor.

"He's stable," she said. "They pumped out his stomach."

"What'd he take?"

"No report yet but I'd guess a bunch of stuff. He on any meds?"

I nodded and then I remembered she couldn't see me and I said, "Yeah." I wasn't certain but suspected that he was taking a big mess of prescriptions: antidepressants, antianxiety drugs, sleeping pills. He hadn't weathered the storm well.

"Some of it hit him," she said, "but he'll be okay. Just, you know, got to deal with whatever made him do this."

She sounded sympathetic, but tired. I asked if I could speak to him. She said he was sleeping.

"He got family?"

Mick had no one and he had nothing. He taught criminology and ran a drop-in center for homeless children. He used to just volunteer there. Then they lost their funding and the director moved on and Mick couldn't stand to let it go so he didn't. His biggest donor was Anonymous and if he'd known who Anonymous was he might not have taken her money.

Mick—my Mick, Constance's Mick—was not going to die or come close to dying alone. I booked a flight for New Orleans the next evening. Something fluttered in my chest, some feeling of life, of direction, of being needed and busy and a part of the human race.

A few hours later, before I started packing, Andray called. It was the only time he'd called me since New Orleans. It might have been the only time he'd called me ever.

"Mick was in the hospital," he said.

"Yeah," I said. "I heard."

"Oh," he said. "You knew."

He sounded disappointed.

"Thanks," I said. "You seen him?"

"While he was still there," he said.

"What do you mean?" I said. "He's out already?"

"Yeah. Let him out this morning."

"Where is he?" I asked. "Is he okay?"

"Home," Andray said.

We didn't say anything for a minute. I didn't know how Andray was going to stay alive another year. He had been shot once since I'd been gone, his fourth bullet diving neatly into the top of his right shoulder and through the other side. No one in New Orleans had called me when it happened. I'd found out from the lama.

I knew I wouldn't have made it without Constance. Andray had me and Mick. Put us together and we weren't a quarter of her. As evidenced by the fact that both Mick and Andray were very close to dead.

"You been okay?" I asked Andray.

He made a noncommittal sound: *Uh-huh* or *I-'ont-know.*

"You see Terrell?" I asked.

"Yeah. Few times," he said.

"He doing okay?"

"Not really."

"Yeah," I said. "But. You know. The only way out is through. That's what they say."

Andray didn't say anything.

I thought about Andray and Terrell all the time. I didn't know if I'd made their lives better or worse when I came to New Orleans on the Case of the Green Parrot. At least I knew that before me, they'd had each other. Now Terrell was locked up and Andray was floating through life alone.

I wanted to say *I will do anything I can to get you out of this.* I wanted to say *I will pull you out of this black tar pit of death and sorrow and drag you to the shore.* The way someone had dragged me out of that black pit.

When you love something so much, the thought of doing it but not doing it well hurts almost more than never trying. Almost. You wouldn't know until you tried it that failing is actually better.

"Well," Andray said. "Just lettin' you know."

He hung up. I rummaged around my coffee table, through unpaid bills and unread magazines and cups of undrunk tea until I found what I was looking for: a little bag of cocaine Tabitha had left here a few nights ago. I opened one of the magazines, the *New Journal of Criminology,* ripped out a stiff subscription card, and used it to scoop out a bump of cocaine and snort it.

I called Mick. He answered, groggy.

"Hello?"

"It's me," I said.

"Me? Ellie?"

He was still high off whatever he'd used to try to end his life. Ellie was his ex-wife, the wife who'd left after the storm.

"Claire," I said. "Claire DeWitt."

"Oh, hey, Claire," he said, disappointment audible. "I'm sick."

"I know," I said. "The hospital called. They told me."

He didn't say anything.

"What the fuck?" I said. Suddenly I felt insulted, as though he had tried to leave this mortal coil only because I was in it. "Seriously?"

He sighed and didn't say anything.

"You want to come out here for a while?" I said. "I could—"

He sighed again and didn't say anything. He sighed like I'd said the dumbest thing in the world, like I understood nothing and never would.

"I have a ticket booked for tomorrow," I said. "I figured I'd come and see if—"

"This isn't a good time for a visit," he said. "Listen, Claire. I don't feel. I. I mean."

"Okay," I said. "Can I call you later?"

"Sure," he said. But I knew he wouldn't talk to me later, either.

"You sure you're okay?" I said. "I mean, I could come and—"

"Yeah," Mick said, clearly not fine and clearly not wanting to talk to me. "I'm fine. I'm totally fine. We'll talk soon, okay?"

He sounded like he was talking to a bill collector. We hung up. I called Andray back. His voice mail picked up.

"Hey," I said. "It's Claire. So I just talked to Mick and he doesn't sound so good. I was thinking maybe you could go see him? See if he's okay? I think they let him out of the hospital too early and I also think, you know. I don't know how safe he is."

Andray didn't call me back and neither did Mick.

I canceled my ticket and didn't go to New Orleans. Instead I did the rest of the coke and cleaned my apartment, meaning I moved stacks of unpaid bills and unopened mail from one table to another. I put unfiled papers closer to the file cabinets and put all my scraps of paper with very important notes on them (*Nate* DIDN'T HAVE THE LEMONADE. *Fingerprints don't match, 1952–58. Sylvia DeVille, DOB 12/2/71, not in system, likely not an abortion.*) in a pile on the kitchen counter. I put the dishes in the sink. When the apartment was cleaner it felt empty and alone, like a tomb I might not escape from, and I got dressed and went out as quickly as I could. It was after midnight. I went to a bar in North Beach and ordered a beer and then a scotch and then another beer, and when a man I'd never met before asked if he could buy me another drink I said yes. He asked me what I did.

"I'm a private detective," I said.

"Yeah," he said with a little smile, thinking he knew, "and I'm a cowboy."

15

AND THEN THERE WAS the Case of the Missing Miniature Horses. I took the case twenty-five days after Paul died. A man named Ellwood James had a ranch near Point Reyes, north of San Francisco, in Marin County. Ellwood James was the cousin-in-law of the district attorney of San Francisco, and he raised miniature horses. It was a surprise to see just how miniature the horses were. The tallest was three and half feet, on all fours. The horses looked a little sad and ashamed that they weren't going to grow anymore. They reminded me of the kids from *Flowers in the Attic,* never growing after being locked in an attic a few years too long.

Ellwood James thought that someone was stealing his horses.

"I started off with one fifty," he said. He sounded like a real rancher, as if he were talking about heads of cattle. "Births, deaths, what have you, six months in I got ninety-nine. Someone is stealing my horses."

My theory was that the little fellows were running away to try to get some big boy genes back in the mix, or maybe committing suicide. I made a mental note to research equine suicides.

He took me around the ranch. Your basic low-security operation. I explained to him that if he wanted to stop the thefts, he needed to put up some higher fences, some lights, and maybe some razor wire. If he wanted to find out who, if anyone, was stealing the little guys, he'd be better leaving things as they were and investing in some surveillance.

Ellwood also bred peacocks.

"Peafowl," he corrected me, using the gender-neutral term. "Peacock's a male, peahen's the female."

He looked up; I followed his eyes to see a ring of vultures closing in.

"Goddamn it," he said. We followed the vultures and walked across the pasture, tiny horses in all colors roaming and grazing. Dandelions and little purple flowers I couldn't name dotted the green grass. The sky was so blue it almost hurt to look at it.

When we'd reached a hundred feet or so we saw what the vultures were so eager for. A dead peacock. Maybe a peahen.

"Goddamn it," Ellwood said again. "Damn things were supposed to live to twenty."

"Maybe she *was* twenty," I said.

Ellwood nodded. Neither of us knew how to date peafowl, that was for sure.

A vulture swooped down and landed ten or fifteen feet from us.

"Might as well let her have it," Ellwood said, and we walked back across the pasture.

"Not much of a job for a private eye," I said.

"I want to know who's doing this," Ellwood said. "A man has his honor. His pride."

I wasn't sure where honor and pride fit into shrinking horses. When we got close to the barn one of the little guys, all black with a glossy coat, came toward me. I crouched down and we looked at each other. He looked sad and wise.

"I see your point," I said to Ellwood. "But what I charge'll cost more than you're losing."

"Money is not an issue," Ellwood James said.

Magic words.

I took the case.

From Ellwood James's place I drove back to the 101 and up to Sonoma County and got off near Santa Rosa and drove out to the Spot of Mystery. The Spot of Mystery was one of those places where a very mysterious house slid down a very mysterious hill and now defied every known law of physics, if you squinted just right. Other highlights included a gift shop, a petting zoo of fainting goats, hot springs, and some extremely tall redwoods with names like Old Buddy and Faithful Susan.

Jake, the man who ran the Spot of Mystery, was a retired police detective from San Francisco. In the cabins behind the main building he ran a kind of halfway house for detectives and cops, men and women who were halfway between one mystery and another. I told him I needed some people for surveillance and he said he would set it up. I trusted him to do it right. I ran down the plan for him and gave him some cash to start paying two people. I would have my assistant, Claude, check in with Jake once a day and monitor the situation.

I went to say hello to the goats. They remembered me from a stint I'd spent with them a few years back. I wondered if they liked what they saw. Probably not. I told myself I didn't care.

That was the Case of the Missing Miniature Horses.

16

ON THE THIRTIETH DAY after Paul died I heard from the cops about the bullets. There were no matches—it was a new gun, or at least one unknown to the national database. I'd been through his house a few times since the day of the crime and found absolutely nothing interesting. Both the cops and I tried fingerprinting the place and got nowhere—Paul and Lydia had people over a lot, and their house wasn't small. There were hundreds of partials, a few clear impressions, but no matches. The stolen instruments, which I thought would be the clincher, still hadn't shown up. Since the murder I'd gotten a rough list from Lydia of what was stolen and I'd sent alerts to every pawnshop and music store I could find. Like a lot of musicians Paul was constantly buying and selling instruments, so it was hard to pin down exactly what was missing. The case had gotten a lot of media attention and been in all the papers, and I figured the thief—who was likely also the murderer—knew that, and was sitting on the gear to sell it when things cooled down.

I went back to Paul's house again. I talked to his neighbors. No witnesses. No one heard anything except the neighbor who'd heard the shot to begin with.

The neighbor's name was Freddie. Freddie was a white man, somewhere between fifty and a million, who seemed like the least happy person on earth. He seemed like a man who had devoted his life to misery.

He had on a worn bathrobe over pajama bottoms and a T-shirt and fake leather slippers that had seen better days, although I think it would be fair to say that none of their days had been exactly good. We stood on the steps of his house. It was foggy and cold. Living in San Francisco was a war of endurance. I knew many people who had, after years of winning, one day lost the battle with the fog and moved back east or down south.

"With the noise around here," Freddie said. "I mean, the Mexicans and now these club kids or hipsters or whatever. And the musicians. Everyone's a musician."

His kind, the cranky-middle-aged-white-men of the world, weren't exactly known for their silence, but I let it go. I also didn't mention that his house was worth approximately a billion dollars and he could easily move to a neighborhood with fewer Mexican club kids if he chose.

"But you knew it was a gunshot," I said.

"Well," he said, "living around here, you learn. You know, the Mexicans."

"And the Salvadorans," I added. "And I think some are Guatemalan."

"Exactly."

"So you went over," I said.

He nodded. "I don't know what I was thinking. What am I gonna do if someone's shooting? But I went, took a look, didn't see anything obvious, called the cops."

It was the world's most boring story.

I hugged myself against the cold. The fog of the Kali Yuga. Paul deserved so much better. He deserved a grand theft, a jewel heist, murder by a crazed fan. Paul deserved to die in a duel, to tumble down the Himalayas, to be mauled by wildcats on the Serengeti. Instead, some asshole wanted his guitars, shot Paul, and took them. He should have been killed in a high-speed chase in a Lamborghini, poisoned by a duchess, taken out with the candlestick in the conservatory.

Or he could have just lived.

"This neighborhood," Freddie said. "I don't know what's going on."

It should have been you, I thought but didn't say. *You should have died and Paul should have lived.*

69

"Maybe the Mexicans will move out," I said. "Go back to Spain."

"Maybe," he said. "I don't think so. I think they like it here."

I looked at Paul's house. Flyers and phone books were starting to pile up by the front door.

Maybe all the Mexicans would move out and Freddie could have his shitty neighborhood back again. Maybe everyone would move out, maybe everyone would die, maybe everyone would realize that life really was as dreary and awful as Freddie told them it was, as it seemed today, and there would be a mass suicide and Freddie could have the whole world all to himself.

Freddie and I stood on his porch and looked at the fog around us. At the Kali Yuga.

"Mysteries never end," Silette wrote. "And we solve them anyway, knowing we are solving both everything and nothing. We solve them knowing the world will surely be as poorly or even worse off than before. But this is the piece of life we have been given authority over, nothing else; and while we may ask *why* over and over, no one yet has been given an answer."

17

AFTER FORTY-ONE DAYS PAUL'S Bronco turned up in an impound lot in Oakland. They wouldn't let me see it. I'd tried looking for it and gotten nowhere. Lydia was barely able to get out of bed the first three weeks, so she wasn't looking. She'd been spending most of her time up in Sonoma County, in a house Paul had on Bohemian Highway. I didn't blame her. No one wanted to live in a murder scene. I'd called her a few times and she didn't feel like talking much. I didn't blame her for that, either.

The car had been found on the Bay Bridge early in the morning the day after Paul died. But with the DMV being the DMV and with Lydia not checking the mail, no one made the connection until now. I'd called and the cops had called, but that's life sometimes.

"It was the alternator," Ramirez told me over the phone. I was home. I'd called him four times before I caught him by surprise by calling from a different phone, a cheap disposable cell. "Probably driving the car, lost steering, got scared, pulled over to the shoulder, and either called for help or flagged down a passing motorist or a patrol car."

While I talked to Ramirez I felt something in my chest and I found the remains of a bag of coke I'd gotten from Tabitha and snorted a bit off the tip of a key.

That night I drove to the Bay Bridge, which I'd driven over many times but never driven *to*. At about the middle of the bridge

I pulled over to the shoulder and put my hazards on. I checked my phone: no reception. He must have gotten lucky with highway patrol or a good Samaritan coming to his aid. There never seemed to be any bad Samaritans. But what did I know?

Back in my car, I did another bump to kill the strong dark thing that was screaming in my chest.

18

ON SUNDAY NIGHTS I usually had dinner with Claude to talk about what we'd done or hadn't done the previous week and would or wouldn't do in the week to come. I didn't have an office—that would only encourage people—and so Claude worked sometimes from his place in Berkeley and sometimes at my apartment. That Sunday, forty days after Paul died, we went to the Enlightened Mistress's place. Claude was keeping a close eye on our miniature horse ops and I gave him an A+. There was nothing to report on the Case of the Kali Yuga—no clues, no hunches, no suspects. Around us a few big Chinese families had Sunday supper. It was damp and cold outside and everyone in the restaurant seemed to have either a hot cup of tea or a bowl of soup in front of them. Some days in San Francisco it seemed like the weather moved inside of you and the chill was something you would take with you wherever you went, forever.

That night I spoke to Lydia on the phone. She was in the house on Bohemian Highway.

She was doing as well as you could expect. She had a lot of friends to help her with the practical stuff. But she said no one talked to her about Paul. About how he was dead now, and gone, and never coming back. Instead they said things like "He's home now" or "He's with the angels" or "His suffering is over now." It was as if, Lydia said, they thought she didn't know he was dead.

"It's like they haven't fucking grasped that he's dead," she said.

"I mean, it's like they think I don't know how bad it is so they shouldn't fucking tell me."

She sounded angry. Most people shy away from death, seal themselves off from widows and widowers and grieving parents as if losing the people you love is contagious. But if death is contagious, I was already infected.

"So I've got a case near you," I said. "Point Reyes. These miniature horses."

"Horses?" she said. "What, did they do something?"

"Maybe," I said. One of them did look pretty guilty, a mini-palomino with murder in her eyes. "How about I take you out for a cup of coffee next time I'm up there?"

"Sure," she said. "Let me know."

"Oh," I said. "And the keys."

No one had ever found Paul's house keys. Was the murderer planning to come back? Steal whatever was left to steal?

"Can I have a set?" I asked. "I wanted to check something in the house again."

"Sure," she said. "I'll mail a set to your place. So, yeah, let me know when you're coming up. We'll get a coffee."

But she said it as if it was just another promise the world was going to break, another bitter cup she'd have to drink.

19

LATER THAT NIGHT I tried Mick again. I called him once or twice a week. He never answered. I got Mick's voice mail. I called Andray. He also didn't answer.

There weren't many people who wanted to talk to me, it seemed. I thought of other people I could call who wouldn't answer. People who were dead or people who were gone or people who hated me or just didn't like me.

It wasn't like anything had happened. I knew Mick wasn't angry at me. He just had never liked me that much to begin with. I knew he kind of sort of loved me, but that isn't the same as liking someone. If I'd been almost dead he'd probably call me and I probably wouldn't pick up. Neither of us was doing very well or really even passing the grade with this humanity business.

I hung up and lit another joint and tried to sleep. I tossed and turned for a while, and when I did fall asleep I had nightmares: Mick was underwater, locked in some kind of glass box, like Houdini. It started off as an act but then he couldn't get out. He didn't have his keys; he'd had them when he'd come in and lost them somewhere inside. His air was running out and he couldn't escape. He didn't have his keys . . .

When I woke up I felt sick to my stomach, a terrible anxiety as if I'd lost something important and irreplaceable. It was three in the morning. I couldn't fall back asleep. I got up and made a pot of chamomile tea with rosebuds and mint.

I went over the case again. The keys. So someone cared little enough about Paul to kill him and steal his guitars, but cared enough to lock the door behind them.

Or maybe they didn't know they'd killed Paul and figured by locking him in the house they'd get a head start. Maybe they'd just shot him and hadn't known how well they'd hit their target. The police would have all kinds of tests and analysis by now that would explain how close or far the shooter had been. They wouldn't share it with me, so it didn't matter. And besides, I didn't particularly trust any of it.

I wrote *Keys* on a piece of paper and added it to my stack of very important scraps of paper on the kitchen counter. I stared at it for a while and nothing brilliant or interesting came to me. Nothing at all. I checked my phone. Paul's sister, Emily, had called again. I deleted her message without listening to it.

There was a message from Kelly. Kelly from Brooklyn. I hadn't heard from her since I was in New Orleans.

Hey, (mumble mumble) it's me (phone drop)—call me.

I didn't call either of them back. I put a Maria Callas record on my record player and smoked another joint and gave up on sleep. Instead I lay in bed and thought about the horses, so sad and crying because they would never grow up, trapped in a living death in their tiny bodies, living in the attic with that cruel grandmother . . .

I stood in the pasture at Point Reyes with the little black horse I'd seen at the ranch, the horse with the glossy coat and wise eyes. It was night, and the moon was round and full behind him. I gave him a tiny bottle of potion and he grew into a big, strapping stallion. He reared up on his hind legs and roared.

"Your science will not confuse me," he roared. "Your lies will not stop me from knowing the truth."

20

Brooklyn

W E'D FOUND ACE Apocalypse's shooting schedule for *The End of the World* in Chloe's room. The next shooting day was Friday. They were filming CC and Vanishing Center at a loft in Brooklyn. We hoped we'd find her before then, but if not we could find Ace at the loft in Brooklyn and see what he knew.

Chloe's room revealed disappointingly few other clues. The razorblade, the shooting schedule, and a few more books. Tracy found them under a pile of dirty clothes in the closet.

They were cheap paperbacks. They had racks of them at the newsstand on Myrtle Avenue. *Miss Mary's Punishment. The Story of a Slave Girl. A Bad Girl Gets What She Deserves.*

We knew about things like that, of course. Men had all kinds of desires, and if you let them, they would take that desire and put it squarely on your back, making it yours to carry. They would hand it all right over to you, this giant mess you could never hope to contain or control. It would take you over, if you let it. And I knew their desire was not always in a straight line, that sometimes it could fold back on itself, eat itself alive. It wasn't enough for them to want some of you; they needed you to want some of them, to care enough to hurt them, or let them hurt you.

But Chloe? Chloe wanting something like that for herself?

Again I had the feeling that I was lost in the woods. No signs pointed the way. No exit in sight, and it was too late to turn back now. All we could do was follow the clues, and keep going.

By ten o'clock that night we'd been to four bars: International, Mars Bar, the Blue & Gold, and Holiday. We'd asked everyone we knew and a few people we didn't; lots of people knew Chloe, but no one knew where she was now. It wasn't until Blanche's, a dive-y bar on Avenue A, that we found anything close to useful.

We was Tracy and I. Kelly was with Jonah. His band was playing in Hoboken.

"Me and Chloe used to be close," Elizabeth said. Elizabeth was a junior at Hunter High School. As we talked she played a Playboy pinball game. She was remarkably good at pinball. "I used to stay at her place all the time. She was a really good friend. From when we were thirteen to, like, less than a year ago. Like nine months."

"So what happened?" I asked.

Elizabeth scowled and slammed the ball around, hitting Bunnies' breasts, stomach, thighs.

"She turned on me one day, is what happened," Elizabeth said bitterly, looking at the game. "One day we were hanging out at her house and she just lit into me. Sounded like my fucking dad."

"So you had a fight?" I asked.

Elizabeth slammed a ball into a playmate's blond head, still on the same quarter. "No. Not even. The weird thing was, we'd been getting along great. When we first became friends, she could be a little bitchy sometimes, but, you know, I could too. And then it was like . . . it was like we got past that, and we were really close. I was staying at her house for the weekend, with her and her mom, and we had all this fun — we watched movies, ordered Chinese food, just being stupid. And then on Sunday night, after this great weekend, she started getting more and more annoyed with me. Like, I did the dishes, and I was doing the dishes wrong. And the stupid VCR got unplugged, and when I tried to put it back together I was doing that wrong. And then — I don't even remember what set it off. Shit!"

A silver ball bounced off a Bunny and fell down through the flippers, ending the game.

"You get a match?" I asked. A matching number on a pinball machine could get you a free game.

"That *was* the match," Elizabeth said. She turned to face us. "It was something ridiculously stupid. She asked if she could borrow this dress, this really cute vintage dress I have—you know the polka-dot one?"

Tracy and I nodded. We did know that dress.

"So I said no, because I wanted to wear it. And she just lost it. She started screaming at me that I was selfish, that I didn't care about her, that I was a bitch—totally crazy stuff."

"What'd her mom do?" Tracy asked.

"She was gone by then," Elizabeth explained. "She went on a date with this guy. We were supposed to go out together and then this guy called and she totally blew us off and went out with the guy. He was, like, twenty-five. Anyway. I never talked to Chloe again. She can fuck herself for all I care. Never apologized or anything."

"What do you think happened?" I asked.

"I have no idea," Elizabeth said. "She can fucking die for all I care. I hope she does die, actually, because she's a fucking cunt. How long has she been missing for?"

"Only a few days," Tracy said. "But we have reason to suspect foul play."

"Good," Elizabeth said. "I hope she disappears forever. I hope she fucking dies. Actually, I hope she's raped first, has an abortion with a rusty coat hanger, and *then* dies."

"Well, okay, then," I said. "Thanks for the help."

"No problem," Elizabeth said, still scowling. "And hey," she called out behind me as we turned to leave. "If you need help —I mean, I fucking hate Chloe. But *you guys*—well, let me know what happens. Let me know if you solve your case or whatever."

"What do you think?" Tracy asked when we were outside on the cold street.

"No idea," I said.

But we looked at each other, and we did kind of have an idea. We just didn't have the words for it.

If you hate yourself enough, you'll start to hate anyone who reminds you of you. And if you stick with it, you'll come to hate anyone who doesn't see how just awful you are.

As we both knew all too well.

We'd had a few drinks but after Elizabeth we didn't feel like having fun, or whatever it was we did. We were quiet and without talking walked to the subway and started the long ride home.

I felt like at any minute I could float away, or shatter apart. There would be nothing left. I may or may not have been real. I might have died. Maybe I had died and no one had noticed or remembered to tell me.

On the subway we dozed, my head on Tracy's shoulder.

"Trace," I said.

"Yeah?"

"If I was dead, would you tell me?"

She reached up and put her hand on my head, stroking my hair.

"You bet I would," she said.

"Would you miss me?" I asked.

"You bet I would," she said. "For the rest of my life. I couldn't live without you, bitch."

21

San Francisco

PAUL'S HOUSE WAS a row house from the early 1900s, not technically a Victorian but dressed up like one all the same. I'd had Claude research the house, and what he didn't tell me in his report I could guess from the scars on the walls. Over the years it had been cut open and ripped apart again and again—first built as a single-family home, then made into apartments, probably during the Depression, then divided into rooms when it was a boarding house in the seventies and eighties, each probably holding a hot plate and a depressed, lonely man. Or woman. As the neighborhood started to gentrify in the nineties, the apartments became bigger again. Than a gay couple bought it and restored it to single-family stature just before Paul bought it, turned the bottom floor into a studio, turned the parlor into another studio for Lydia, and lived in the rest of the house.

A few days after I spoke with Lydia, a set of keys in a white envelope arrived through my mail slot. I noticed they weren't Paul's or Lydia's—they were a new set from a hardware store. That evening I drove over to the Mission and let myself into the house where Paul died.

The police had come and gone. I'd snuck in a few times while they were investigating but they'd shooed me away when they found me. Of course, technically it was Lydia's house and I could go in anytime she said it was all right. But the police didn't want me there, and I was trying to play nice, hoping to stay in the loop in the unlikely event that they actually found something. Now their investigation was dying down and I could have it all to myself.

When I got to the door I noticed the lock looked good. If someone had picked it they had done a nice job—no scratches, dents, or dings. The key Lydia'd given me fit nearly perfectly in the lock, with the usual scratchiness of a new key. The door was intact; the windows around it clearly hadn't been broken recently.

So how did Paul's killer get in the house?

Inside was quiet and dark. The cops had covered it and Lydia's friends had been in and out, getting stuff and helping her with papers and money. But it felt still. The things had been moved since Paul died, but the energy remained untouched.

The entrance opened up onto a kind of hall/foyer with a parlor on one side and a living room on the other. Dusk cast long shadows across the floor. I flicked on the lights and saw I was stepping on a pile of mail. I picked it up and put it on another pile of mail on a table near the door.

It was almost exactly as it had been the night he died. Lydia's coat was still hanging over the banister where she'd tossed it that night. Everywhere in the house were records, CDs, small musical instruments like maracas and reindeer bells, books about music: *Ethnomusicology of Northern Peru; Vintage Guitar Price Guide 2007; Narcocorridas: A History; Protest and Harmony in French Folk Music.* The house was clean but not neat. Vintage furniture, framed music posters, thrift store paintings of cats and dogs: it looked like two much younger people lived here.

The parlor was Lydia's studio, where she kept her instruments, practiced, and recorded ideas. I went in and glanced around. It felt like nothing. Lydia hadn't played much in the months before Paul died and, obviously, since. She said she'd lost inspiration. I wasn't sure what that meant. In the studio there was a light layer of dust over everything. Her guitars were locked in a safe that was bolted to the wall; she'd grown up in a rough neighborhood and no one was taking what was hers. A door in the hall led to the staircase to Paul's studio downstairs. The padlock had been open when the police got here the night Paul died; Detective Huong had arranged for a locksmith to come and lock up the rest—she didn't want Lydia to lose what was left to regular thieves.

Huong was okay. For a cop.

Lydia said the thief could have picked the padlock or Paul could have left it open—it wasn't a great lock and Paul wasn't careful about using it. She'd tried to tell him, she'd told me bitterly over the phone. As if it would have mattered. *I tried to tell him about that fucking lock. That that fucking lock was no good.*

The keys Lydia gave me included one for the padlock. I opened it and went down to the studio. It was full of musical detritus: castanets, guitar cords, a harmonica, a laptop computer, an old-fashioned reel-to-reel recording device. The brand names spelled a melancholy poem: Vox, Harmony, Voice of Music.

Paul had owned eighteen guitars. Ten had been out in stands when the crime occurred; five had been stolen and five had been left behind. The other eight guitars were in a locked closet; those hadn't been touched. No time in a smash-and-grab.

Five guitars stolen and five left behind. The obvious reasons the thief didn't take them all were time and attention—not enough of the first and wanting to avoid the second. But the obvious was not always true.

Five stolen: an acoustic Favilla, a Gibson J-2000, a Lucite Dan Armstrong, a Les Paul, and a Telecaster. Five left behind: a Teisco Del Ray, a plastic Maccaferri, a Japanese-made little western number with cowboys painted on the front, a two-toned green Gretch Anniversary model, and a Guild acoustic.

Why those five taken? Why those five left behind?

You'd think someone who knew guitars would have taken the good stuff and left the crap, financially speaking. Or a random thief would have just grabbed five, maybe recognized the big names like Gibson or Fender but otherwise just taken his chances.

But what was actually stolen was somewhere in between.

The guitars were worth between about two hundred bucks and two grand. I figured the thief had guessed what was worth the most and he'd been wrong. I'd got a list of what was taken and what was left from Lydia and I'd had a few different guitar dealers look the list over. The values were not obvious. Most people would have expected the Les Paul to be gold, but it was a fake, worth only a few hundred bucks. The stolen Favilla didn't look so special but it clocked in at about six hundred. Of course, our thief, who was likely also our murderer, would get much less than that. But he'd get something. The stolen Korean-made Telecaster was only worth two or three hundred, but the Teisco he'd left behind was worth close to a grand, and the Maccaferri, which looked like a worthless plastic toy, would bring in at least six hundred bucks. The Gretsch, which was beautiful but not famous, was worth close to two grand.

Maybe the thief had just grabbed five guitars at random. Maybe he was someone who thought he knew guitars but wasn't as knowledgeable as he thought. Going by that I could put half the men in San Francisco in a lineup, along with a quarter of the women. Or maybe the thief knew something I didn't.

You couldn't exactly call it a clue, but it was something.

Upstairs were two bedrooms and a bathroom. I went to the bathroom and looked through the medicine cabinets. Lydia had left a bottle of Vicodin, twelve strong pills left. I put the bottle in my purse.

One bedroom they used as intended, the other held clothes, shoes, and occasionally guests. Both Lydia and Paul were sharp dressers, and they had tons of clothes. Scattered around were more CDs, more books, guitar picks and pick guards and pick-ups. On top of one dresser in the first bedroom were three coffee cups and two books. One cup was vintage, from Tahoe; in it was a twenty, two singles, and a few dollars in change. In another, a souvenir cup from Las Vegas from the same era, was a paperclip, two guitar picks, a cheap sandalwood *mala,* and a roach from a joint.

It was where Paul emptied his pockets. Nearly every man has a spot like this one. Everything here was Paul's, used to be Paul's, had been touched by him.

I put the thought aside and looked at the last cup, from the Spot of Mystery in Santa Rosa. In it was a little collection of business cards. I flipped through them: A Vietnamese restaurant in Alameda. A guitar store in San Rafael. A stamped card one-tenth of the way toward a free smoothie in Oakland.

Nothing jumped out at me. Nothing spoke to me. I put the cards in my pocket. The bed was unmade, sheets wrinkled and tossed. I imagined Paul sprawled across it, asleep, sun streaming in on his last morning, blissfully unaware of what the night would bring.

I left the bedroom and started to walk down to the kitchen and then, suddenly spooked by being in a dead man's house, I ran. I ran into the kitchen and looked out the window to remind myself there was still another world out there. But the overgrown backyard didn't convince me. In my pocket I found the very last of my cocaine. I used a butter knife to scrape out what was left, snorted it, and then licked my finger and ran it through the bag and then over my teeth. I stood for a minute letting my chemicals acclimate themselves, and then went back to work.

I went back to the living room. The body had been found here. Someone had tossed a carpet over the bloodstain on the wood floor. I pushed it aside.

I sat in a chair and looked at Paul's blood.

No, I corrected myself. The victim's blood. Paul was gone. There was no Paul and maybe never had been. Only the victim, *a* victim, the role he was apparently born to fill. All his life he probably thought he was something else, something so much more interesting: friend, husband, lover, musician. But in the end he was a victim.

I let my mind clear and I looked at the blood, the blood that had once been red and blue and alive and was now dead and brown.

The cops can only do so much. Even if they mean well, even if they're geniuses, they have fifty or so cases and limited overtime and wives and husbands and children and mortgages. That's why you hire a private eye. Because if she's smart, the private eye has none of those things.

I knew the cops had looked under the sofa and looked through the desk and in the corners and through the laundry hamper. But there were secrets to find.

First I went to the kitchen and looked through the refrigerator. Nothing was out of order—soymilk, rotten vegetables, half a chocolate bar, everything you'd expect. I checked the freezer: ice, frozen vegan burgers, miscellaneous uninteresting foodstuffs. I went through the kitchen cabinets, the dish rack, the dishwasher, the spice shelf.

Nothing. This was the fourth time I'd done this, maybe more. There was nothing the first time and nothing the last time and nothing this time.

From my bag I pulled a penlight and I got down on the floor and looked under the furniture. Nothing. I looked through the sofa. I'd looked through it before, but sofas were complicated creatures. They were like slot machines. Things would go in and in and in, but most of them would disappear. Only occasionally would anything come back out, and only for those with dedication and luck and a good understanding of how the machine worked.

I'd searched the sofa before. Now I *really* searched the sofa. First I took off all the cushions and pillows and piled them a few feet away. I looked at the sofa carcass, its tight crevices and narrow valleys. I went to my car, opened the trunk, and after some rummaging found my slim jim, the tool locksmiths use to open a locked car door, a very thin, long piece of metal about an inch wide. I took the tool and went back to the sofa. First I reached my hand into the crevices around the edges. Next I went through the same crevices, as slowly as I could, with the slim jim. The first thing I found was a corn chip. I picked it up and put it aside. Next I found a few quarters and then a nickel. I was toward the back when the tool hit something hard and solid.

I felt a current run up from the small, solid thing through the tool and into my hand and I knew: It was a clue.

A clue is a word in another language, and mysteries speak the language of dreams. Mysteries speak the alchemical language of the birds. There is no dictionary. Not even for me.

I gently extracted the locksmithing tool and set it aside. The tool was hard, and I couldn't risk damage. Instead I stretched my arm out as far as it would go, painfully pulling my shoulder a little from the socket. I moved my hand as best I could in the tight fit, and after a few seconds I found it: something small, hard, round. Slowly, carefully, I pulled it from the sofa and up to the light.

It was a poker chip.

Paul didn't gamble. I took him with me to Reno once. For a case I had to pick up a suitcase full of cash from a doctor in Reno who dealt in tranq prescriptions and homemade liver tonics and deliver it to a woman in Needles, Arizona—a long story, but that was the only way the Case of the Dove with Broken Wings was ever going to be resolved. Since I had to stay in Reno overnight I figured I might as well have some fun doing it. I played a little craps and an hour or two of baccarat, but Paul didn't play anything, not even slots. He said he didn't know how and besides, he was having fun just watching.

After a while I realized the real reason he wasn't playing. He wasn't worried about losing. He was scared that he would win. Paul was embarrassed enough about being rich. The last thing he wanted was more money.

I put the chip in a little plastic bag and put it in my purse. I was done for the night. I'd already been here for two hours and I was fairly certain I'd gotten what I'd come for. I stood up, dusted myself off, used the bathroom, washed up, got my coat, and reached in the pocket for my keys—

Keys. That reminded me. I went and looked at the front door. You didn't need keys to let yourself out, but you did need them to lock the door behind you.

I stopped and lay down on the sofa and tried to puzzle it out. Whoever killed Paul didn't *have* to take his keys. But it seemed like he had anyway.

Paul let himself in. Maybe the killer came in with him. Maybe the killer knocked. Or maybe the killer was already there.

Somehow the killer got in.

He—or she—killed Paul and left, locking the door behind him. Or her.

Why would he lock the door behind him? I mean, you kill a man, take his things, and split. Are you worried someone else will steal *more*? That your awesome crime scene will be spoiled?

Something knocked around in my brain. It almost came to the surface but then fell away, dissolving back into the currents of grocery lists and half-read books and misconceptions, the sad little graveyard where thoughts go to die.

I reached in my pocket for more coke and came up with the empty plastic bag. I licked it clean.

You figure this: The neighbor hears the gunshot, fucks around for a minute or two, calls the cops, throws on a robe, goes over to check Paul's place, finds that it's locked, and so the neighbor waits for the cops. This all takes three to seven minutes. Plenty of time for someone to kill Paul, lock the door behind them, and disappear.

Then why didn't it sit right with me?

I got out my phone and called Officer Ramirez.

"Hi," I said. "It's Claire DeWitt."

"Seriously?" he said. "Today?"

"Nah," I said. "Just kidding. Someone you actually like is on hold. But while I've got you: Paul Casablancas. Are you absolutely sure the door was locked?"

"Yeah," he said. "I was first on the scene, as far as I know. It was locked."

"Could the killer have been in the house? Not *were* they. But would it even be possible?"

He thought about it for a second. "No," he said. "Well, yes. Possible? Sure. They couldn't have gone out through the front door, 'cause we had a guy there while I looked inside, just for that reason. But could he have, say, snuck out through a back window, closed it behind him, and somehow broken into or, you know, scaled another house to get out from the yards and back on the streets, all without a dozen cops noticing—sure, that's possible. It's within the realm of human possibility, I guess. We searched the backyards, but if he'd done it fast enough, before that—yeah. It's possible. Extremely fucking unlikely, though."

"Extremely unlikely," I repeated.

"More than unlikely," Ramirez said, "but I don't know the word for that."

"Me either," I said. "I'm gonna have to look that up."

"Well, I don't think that happened," he said. "I think we would have seen or heard or vibed or otherwise been aware of the perp."

"Could he have hid in the house?" I asked. "It's a big place."

"Could?" he said. "Sure. Could he, you know, had a false panel and been hiding in the wall? Sure. Coulda been living in there for years. But did the officers do a thorough and reasonable search of the house? Yeah. You bet. Saw it myself. I don't think he was there."

He stopped and took a sip of something. Probably coffee.

"Or she," he said.

"Or she," I repeated.

"Yeah," he said. "That's what I said."

"Right."

Ramirez said *okay* and *goodbye* in a way that sounded like *go fuck yourself* and got off the phone.

22

I DROVE BACK TO MY apartment, where I took a shower and got dressed and read the new issue of *Detective's Quarterly*. Alex Whittier was on the cover. Professor of criminology at Northwestern. There was a transcript of his latest talk: the scientific method of solving et cetera. Or something like that.

A few hours later I got back in my car and drove to Japantown, where I met an old friend, Bret, at Fukyu in the mall for a late dinner. He'd already ordered for us. He knew what I liked. That was Bret's hobby: he knew what women liked. Bret was in his fifties and the richest person I knew. I didn't need money, but if I did, I knew I could always ask him. That counted for something; you couldn't say that about every rich person. He was born rich and he loved money, so he just kept getting richer.

After dinner we walked around the mall. Bret was born in Italy and had lived all over the world. He stopped at a little sweet shop and ran in to talk to the woman inside in Japanese. When he came out, he had a little box, and a look of triumph on his face.

"This is the thing!" he said with a big smile, and I didn't know what he was talking about, but I smiled too. He explained that it was a special little pastry he hadn't had since he lived in Kyoto. Happiness is contagious, and Bret seemed impossibly, always, happy.

Later, though, in his house, as the sun came up, I couldn't sleep and his happiness had worn away, fought off by my natural immunity. "Happiness," Silette wrote, "is the temporary result of denying the knowledge one already has." Far be it from me to deny the clever and glamorous truth for a stupid thing like happiness. The truth that was so fucking important, the truth that we were all supposed to give up our lives for, give up our happiness for. This truth we detectives, we Silettians, were supposed to love so much. To think some other girl, some poor sweet sap who didn't know any better, might actually be enjoying herself right now.

I sat in a silk-covered window seat and looked down to the city below. Bret slept a happy sleep in his giant bed. In a drawer next to him I found a big fat bag of coke. I did a small fingernail's worth, then stuck the bag in my purse. He knew what he was getting himself into when he invited me over. Bret's San Francisco house was at the top of Pacific Heights and you could see the entire world from his bedroom. I opened the window and leaned out. The fog was damp and the streetlamps glowed. I took his special pastry from the bedside table where he'd left it, half eaten, and dropped it out the window and watched it fall slowly in the pink dawn to the black street below and then, in pieces and layers, tumble down the hill toward the bottom. A fat, smart crow swooped down, landed next to it, and started picking up the pieces for breakfast. After that I got dressed and walked back to the garage where my car was parked. The bill was fifty-two fifty and the cashier expected me to argue but I didn't.

After I got my car, I didn't drive home. Instead I drove around the city, watching the sun break neighborhood by neighborhood, sniffing little scoops from the big bag of cocaine. At six or seven I went home and took one of Lydia's Vicodin. I crawled into bed and fell asleep watching *Craig Kennedy, Criminologist*. Craig always solved his case in thirty minutes. Every week the same sets, dressed up a little differently, and most of the same actors, in different clothes, played out different stories on the screen. Which maybe wasn't so different from every mystery. Just shorter.

After a restless sleep I got up the next day and made green tea and watched more TV. I talked on the phone to Claude and Tabitha. Later I sat on my floor and shuffled the business cards I'd taken from Paul's dresser. I shuffled some more and then I pulled one.

The guitar store.

I went to the file for the Case of the Kali Yuga and looked at the list of missing guitars. Five of them. The language of guitars sounded like a pornographic story translated from another language: whammy bars, f-holes, double-cutaway, fretwear, tailpiece, binding, belt-buckle rash, wall hanger, case queen.

I called Jon, the guy from the guitar store, and left a message. I told him I wanted to talk to him. I didn't tell him I didn't know what I wanted to talk about.

I didn't know why I didn't tell Lydia about the poker chip.

I only knew that I didn't.

23

Brooklyn

I WOKE UP THE NEXT DAY thirsty and hungover. I stumbled into the cavernous kitchen, designed for full service, and put on a pot of coffee. My blanket was wrapped around my shoulders. The heat was either broken or we hadn't paid the bill. I turned the oven on.

"You making something?"

I turned around. My mother was there, looking as hungover as I felt.

"Just warming up," I said.

"Yah," she said. "Make Mommy a cup of coffee, will you?"

"It's already on," I said.

She looked relieved. We both sat at the big wood table. My mother, Lenore, was still a shockingly, unearthly beautiful woman. Her blond hair was in a dated flip and she had on smudges of last night's makeup, but it didn't matter. She had high cheekbones and perfect tight skin you could bounce a quarter off of. Her blue eyes shone. Her Austrian accent had been finely tuned in boarding schools all across Europe, as one after the other kicked her out. Men would stop cars in the middle of the highway for her. Men would give up fortunes for my mother. Men had done those things, and more, as she liked to remind us.

But then she fell in love with my father. And, according to her, that was when her life started its slow, long spiral down.

Over the mantel was a clean patch, outlined in gray dust, where a Warhol silkscreen of my mother used to hang before she sold it a few years before. We looked at the empty spot.

"Ach," my mother said. "The car."

My mother had a little yellow Karmann Ghia. At least twice a year it was towed—reading street signs and feeding meters was exactly the kind of drudgery Lenore had no time for. The drudgery of getting the car back from the impound lot at the Navy Yard would be someone else's problem.

One morning a few months later an Italian man would show up at the house and scream at Lenore for an hour in Italian, while she screamed back. Then the man would drive away with the car, which I would never see again.

She went to the window. She'd parked in front of a fire hydrant a few yards down from the house. We had our own driveway, but it had been blocked by an abandoned car for a few weeks.

No one had noticed yet, not the car in our driveway or the Karmann Ghia parked in front of the hydrant. Traffic enforcement wasn't exactly patrolling our neighborhood regularly. The street was gray, with old black snow hardened in little piles here and there, trash scattered around it.

"Baby," Lenore said. "Could you?"

She looked ready to cry.

"Sure," I said. "After some coffee, okay?"

She nodded. She looked at me, a long look, like she was really taking me in.

"What?" I said, annoyed.

"You okay, right?" she said. "Everything okay?"

"Of course," I said. "Of course everything's okay."

She stood up and came toward me—I thought she might hug me and I stiffened, but instead she only put her hand on my head.

"Yah," she said. "You always okay."

Her voice sounded bitter, like I had done something wrong. Her hand tightened on the top of my head, as though she were a hawk and I were a mouse she'd found. For a minute I thought I might fall off my chair.

Lenore squeezed my head. I felt her fingernails dig in.

Finally she dropped me.

"Gimme some money," I said after a minute. "I'll get the boys down the block to move the car already."

That night Tracy and I took the subway downtown to follow up on our last, best clue—the movie Chloe was supposed to see before she vanished. We took the G to the F to the East Village. New York City wasn't all that big for us—Brooklyn, parts of Queens, and Manhattan below Fourteenth Street.

It was less than ten miles from our house to Second Avenue: on the subway it took sixty-seven minutes to get downtown. I read the *Cynthia Silverton Mystery Digest,* checked out from the bookmobile that morning. Tracy had read it already. She picked up a copy of the *New York Post* that someone left on the bench.

"Fucking Koch," she said. "Switch with me."

"No," I said.

Every month brought exactly one good thing, more regular than a period: a new *Cynthia Silverton Mystery Digest.* We didn't have much of a library in our corner of Brooklyn—a pale-brick storefront that was perpetually closed for renovations—but we did have a bookmobile: a shining airstream-type trailer some do-gooder stocked with comic books, romance novels, detective stories, a few Sweet Valley High paperbacks, and the *Cynthia Silverton Mystery Digest.* The *Cynthia Silverton Mystery Digest* was a five-by-seven magazine featuring the exploits of teen detective and junior college student Cynthia Silverton. Each issue featured a Cynthia Silverton story, a True Mystery Not Quite Solved, true-crime tales, and alluring advertising for home-study courses in private detection and fingerprinting and important detection tools. I already had the Cynthia Silverton Spy Camera, a tiny fourth-rate imitation Minox that fit in the palm of my hand, and the Cynthia Silverton fingerprinting kit, which had started us on the road to ruin.

This month's unsolved mystery was the Case of the Murdered Heiress. Lana Delfont was found murdered in her Park Avenue apartment. The door was locked from the inside. Who could have done it? And why didn't the killer steal her famous diamonds, but instead carefully arrange them on her body?

"The daughter did it," Tracy said.

"Yep," I said. "The earrings."

"Exactly," Tracy said. "No one but a daughter would put earrings on her mother like that."

"No one but a daughter would stab her mother that many times," I said.

Tracy nodded. She didn't have a mother—hers had died in an accident when she was two—but she'd heard.

Finally the train pulled into the station and we bundled up for the cold outside.

That evening we went to Theatre 80. At the counter was a bored punk girl with pink hair and a leopard sweater. SUNSET BOULEVARD, the marquee exclaimed. THREE NIGHTS ONLY.

"Hi," I said to the girl through thick plastic. "Can you tell me what was playing here last Saturday night?"

"Five dollars," she said.

"I'm not trying to buy a ticket," I said. "I'm trying to ask you a question. Do you know what was playing here last Saturday night?"

The girl pointed to my left. I turned. I didn't see anything.

"Can't you just answer my question?" I said.

The girl pointed again. Then she turned around.

"Why are you such a cunt?" I asked.

She shrugged.

"Fuck you," I said. "Cunt."

She turned back around and gave me the finger.

"Fuck you, whore," she said.

"Look," Tracy said. On the wall to my left was a poster for *Belle du Jour*. Underneath, a little card said *Saturdays 8-10-12*.

"I never saw it," Tracy said. "What's it about?"

We got a slice at Stromboli's across the street and I told her about *Belle du Jour* and the fat man with the pet crickets and the gangster with the gold teeth. After pizza we walked over to Sophie's, the bar across the street from Reena and Chloe's place. In Sophie's we got dollar pints of beer. Someone put the Pogues on the jukebox. At the bar an old man muttered to himself, angry and suspicious.

We walked over to the horseshoe bar, where by now Chloe's ex, Ben, would be on his shift.

Ben was just starting when we ordered our first round of drinks. As far as I could tell, Ben was perfect. He was twenty-one. He had short brown hair and wore Levi's and a shirt with the sleeves rolled up to reveal perfect olive forearms, one tattooed with a broken heart and the words LOVE KILLS.

We both knew who he was, but he didn't remember us. He didn't seem to care, either.

"Yeah," he said bitterly when we said we were looking for Chloe. "I have no fucking idea where she is, and if I did, you're the last people I would tell."

"What?" I said. "Why?"

"Who do you think we are?" Tracy said.

"I know exactly who you are," Ben said, and walked away to perform some imaginary bar task.

Tracy and I looked at each other. Another mystery. We walked around the bar to where Ben was.

"We're detectives," Tracy said. "Reena asked us to help find Chloe. She's really worried about her."

Ben opened his mouth and then closed it, looking confused.

"I've known Chloe for, like, a year," I said. "We've met before. Like, a million times. That time at Gas Station when Vanishing Center—"

"Oh," Ben said. "Oh! Oh! Shit." He shook his head. "I am so sorry. I didn't recognize you at all. No, you, you're—I am so sorry."

I said it was okay. He asked why we were looking for Chloe. I told him Reena had hired us. Chloe was missing. No one had seen her since last Thursday.

"Fuck," Ben said. "Reena did call me, but I figured. Well. You know."

"No," Tracy said. "We don't."

"You don't know?" he said. "You don't know about Chloe?"

We shook our heads. Ben looked at us and sighed. He closed his eyes and drew one hand down his face, like he was trying to wipe something away that wouldn't come off.

"Dope," he finally said, opening his eyes.

"What?" Tracy said. "Chloe? Heroin?"

Ben nodded and opened his eyes. "I thought you were her stupid little dope friends. Some of them have been in looking for her."

"Wait," I said. I got out my notebook and my pen. "When did Chloe start using?"

Ben raised his eyebrows. "Six month ago, maybe. Maybe longer —I don't know anymore. She made these new friends. That's who I thought you guys were—sorry about that. This whole crowd of little fucking sluts, fucking skeeves. These girls, Soon Yi and Nico, and all those trashy little sluts they hang out with."

Soon Yi, I wrote down. *Nico. Trashy little sluts.* We knew them.

"How about those other trashy little sluts?" I asked. "Know any of their names?"

"Hmm," Ben said. "One of them is called Cathy, she's this girl from the projects. And there's Georgia, this little girl who I actually think is homeless—I think she stays with Cathy most of the time."

We knew Cathy and Georgia too.

"Is that why you guys stopped seeing each other?" I asked. "Dope?"

Ben nodded. He looked sad and I was sorry I had asked. I was sorry I'd had to ask.

"I was so in love with her," he said. "I was going to—I was hoping we would, you know. I thought we'd stay together. I mean, I know she was young, but she was so fucking mature. She was, like, you know, a regular person. Not like a kid at all. And then she started *that*. I wasn't mad at her. Not at first. I thought she was just experimenting, just trying, and hey, I've done it. I've done pretty much everything. I couldn't really tell her not to. But then. You know how it goes. It was every weekend and then every night and then every day."

"You broke up with her?" I asked. "Or did she end it?"

"Neither of us did, really," Ben said. "That's the fucked-up thing. We just stopped. She started spending less and less time with me and then when she did, we were fighting."

"About drugs?" Tracy asked.

"Yes," Ben said. "No. Everything." He sighed. "When I first met Chloe, she was this amazing, smart, together girl. She had a great job, her own place, totally responsible. She seemed totally, you know. Totally sane."

"And then?" I asked.

"And then it started to, like, unravel," Ben said. "Not just the drugs. Hanging out with those fucked-up girls, going out too much, not paying bills, not returning phone calls. It was like she was starting to fall apart around the edges. Or like she never was that responsible, together girl at all. Like she was always this totally fucked-up chick underneath and she had just done a really good job covering it up all this time. And she just couldn't do it anymore. I mean, God, fuck, I felt terrible."

"You tried to help her?" Tracy asked.

"Of course," Ben said. "I tried talking to her, yelling at her, telling her I loved her, everything. But she just kept, like, running away. What I said mattered less and less."

"When was the last fight?" I asked.

"The last fight," Ben said. "Well, one night I came home and she was there with a bunch of her little skeeve friends. And they were getting high, right there in my place. Just sitting around passing a little bag of dope like it was nothing. Nodding out on my living room floor. *Mine.* And I—you guys don't know this, but my mom is an addict. And I have a rule in my house, which is *No drugs.* Like I said, I've tried everything, and I don't judge. But that's the house I grew up in, and that's not the house I want to live in anymore."

We nodded. We both understood that.

"So I kicked her friends out," Ben went on. "And Chloe, well, she was high. I guess I should have let her sleep it off or something. But I was, you know, freaking out. So I just lost it. I just started yelling at her. *I love you, what the fuck are you doing. What happened to you.* And she just *laughed.* She sat on the floor, her eyes all, like, rolling back in her head and shit. And she was *laughing.*"

Ben shook his head. There was something else. Something he wasn't saying. I saw it in the way he wrinkled his brow, the way the whites of his eyes dimmed.

"She said something," I said. "Something to you."

"Yeah," he began softly. "She said. She said. She said she knew I never really loved her anyway. And then I really lost it, and I threw a glass at her—not at her, but at the wall above her. Because, she had to know—I mean, I had done everything. Everything I could." He frowned again. "Everything I knew about, at least. I mean, what the fuck do I know about love?"

We sat at the bar and didn't look at each other's eyes. For the first time I noticed the tattoo on his arm was still dark, and nearly new. LOVE KILLS.

"There's this book," Tracy said, looking at her shot glass. "This guy, he says, 'The teller has no responsibility to make the listener believe in the truth. Each must take the words and make them their own. No one can do this for another.' That's what he says in this book we like."

This book we liked. Like this air we breathed, this sun that shone on us.

Ben frowned and looked at Tracy.

"You think so?" he said.

"Absolutely," Tracy said.

Ben and Tracy looked at each other and something passed between them—a secret handshake, a code word. The moment passed as quickly as it'd come. Ben poured us each a shot of tequila and knocked on the bar, telling us in the ancient code of bartenders that the drinks were on the house. We thanked him and we threw back our shots and he poured us another round.

"So," I said, bringing us back to topic. "That was the last time you saw her?

"Yeah," he said. "I left the apartment and stayed out pretty much all night. When I came back she was gone. The next day I changed my locks. A few weeks later, I changed my phone number. I never wanted to see her again."

"So the skeeves and whores," I asked. "They've been around looking for her?"

"A few times," Ben said. "They didn't seem concerned or anything. Just mentioned they hadn't heard from her."

None of us said anything. A customer came in. Ben left to get him a drink and came back.

"Tell me something else," Tracy said. "Tell me something about Chloe."

Ben took a deep breath.

"I loved her," he said. "And I never want to see her again as long as I fucking live."

A few more customers came in and Ben left to take care of them, finishing his second shot before he did.

"You know where we can find them?" I asked Tracy. "Cathy and Georgia?"

"Maybe," Tracy said. "Got some quarters?"

I dug some change out of my bag and Tracy went to the pay phone in the back. She came back twenty minutes later with information.

"Chris Garcia, this guy I know who slept with her a few times, says Cathy hangs out at Cherry Tavern."

"And where Cathy is," I said, "Georgia will be nearby."

I knew Georgia. I hated Georgia. I thought of her pretty face and her dark eyes and something in me burned hot.

Sometimes it seemed like every teenager in New York was separated by only two or three degrees. Like it was a secret world you gained admittance to at fourteen and left at twenty, swearing never to repeat what you'd seen. No one would believe us, anyway.

24

San Francisco

FIFTY DAYS AFTER Paul died I drove across the Bay Bridge to Oakland. I passed the spot where Paul had left his car and thought I might feel something and I didn't. Or so I told myself. Traffic on the highway was bad and I got off at the wrong exit and ended up stuck in traffic in downtown Oakland. It was like downtown Brooklyn — a lot of beautiful old buildings, built for the respectable middle-class shopper, now filled with "New York style" clothing stores and shops that sold gold teeth and fish-and-chips restaurants and, now, medical marijuana joints. A few old holdouts like I. Magnin somehow held on by their nails.

Homeless people congregated under an awning at Broadway and Thirteenth, trying to stay dry as it started to rain. A few blocks farther a man in a wheelchair weaved in and out of traffic, asking for change, his wheels slippery on the wet pavement. He knocked on my window. I didn't want to open it.

He kept knocking. The light changed but I didn't go — I wasn't sure how close the man was, if the wheels of his chair intersected with the wheels of my battered Mercedes. He was annoying, but I didn't want to kill him.

"Bitch!" he spat. "Bitch. In your fancy car. You give me some money."

I looked around. From the sidewalk two cops watched. They

didn't do anything and they didn't look like they would anytime soon.

The man banged on my window.

"Bitch!"

People behind me honked.

"Bitch! You give me some money, bitch."

I leaned on the horn. The man didn't seem to notice and didn't move.

"Fuckin' bitch in a Mercedes. You gonna give me something."

Behind me more horns honked. Finally the cops stepped toward us.

The man wheeled himself away, screaming in the rain.

I wound my way through downtown, made a few more wrong turns, and finally righted myself going up the mountain. Sick of my car, I stopped at the first park entrance I found, parked, and entered the woods by a hiking trail.

The rain stopped. In a half mile I veered off and followed a deer path up a hill. Mushrooms bloomed on either side of the trail. I didn't see another person until in ten or fifteen minutes I heard a woman's voice, singing lightly in Spanish. After a few more minutes I came across a group of ten or twelve people in a clearing, about half of them indigenous people from somewhere in the southern part of the Americas—my guess was Peru, although I wouldn't have bet on it. Most of them were lying around not really doing anything, but two of them, a tiny indigenous woman and a tall white woman, were standing.

The indigenous woman sang. The white woman said, "As the medicine starts to take effect, you might start to see things. These things might seem real, or they might not. But try to remember what you see. No two people will see the same things. These are private communications to you from the spirit of the vine."

I climbed higher up the mountain. Near the top I veered off to another trail, this one fainter. In half an hour or so the trail took me around the mountain to the other side. No one was around; no one I could see, at least.

Finding landmarks in the woods wasn't easy for me. I'd lived most of my life in cities, and most trees looked alike to my untrained eye. But after a few wrong turns I found the spot I was looking for, a ring of redwoods around a giant stump, blackened and hardened by fire. When a redwood dies five or ten more grow in a circle around the remains of the mother. It's how they reproduce. This grove had been hit by fire, maybe back in the Oakland fires in the eighties, maybe a hundred years ago. A few trees in the circle had holes burned in their bases, caves big enough for a small person to curl up in. But they were still strong.

Sitting on a big rock nearby was the Red Detective.

"Look at you," he said. "You got so many lies on you, you ain't even know the truth no more."

I shrugged and sat next to him.

"You wanna read cards?" he asked. "Or you just wanna sit?"

"I think I just wanna sit," I said.

"Too bad," he said. "I wanna read cards."

From his pocket he pulled out his dirty old Rider-Waite tarot deck and shuffled and pulled a card. The Moon.

"Told you so," he said.

"Thanks," I said.

The Red Detective was not ever actually a detective, not in the way most people think of it. He never had any clients or solved cases. Instead he'd spent most of his life on the other side, committing crimes and getting caught for it. He had a heavy southern accent that showed his parents' origins in Louisiana—a southern accent is common in Oakland, where it seems half the population can trace their roots to Louisiana or Alabama. By the time he was thirty-three, they say, and I don't know if they're right, he'd spent more than half his life in jail. He was out for three months when they got him for murder, first degree. It was a life sentence, no questions asked, if he lost the trial.

After that the story gets dim. In Oakland they say he knew how to work roots and that he "fixed" the judge, who threw the trial out on a technicality. In Berkeley, of course, they say that's racist. They say he used his intellect to find a technical loophole the judge and all the lawyers had overlooked, that his brilliant mind, honed from years of jailhouse lawyering, outlawyered the law. In San Francisco they say it was a woman, that the Red Detective was a pimp and one of his women worked on the judge until he gave in and found a reason to throw the case out.

The Silettians have another story. The Silettians say that in prison, the Red Detective read *Détection*. And although the book makes sense to almost no one else, it made sense to him. And using what he learned in that book, combined with his army of prison and street acquaintances, he found the real killer—because he had not, after all, committed the murder he had been charged with, although surely he had committed others.

But Silettians don't worry about justice. That's for courts and judges. Silettians worry about one thing only, and that's the truth.

In any case, the Red Detective was now free. Of course, he wasn't the Red Detective back then. He was, maybe, just Red. Free, but, the story goes, with nothing—no friends, no family, no money, no place to stay. First he stayed on the streets of downtown Oakland for a while, moving in and out of shelters, following the clues to learn what the streets had to teach him. Slowly, a few blocks at a time, he started moving up the mountain.

I'd met him on the Case of the Washboard Killer. I'd heard about him for years but had not exactly believed he was real. Back then he was not quite up the mountain and into the woods. He was still in downtown Oakland, huddling under awnings to stay dry. He pointed out to me the clue I'd so stupidly missed: the killer had dirt under his fingernails long after he claimed to have left the park. Sometimes we are so blind. He didn't talk to most people and wouldn't have talked to me at all except he knew who I was; he and Constance had exchanged letters when he was locked up. I set the Red Detective up in a little place in Berkeley for a while, but he didn't dig it at all. That was when he started to see that the woods were the place for him. He never thanked me, but he never forgot me either, and if I needed a pair of fresh eyes on a case he was always around.

"This missing girl case," he said. "That's why you come up here all in a funk."

"It's not a missing girl case," I said. "It's a murder case."

"Every case is a missing girl case," he said. "There's no murder case, robbery case, missing girl case. Every case is every case."

I nodded.

"I see that," I said. "I do. There's a lot going here. Definitely robbery. Definitely murder. But I don't see a missing girl case."

"You find that girl," he said, "you solve your case."

"Thanks," I said. "That's extremely un-fucking-helpful."

He laughed.

"Good luck," he said, still laughing a little. "Good luck with that missing girl."

25

THE NEXT DAY I turned the poker chip from Paul's house over to Claude. The chip was for fifty dollars. It didn't have a casino name on it. I asked him to look into it.

"Right," Claude said. "Of course." Then he blinked. "No. I don't really understand what I'm supposed to do with that. Sorry."

"Start with where it came from," I said. Then I realized Claude didn't know how to do that. "The first thing to look for is a maker's mark of some kind. So go over the thing with a magnifying glass. There's a few reference books on poker chips for collectors. They'll have them at the big library at Civic Center. So go there next. And if that doesn't pan out, I know a guy."

"A guy?" Claude said.

"A guy," I said. "But he's the last resort." The poker chip man could be unpleasant, and besides, I figured Claude could use the practice. Claude was excellent at library research, but he was still working on putting all that research together into a narrative that was not only possible but true. They aren't teaching that in school these days.

"Okay," Claude said. He sounded relieved to have some clear instruction at last. "I'm on it. Oh, and I got that address you wanted. It's in your email."

"Just tell me," I said.

"I don't remember," he said.

"You do," I said.

"I'll get it wrong."

"You won't."

He sighed, and gave me the address in Concord.

It was dark when I parked my car on Hemlock Drive in Concord, a bland East Bay suburb. Number 404 Hemlock was a low-slung little suburban number with a patch of green lawn in front. I got out and rang the bell.

A man answered the door who looked pretty much like I expected. He was white and forty-ish and strong and wore blue jeans and a T-shirt.

"You Craig Robbins?" I asked.

"You are?" he said, wary.

"Claire DeWitt," I said, flashing my ID. "PI."

He looked at me blankly.

Craig Robbins worked for the city towing cars—cars that were stuck, cars that were abandoned, cars that died, and, in Paul's case, cars whose owners died.

"I'm investigating Paul Casablancas's murder," I said. "You found his car."

"I did?" he said.

"You did. Ford Bronco. Old one. You found it by the side of the Bay Bridge, four fifty a.m., forty-nine days ago."

Craig wrinkled his brow. "I *did,*" he said, surprised.

"What was the trouble with the car?" I asked.

"Alternator," he said. "Guy probably either called highway patrol or hitched a ride. Got no records. He was long gone when I got there."

"How did the car feel?" I asked. "When you went inside to check it out. How did it feel?"

"Feel?" he said. "What do you mean, feel? Like, did it feel like leather?"

"No," I said. "How did it feel?"

He frowned. "I don't know what you're talking about," he said. "I'm not following. I didn't really feel it."

"What I mean is," I said, "what did it feel like?"

"I didn't, like, put my hands on it with any intent," he said. "I just got in and got out."

"When you were in the car," I said. "What did it feel like?"

"Like a car," he said, sarcasm creeping in. "It felt like a car."

I looked at him. I looked at him until I saw the shadows underneath his eyes, shadows he'd been trying to hide with his sarcasm and his cheap defenses.

"Look," I said. "I'm the only person you can tell this to. You can pass it on over to me and get rid of it, once and for all. Me and no one else. And if you don't, if you choose to hold on to it and pretend it doesn't exist, you will be stuck with this for the rest of your life."

He looked at me. "You're crazy," he said. "I think you should go. I think you should go now."

"What did it feel like?" I asked again. "This is your last chance. Your last chance to get rid of it. Forever. For the rest of your life."

Craig Robbins made a face and sighed and looked around and scowled and then finally said: "It felt . . . dark. Like a very dark place. It felt like a place where you could get lost. Where people could forget about you and . . ."

Craig Robbins started to cry, angry tears forcing their way out.

"It felt," he choked out, "like being lost in the woods."

26

IN CONCORD I GOT *pupusas* and plantains in a Salvadoran restaurant and then drove back home. Back at my place I lit a joint and watched *Law and Order*. During the third episode the phone rang. I let the machine get it.

It was Kelly again.

(Mumble mumble) are you there? I know you're there. Pick up. Pick up. Pick up.

I did.

"Hey," she said when I picked up, as if we spoke every day. "Do you remember the bookmobile?"

"Yeah," I said. "Of course."

"The Cynthia Silverton books?" Kelly said. "Or comics or whatever you call them?"

"Yeah," I said again. It stung a little that she asked, for some reason. That it didn't go without saying. That maybe our life together had been as ephemeral as all that.

"Go look online," she said. "Look for Cynthia Silverton. Then call me back."

She hung up.

I made a cup of green tea and thought about what a bitch Kelly was. How she'd always been a bitch.

Then I did what she said.

At first I thought I'd spelled it wrong. I tried it a few different ways and realized I'd been right the first time.

There was one short entry in an online directory of printed comics, which was stolen and republished thirty-eight times:

> Cynthia Silverton: limited run comic privately printed in Las Vegas, Nevada, 1978–1989. The adventures of Cynthia Silverton, teen detective and junior college student. Extremely rare, but of limited value.

And one blog post, above a photo of the comics themselves:

> *Complete set of the* Cynthia Silverton Mystery Digest. *Or so I think. There's little information to be had on these obscure 70s/80s mystery comics. No reference in Grafton or Heinz. Teen detective Cynthia Silverton of Rapid Falls solves mysteries, fights her nemesis, Hal Overton, and attends junior college, where she studies criminology. Bizarre and wonderful.*

In a few minutes online I had the blogger's phone number and address, and when I was done I didn't call Kelly back. I got in my car and drove over to Oakland to meet Bix Cohen, blogger.

Bix Cohen lived in a big apartment in the high-crime part of Oakland, where heroin addicts roamed free and glass windows were there for breaking. It was dull and drizzling when I got there. He lived in a big industrial building surrounded by abandoned lots, empty except for random pieces of furniture and broken glass and the other strange things that accumulated in urban blank spots—weeds, dirty pieces of clothing, used condoms, fast food wrappers, unidentifiable pieces of plastic and leather.

On his block were three other cars, two of which looked old: an '85 Merc and a '91 Olds. The hood on the Merc was popped. I figured the third, a little '98 Honda, was Bix Cohen's. I pulled up in front of his house and took out my phone and called him.

"So you're *who?*" he said again after a few minutes.

"Claire DeWitt," I repeated. "I'm a private eye. And I think you can help me with a very important case."

"Wow," he said. "You're sure you have the right guy? I'm not really important."

"Don't sell yourself short, Bix," I said. "You could be the key to the whole thing."

"Well, okay," he said hesitantly. He wasn't buying it. Most people wouldn't know the truth if it bit them in the ass and paid for the privilege. I could hardly blame them. "So you wanted to meet sometime?"

"Sometime like now," I said. "Like right now."

Bix came downstairs and he didn't trust me at all. Smart man. He was early-thirties-ish. He wore glasses and a black T-shirt and jeans. I guessed he worked in a bookstore and I guessed close: he was a book dealer. He stood at the doorway without the door fully open, as if that would prevent me from coming in.

"I don't understand," he said. "No one else has them?"

"No one," I said.

"I don't know," he said. "I would feel better meeting in a public place."

"Of course," I said. "I understand that completely. But I would feel better seeing the books right now."

We looked at each other. I liked Bix. He had more spine than I'd imagined.

I took out my wallet and started slowly taking out one-hundred-dollar bills.

After one he didn't budge. Two and he shifted in place a little, wobbling from one foot to the other. Three and he sighed deeply.

"How's the book business these days?" I asked.

"Fine," Bix said, staring at the money.

I held out two hundred-dollar bills to him. They were nice and new from the bank. Little things mean a lot. No one's giving you jack shit for a pile of crumpled fives and tens.

"Two to let me see them," I said. "All to buy them."

He took the two. "Okay," he said. "Fine. Come on upstairs."

I followed him up the stairs.

Bix made tea. The apartment was huge by Bay Area standards —over twelve hundred square feet, probably close to fifteen hundred—and full of books, magazines, and other things on paper. Bix also collected other strange things; a collection of glass eyeballs filled one shelf, old teapots in the shape of monkeys, cats, and other animals filled another. On a big wooden table were stacked the Cynthia Silverton books, one hundred and eight of them. I looked them over. They were the right books, all right. Just glancing at them brought a flood of memories. Passing them around classrooms with Tracy and Kelly. Having one stolen on the G train and fighting with the girl who took it. Lying in bed reading about Cynthia's struggles with Hal Overton, her nemesis.

"Where'd you find 'em?" I asked.

Bix sat on an old red velveteen sofa in the living room and crossed his legs.

"Honestly?" he said.

"Nah," I said. "Let's have the bullshit talk first."

"I found them in the garbage."

"Honestly?" I said.

"For real," he said.

"What do you want for them?" I asked.

"Oh," he said right away. "They're not for sale."

That means expensive.

"I'll give you five hundred," I said. "Right now. For all of them."

He made a face like he was about to break up with me. "I don't think so," he said.

"A thousand."

He made the face again.

"Two grand," I said. "I can come back in an hour with it."

He made the same face.

"You own this place, don't you?" I said.

He smiled. "Yeah," he said. "I own the building. I bought it from the city in this homesteading deal for like five bucks."

"You know I'm a private eye," I said. "We could barter. I can find out pretty much anything. About anyone."

He shrugged. "I feel pretty good about what I know," he said. "Unless you can solve, like, you know, who Kasper Hauser was and who killed Kennedy, stuff like that."

"The crown prince of Bavaria," I said. "And E. Howard Hunt."

"Wow," he said. "Huh. But now, you know, there's nothing to barter with."

"I could dig up dirt on you," I said. "Blackmail is always a possibility."

"Yeah, well, hmm," he said. "Good luck with that. I'm not famous or anything. I mean, I could be out there fucking dogs in the street and I don't think anyone would really care."

"Except the dogs," I said.

"Oh, sure," he said. "Of course. Good point. And you know, I would never fuck a dog. That would be, just. I mean, I *like* animals. Not like that. In a good way."

"I didn't really think you would," I said. "Good tea."

"Thanks," he said. "It's picked by monkeys in Thailand. Or so they say."

"Wow," I said. "I guess it's good that they have jobs."

"Yeah," he agreed. "I guess. Although, not having a job is kind of nice too."

"I bet," I said.

We looked at each other.

"You can read them here," he said.

"You sure?" I said.

"Sure," he said. "Only not now. I have a date."

"I could stay when you go out," I suggested.

"I don't think so," he said. "If you don't leave, I'll call the police. All I have to do is press the button." His phone was in his hand, 911 already dialed in. Bix was a smart cookie.

"Okay," I said. "Tomorrow?"

"Another day," he said.

"Tomorrow's another day," I said. "Hopefully a better one."

"Another day," he said. "I think we need to leave it at that."

"Can I ask you something?" he said as he walked me downstairs to lock the door behind me. "Is India Palace good for a date?"

"Do you want to get laid?" I said. "Or do you just want to talk?"

"Are both an option?" he asked.

"You'll be fine with India Palace," I said. "Let's see how you do tonight and we'll talk about the next step."

"Cool," he said. "Thanks."

"Tomorrow?" I said.

But Bix wasn't stupid. "Another day," he said, and shut the door behind me.

27

THAT NIGHT I DREAMED ABOUT PAUL. I dreamed about the first night we'd spent together, only in my dream we were on a boat, floating in a deep black sea, the two of us alone. When my clothes were off and he saw my scars and tattoos and bruises for the first time, he wanted to ask about each one. But I didn't want to talk about how I'd been shot and marked and cut. His body was smooth and unmarked except for a few bad teenager tattoos and one neat, barely visible surgical scar, the kind rich people have, where an appendix used to be. He put a hand on my foot, over the four-leaf clover I'd put there myself long ago in Los Angeles. It was faded but still there, just barely.

"I bet there's a good story behind this one," he said, smiling.

"There's a story," I said, and I smiled back, but I didn't tell him. I let him think what he wanted. It wasn't really the kind of story you tell someone you like.

In real life, when Paul asked about the clover, I got out of bed and lit a joint, and when my phone rang I answered it, happy for the distraction. It was a case. Always a case. When I came back to bed that conversation was done. Something else was done too, done and gone. Something I'd killed.

In my dream I stayed in bed, on our boat, just the two of us, his hand on my foot, and I let the phone ring and we looked at the clover together and I said, *When I put it there I dreamed of you. Of this night. I put it there for you.* I handed him my heart, bloody and bruised.

Go ahead, I said. *Take it. It's yours.*

28

I T WAS SUNDAY AND that night I had my usual appointment with Claude for seven o'clock. He rang my buzzer
at 7:14. There was no automatic entry in my building—I
wouldn't have lived there if there were—so I went down to let
him in. He was sweaty and wearing a soccer outfit.

"I'm sorry," he said. "Game went late."

I looked at him. "You play soccer?"

Claude gave me a tight smile. "Every Sunday," he said. "Since
I was a kid."

"Really?"

"Really," Claude said. "Every week. I think I mentioned it before."

"I don't know," I said. "You sure?"

Claude's smile got wider and tighter and showed more teeth.
He had really good teeth.

"Well, anyway," he said. "I'm sorry. I didn't have time to eat,
and I'm starving."

"Name your poison," I said. "I'm buying."

Claude chose the Enlightened Mistress's place. We talked about
Paul. We had other cases going on but they weren't very interesting. The Case of the Misunderstood Manager—the guy'd hired
us to prove he didn't steal twenty grand, which I was pretty sure
he *had* stolen. But he was spending most of it hiring us to prove
otherwise, so I didn't feel too bad about it; apparently the universe decided to use him as a conduit for my money. And the Case

of the Confused Academic—a college professor had hired me to find out if his wife was cheating, not work I ordinarily did, but he offered me a ridiculous amount of money and I took it. A mistake. I'd told him a dozen times his wife was not actually cheating, but he kept throwing more money at me to keep digging. He had an inheritance, but not one big enough for this particular habit. Soon I would cut him off—these situations can turn unwholesome fast. Maybe I'd have a talk with him and his wife, try to iron it all out. Maybe not. And the miniature horses.

That left Paul.

"I want us both working on this full-time," I told Claude. "Forget about everything else. This is our case."

"Sure," Claude said. "What do you want me to do?"

"Good question," I said.

I got the lemon chicken. Claude got the beef and broccoli and wonton soup. He still had his little soccer outfit on.

"So who do you play with?" I asked.

Claude stopped with a wonton halfway to his mouth.

"Excuse me?"

"Soccer," I asked. "Who do you play with?"

"A bunch of guys from Berkeley," he said. "Mostly international students. Not too many Americans are into it."

"How'd you get into it?" I asked.

"My parents are from Europe," he said. "My dad is Nigerian-French. My mother is Vietnamese-French by way of Oslo. They moved to Berkeley when I was a kid."

"Wow," I said. "They should open a restaurant. I would eat there."

"Well, they're both academics," Claude said. "My mom does philosophy-literature stuff and my dad does, like, theoretical physics slash philosophy. They kind of let him write his own ticket in terms of a job description."

"I'd still go to the restaurant," I said.

Claude nodded. "I probably would too," he said. "As long as someone else was cooking. My parents didn't do, like, parent stuff."

"Mine either," I said. "So are you, like, an American? Have I been fucking up your payroll this whole time?"

"You 'pay me' off the books," Claude said, making quote marks in the air. "As it were. And yeah, I've been a citizen since I was five."

We ate in silence for a few minutes.

"Any siblings?" I asked. I was still hoping against hope for a Nigerian-Vietnamese-French-Oslosean restaurant to come from this family.

Claude sighed. "No. No siblings. Are you okay?"

"Yeah," I said. "Of course."

We finished our meal and I told Claude to keep going with the poker chip. It wasn't much, but it was something.

As Silette wrote: "Information is what paupers trade in when they have nothing left to sell."

29

THE NEXT DAY I WALKED across Chinatown to City Lights Books on Columbus. Mike was behind the counter. He was about forty-five, with long gray hair and tattoos up and down his arms, most of them names and logos of bands; the Misfits, the Cramps, the Clash. I'd met him about five years back on the Case of the Kleptomaniacal Occultist, and although we hadn't planned to keep in touch, he worked in the closest bookstore to my house, so we had. Mike was sarcastic in a way that he thought hid his battered heart but that actually laid it bare.

"Claire," he said. He looked semi-amused whenever he saw me, as if my existence was a smirk-worthy joke. Which maybe it was.

"Hey, Mike," I said. "How's life treating you?"

"Not as well as some people," he said. "Better than others."

"That's a good attitude," I said. "Do you have this new book called *An Outback Full of Clues*? The subtitle's *The Story of Australian Detection*."

He looked up the book in his computer. "Shame about Paul Casablancas," he said. "Didn't you guys used to date?"

"Briefly," I said.

Mike frowned. "I thought you guys were, like, a thing."

"We were friends," I said.

"I heard you were in charge of the investigation," Mike said. "We don't have a copy. I'll see if I can order it for you."

"Well, I'm in charge of *my* investigation," I said. "Not anyone else's. Yeah. Let's see if you can order it."

"Isn't that like some breach of ethics?" he said. "Like a doctor operating on himself? It isn't shipping for a few more days."

"Well, maybe," I said, thinking of the times when I'd given myself a few quick-and-dirty stitches on bad days. "But I'm doing it anyway. And I thought it came out last week."

"You knew Lydia, too, didn't you? Shame," he said again. "I knew them too. Both of them." He typed in a few more words. "Publication delayed. But we'll get it as soon as anyone does. I can hold a copy for you."

"I didn't know you knew them," I said.

"Haven't seen her in years. She's not exactly a book person. But we were both in bands, you know, back then. You probably heard of us. The Percolators."

"Oh, right," I said. "Wow. That was you?" I'd never heard of them. "And that was when Lydia was in the . . ."

"The Tearjerkers," he said. "Her first band. Or her second. But, you know, that was the band that got kind of big. Kind of. We opened for them a few times at the Ritz. Back then Lydia didn't look at guys like me. And I'm sure she still doesn't."

"What kind of guys did she look at?" I asked.

"Well, back when I knew her—in the eighties and nineties— she fucked rock stars. And rich guys."

Men always said that about girls like Lydia, as if they had the right to fuck them, and the girl had wrongly allowed someone else in.

"Really?" I said. "Like who?"

Mike shrugged. "I didn't know any of them. You know who knew her well, who's still around?" he said. "Delia Shute. That woman who makes those fancy Barbie dolls? She had a big show at MOMA last year?"

I nodded. I'd heard the name.

"She'd know. Didn't Lydia give you her name?"

"Oh, yeah," I said. "She did."

When I left the bookstore I drove up to San Rafael in Marin County. I parked in a parking lot off Fourth Street and walked around town a little. In a bookstore a woman was reading tarot cards. In front of an Indian restaurant a waiter yelled at someone on the other end of his cell phone.

In the guitar store, Jon, the owner, was stringing up a mahogany Favilla behind the counter.

"Hey," he said. "Claire. Sorry I didn't call you back. I was actually just about to. You didn't need to come all the way here."

"It's okay," I said. I looked at the guitar. "You know one of Paul's stolen guitars was a Favilla, right?"

"Wait," he said. "I thought that's why you called."

"No," I said. "I called just because I did. Why did you think I called?"

"I could have just explained," he said. "It's the tiniest thing. You didn't have to come here."

"I'm old fashioned like that," I said. "No worries."

"It was totally not worth the trip. Do you have my email?"

"I like to talk to people in person," I said. "Let synchronicity get involved. See what fate has to say. Keeps things lively."

"Right," he said, eyebrows raised as a shorthand way of saying *I think you're an idiot.* I was used to it. "Well, this *is* Paul's guitar. But he sold it to me like a year ago. I didn't realize because I'd totally forgotten about it—it was kind of trash and basically needed a whole lot of work, so I'd put it in the back and totally spaced it. He traded it along with a Tele copy for a Mayqueen. I never would have bought it, but we did a trade, and, you know, it was Paul. But I knew there was something off about that list, so I checked my records. I'd totally forgotten. Sorry it took me so long."

I'd sent him the list of missing guitars as soon as I had it. Jon and Paul, like most of their friends, constantly bought, sold, and traded instruments with each other. It was almost a communal collection, with guitars, effects, and amplifiers floating around from one to another, going out with the tide on eBay and coming back in at night, sometimes years later. It was entirely understandable that Lydia would have made a mistake on the list —after all, she was part of the ever-rotating ownership. Or used to be.

But for some reason I felt a sick flutter in my chest and a horrible rush of déjà vu that made me want to cry for something I had forgotten, something I couldn't remember but I knew had broken all of our hearts . . .

It was a clue. The Clue of the Missing Guitar.

Suddenly I felt like I was going to cry, and I missed Paul like hell.

"Do you have a bathroom?" I asked Jon. He pointed me behind the counter. In the bathroom I pulled an almost new bag of cocaine from my pocket. I'd bought it from Tabitha the night before. I did a quick bump on each side and went back to Jon.

"So five guitars were stolen," I said, working it out. "There were five empty stands. And one was not the Favilla."

"Right," John said.

"Any ideas what it might have been?" I asked.

Jon shrugged. "Could have been anything. I looked through some old receipts and nothing jumped out at me. Whatever it was, I don't think he got it here."

"A missing guitar," I said. "We have a missing guitar."

"Yeah, that's about it," Jon said. "Sorry you came all this way. I mean. Well."

"Yeah?" I said.

"Nothing," he said. "Just sorry you came all the way up."

"You were going to say something," I said.

"No, I wasn't."

"Right. I'm actually not sure if you knew you were," I explained. "I think it was just going to come out, after 'I mean'—"

"I don't understand what you're saying," Jon said. "Are you making sense?"

"There's something you're not telling me," I said.

"There's lots of things I'm not telling you," Jon said, a bit snarky. "I mean, do you want to know what I had for lunch?"

"Absolutely," I said.

"I don't think so," he said, and turned back to his guitar. Paul's guitar.

"When you want to tell me," I said, "call me. Okay?"

Jon looked up. "What I had for lunch?"

"No," I said. "Whatever you wanted to tell me about Paul."

"Uh, okay," he said, looking away, like you do when you talk to crazy people.

"Promise," I said. "Promise me you'll call when you have something to say."

"Right," Jon said. "Absolutely. I promise. I kind of have to, uh. You know."

I was pretty sure he meant he had to go talk to less crazy people now, and so I left. I walked to the corner. Then I stopped, turned around, and went back to the store. Jon pretended to smile when I came in.

"Are you sure you don't want to tell me something?" I said.

"No," he said. "Nothing to tell. Really."

"You have my number," I said. "You know you can call me. Anytime. Do you have my email?"

He promised he did and turned back to his Favilla. He ignored me. He ignored me until I left.

30

I DROVE BACK HOME. In my apartment I did another bump and called Bix Cohen to see when I could come look at the Cynthia Silverton books again. He wasn't in. I wasn't tired. I flipped through some books Claude got me on miniature horses. Nothing on suicide rates. That didn't mean it didn't happen.

I looked at the list of Paul's guitars. Five empty guitar stands. Five missing guitars.

One of them was not the Favilla.

Then what was it?

I called Claude and explained to him what I needed. He would go through Paul's collection, his receipts, photographs—whatever he had to do to identify the missing guitar. He added it to his list of chores.

After midnight my phone rang. I was watching Iggy Pop videos on YouTube and trying to research miniature horse suicides. I knew who it was even though I didn't recognize the number.

"Okay," Jon said. "Okay. The last time I saw Paul was a little strange, to be honest. I think I saw something I wasn't supposed to."

I felt a prickle on the back of my neck and I halfway didn't want to ask but I asked anyway: "What'd you see?"

"Well, it was in San Mateo," he said. "This Korean restaurant. Tofu House. I know it sounds vegetarian but it isn't—they just have a lot of tofu. Anyway, I stopped there before the airport and I saw Paul there, with a girl. A woman."

"Which one?" I asked. The prickling feeling spread to my upper back, in between my shoulder blades.

"Which Tofu House?" Jon asked. "I think there's only one in San Mateo."

"Never mind," I said. "*With* her? Or with her?"

"*With* her," Jon said, "I think." And somehow I knew what he thought was true.

Maybe two people in love were like two trains, racing toward each other. With a whole town of saps in the middle, not hearing the whistle blow.

31

T HE NEXT DAY I drove over to the Haight and went into
Amoeba Music. In the discount vinyl section I found a
forty-five by the Percolators. They had nothing in the
bins by the Tearjerkers.

"Yeah, they're pretty collectable," the kid at the counter told
me. "Oh, snap, check it out. We do have one." He turned and
looked behind him, where the expensive, rare records were dis-
played against the wall, safe from grubby and thieving hands.

After looking for a minute he found another forty-five. I held
out my hand.

"Uh, it's one fifty," the clerk said, hesitant. "One *hundred* and
fifty."

"I'll be careful," I said. He handed me the record. The cover
was a series of cutouts, like a ransom note, except in addition to
letters there were parts of a woman's body. *Cut to the Bone,* the
record was called. On the B-side was "Never Going Home." It
looked like it had been put together in someone's basement.

"That was before they got big," the clerk said, which I'd
guessed. I bought both records.

Back at home I listened to the Percolators first. I was surprised
that they were good. After that I put on the Tearjerkers. They
were even better.

I tried to single out Lydia's guitar and listen to just that, but
I couldn't. I looked at the forty-five sleeve while the song played
again. *Cut to the bone.*

Recorded at Skylight Studios, Oakland. Mixed and engineered by Kristie Sparkle. Lydia Nunez: Guitar; Nancy Garcia: Bass; Elia Grande: Drums. Special thanks to Delia Shute.

I googled Nancy Garcia. She was dead. Cancer, family, too young, et cetera. Elia Grande lived on a commune in Minnesota. She, maybe, would get an email. Kristie Sparkle was an herbalist living in Marin.

Delia Shute was not easy to track down. It was easy to find her work. She took pictures of Barbie-type dolls who reenacted great scenes from history. She didn't have a listed phone number. Her gallery didn't agree to pass on a message and they didn't fall for my brilliant ploy of calling with a medical emergency for Delia's cousin in Greenland who—

"We have no way to get in touch with her," the owner told me, firm and barely polite. "We are absolutely unable to pass on any message at all, under any circumstances. I'm very sorry, but there's nothing we can do to help. Nothing at all."

It's easy to find businesses who don't care very much about their customers. Delia Shute's bank was pretty good and her insurance company was surprisingly cautious, but her cell-phone provider just didn't give a shit. There's a certain tone of voice that registers as "official" to young people because they've heard it in the movies. They'll fall for it like Sinatra for Ava Gardner. *I have a warrant. National security. Reference number (redacted).* After barking a few commands and clichés, I got her address and phone number.

On a foggy afternoon I rang Delia Shute's buzzer. Her block in SoMa was quiet during the day. There was a bar on the corner called the Manhole that was probably loud on the weekends.

Delia opened the door and looked at me. She was about forty and thin and heavily tattooed, in multiple layers—one whole sleeve seemed to be a coverup of some kind, although I couldn't tell what was underneath without being obviously nosy. It was cold, and she wore black yoga pants under a red vintage housecoat with a nautical pattern of ropes and anchors on it.

"I thought you were the UPS guy," she said. She looked a little confused, as if she couldn't exactly grasp how I wasn't him.

"I'm not," I said. "My name is Claire DeWitt. I'm a private eye."

Everyone loves a mystery. She lifted an eyebrow.

"I'm investigating the death of Paul Casablancas," I said. No matter how many times I said it, it never seemed completely real. I didn't want it to. "I heard that you used to know Lydia Nuñez."

She nodded. "I did."

We walked up three flights of wide slate stairs and she let me into her loft. She had nearly the entire floor of a big old industrial building. I figured she'd bought it when she was young, for a steal, and she had. She was working on her dolls when I got there, this time building a scene from the Russian Revolution. I had to admit, the dolls were pretty stunning.

She showed me the Russian Revolution dolls and a scene from Luna Park, in Brooklyn, she was just starting. We talked Coney Island history for a while—Hottentots, housing projects, elephants, tattoos.

"So you're friends with Lydia," she said.

"Yes," I said. "I was also friends with Paul. I introduced them, actually."

"Fucking shame," she said, shaking her head. "Paul fucking rocked. He was the best. Once he came and picked me up when my car broke down in El Cerrito. Hardly even knew him. I used to go out with this girl Beth, they were friends. Then, like, years later we did this art project together for SF-MOMA. He wrote the music and I did this performance thing. My part was awful but his was wonderful. Fucking great. I still have the music somewhere."

"He was a great guy," I agreed.

"So what do you think?" she said. "Got any suspects, or whatever you call them?"

"No," I said. "Pretty much none. That's why I came to talk to you. Trying to dig into the past a little, just because, you know, there's nothing."

"I thought it was a robbery," she said. "You think it might have been personal? Like someone actually killed him on purpose?"

"Maybe," I said. "It sure looked like a robbery. But I'm just checking everything out."

"Well, Jesus Christ," she said. "I bet you are. Fucking shame," she said again.

"So how did you know Lydia?" I asked.

"We were kids together," she said. "Teenagers. You know. Partied. Slept around a lot."

"What was she like back then?" I asked.

"Beautiful," Delia said. "Hot. You want some tea?"

"Sure," I said. "Green, if you have it."

She stood up and headed toward the far wall, which was an undelineated kitchen.

"Yeah," she said. "I'm doing this Chinese herb thing. No black tea or coffee."

"Liver heat?" I guessed.

She nodded. "You too?"

"Yeah."

"Fucking liver," she said. "It's like the Chinese equivalent of, you know, take two aspirin and call me the morning. Except no one says that anymore."

"Right," I said. "Except it's like, avoid eating everything good, take six weeks' worth of herbs that taste like shit, and *then* call me in the morning."

She laughed. "It's like, give up everything you like, stop getting angry, and then call me next month."

The water boiled and she made us each a cup of green tea with roasted barley. Cooling for the organs. We took our tea over to a table near the windows and sat down.

"So," I said.

"Yeah," she said. "Right. Well, you know, we were kids. We didn't really have, like, families. I grew up in Emeryville, which is kind of a shithole. I guess now it's a shithole with a big mall and Pixar. My parents were kind of in a cult. A new religious movement. Let's put it like this: it was a cult in the common parlance."

"What kind of a cult? What did they believe?"

"Nothing too awful," she said. "It was like this pseudo-Buddhist thing. They meditated a lot, they were pretty spaced out. The kids pretty much roamed wild. They didn't hit us or anything. They just meditated all the time. This guy Carl was the leader. He was from New Jersey."

I made a face.

"I know, right?" she said. "I mean, who follows some guy from New Jersey? He wasn't even in the CIA or anything. He wasn't very charismatic. It's not like you couldn't escape his iron will or anything. He liked to eat Dover sole for dinner. That was the only time he got pissy—when he couldn't get his fish for dinner. Like with almonds, how they make it with butter like that? And then everyone had to change their name, for, like, this numerological thing, and they had this whole thing about eating seeds. I actually still do that, I think they were kind of right about that. You know, it's like everything in the plant is already there, right? Anyway. It was like the world's most boring cult. So, yeah, Lydia. We were fifteen or sixteen when we started hanging out. Are you from here?"

"Brooklyn," I said.

"So you know," she said. "You were a bad girl." You didn't have to be a detective to guess *that*. "Fake IDs. Sneaking into shows. Shoplifting. Guys. Normal stuff. You know. We were poor. Well, not exactly poor. Broke."

"How did you guys meet?" I asked.

"Around," she said. "Going to bars and shows and stuff. She was from Hayward but her parents kicked her out and she was always bumming around—oh, I remember now, we actually met, like, specifically. She was staying with my friend Deena in the Castro. With Deena and her mom for a few months. So we started hanging out and then she stayed with me for a while. At the time it didn't seem like a big deal—honestly, it seemed kind of glamorous, you know, being so young and on your own. Looking back it looks fucking horrifying. It looks like her parents were out of their minds. Which they were."

"What was their deal?" I asked.

"Jeez," Delia said. "Well, her dad had this whole other family, who he had no bones about making clear he liked better. And the mom, she was like this religious nut. Went to church all the time, thought Lydia was, you know, this fucking sinner. Which, believe me, she very quickly became."

"So, you guys got into trouble?"

"Oh, yeah," Delia said. "Look, if I had a kid . . ." She paused and sipped her tea. "I mean, I wouldn't suggest what we did, how we lived—I wouldn't recommend that to anyone. But honestly, it was a fucking blast. I don't regret any of it."

"How did you live?" I asked.

She gave me a look like I was being a little stupid, which I was.

"You know," she said, and I did. "Drugs. Guys. Music. I mean, Lydia was gorgeous, she was smart, she was fun. Guys would literally follow her around. That was another good thing about the cult. They were big on the idea that things always change, and you don't want to get, like, stuck or attached. So I knew it wasn't going to last, and it didn't. Your body, just, you know. You can't keep that up. You don't have the energy and you're not getting the attention. Lydia and me, we started young. By the time we were twenty-four, twenty-five, we were feeling it. We were pretty burnt. I got more into my art, she got into her music. We were lucky. A lot of girls didn't have anything else. They didn't age so well."

"So Lydia was pretty into music?" I asked. Of course, I knew Lydia was into music. I just wanted Delia to keep talking.

"She was obsessed," she said. "Most of the girls we knew just slept with musicians, but she was no joke. She knew everything, had this huge record collection, would travel anywhere to see someone she liked. And she was good. Really good. I think she's so pretty that people sometimes forget she's actually a hell of a guitar player."

"But?" I said. There's always a *but*. If there wasn't we'd all be perfect and no one would ever kill anyone and we wouldn't need detectives.

"But what?" Delia said.

"So it sounds like you both came out pretty okay," I said.

"Yeah," she said. "I think so." But there was a hesitation in her voice.

"So you guys still hang out?" I asked.

"No," Delia said. "Not for a long time."

"Why?" I asked.

"She slept with my husband," Delia said. "That was, like, ten years ago. He's not my husband anymore."

"And she's not your friend anymore," I said.

"Well, no," Delia said. "I don't hate her or anything. But we're not friends anymore, no."

"You sound not very mad," I said. "Considering."

Delia shrugged. "It was complicated. I guess—well, I guess it wasn't entirely unexpected."

I didn't say anything.

"Lydia liked men," she said. "Well, I don't know. She liked being liked by men. Let's put it like that. I mean, that shitty childhood. It kinda catches up to you. It's kinda like—I mean, I don't mean this literally, but let's say there's some kind of, you know, receptor in your body for receiving love, right? Love and affection and all that good stuff. And Lydia, with all that fucked-up stuff with her parents—it's like those receptors were just never turned on. Like, she could never, ever get—I don't think I'm making any sense."

Delia stood up and got us each more tea.

"I don't know what I mean," she said as she poured. "I guess I just want to still like her in some way. I mean, we were *close,* you know? Like teenage girls are close. And you know, I'm kind of an angry person, but I'm not really into hating people. So I don't know—I guess I made up this whole story about how it wasn't entirely her fault. 'Cause the thing about Lydia is, she never really believed that anyone loved her. Or even liked her, to be honest. She just could not believe that. Not me, not any boy, no one. I mean, here she was—*is*—so smart, so beautiful, so talented, so many people in love with her. It was like—you know when you haven't watered a plant in too long, and then you try to water it and the water rolls right off?"

I did know, having killed many plants.

"Like that," she said. "I think that's a better metaphor than the receptor thing. That didn't quite work. Like a plant that got too dry and it couldn't take any water at all. Not if you fucking drowned it. Anyway. Guys would freak out for her. Girls wanted to be her friend. Still do, I bet. And you know, she could buy it for a little while. She had no problem believing that people wanted to be with her or sleep with her or whatever. But when it came down to it, she was one hundred percent sure that no one could love her, not really," she said.

"Do you think Lydia cheated on Paul?" I asked.

Delia shrugged. "I wouldn't know. We hadn't talked in years. But in general, did she cheat? Well, she always did before."

Delia lit a cigarette and looked out the window. I followed her eyes. Outside was a woman who might have been a streetwalker or might have just been walking down the street. The woman stopped and queried a passing car. The man in the car and the woman came to terms and she got in. Maybe she was just a woman doing her grocery shopping who ran into a friend.

Mysteries never end.

"Paul was a good guy," Delia said. "He deserved better. Do you think it's true that, like, someone's soul can't rest until you find who murdered them? Until there's some justice? I read that in a book once. I don't know if I believe it."

"I don't know," I said. I knew there was something set off its axis when a person was murdered. I didn't know if it was a soul or just some pocket of the universe that needed to be set right. I tried to imagine Paul's soul but all that came to mind was a ghost like a child would imitate for Halloween, a lonely thing under white sheets, holes cut out for eyes.

Boo, the ghost said. I scared you.

32

Brooklyn

CHERRY TAVERN WAS a few blocks away from Ben's bar. It was a disjointed spot on Sixth Street; the lights were too bright and there weren't quite enough tables and the room was a strange shape. A dozen skinheads checked us out as we went to the bar and ordered bottles of beer. Tracy and I got our drinks and soon were joined by a big kid we knew named Al from Queens, who looked scary but everyone knew was just a sweetheart. Unless he drank too much. In which case he did become scary and was not so sweet anymore. But tonight he was sticking to beer. I went to the bathroom and when I came back Tracy was already questioning him.

"Yeah, I know Cathy," he said. "I think she's actually here."

"Here?" I said, sitting back down. "But we're here." For a second it crossed my mind that I was not, in fact, here. Or maybe I was here, but somehow it was a different here—a different piece of here, or the same here in a different time.

I closed my eyes and for a quick flash I saw a woman drowning in dark water, like the Anima Sola burning in flames. Instead of helping her I put on a thick pair of glasses and watched her drown.

I opened my eyes. Al was looking at me like I was an idiot.

"The *men's room*," he said.

"If you talk to me like that again," I said, "I will break this fucking bottle in your face."

Tracy laughed.

"All right," Al said. "Jesus. Let me buy you a beer."

"It's cool," I said. "Let's just not do it again."

We finished our drinks and went to the men's room. Tracy knocked first. A girl's voice called out, "Fuck *off*." We opened the door and went in.

The men's room was actually two rooms. First was a kind of bathroom antechamber with a sink and a few chairs. Through another door was the regular bathroom, which men used for its intended purpose. In the antechamber were two girls passing around a little bag of cocaine and a house key to imbibe it with. One of the girls was Cathy. The other was Georgia.

"Tracy!" Cathy said. "Oh my God! I was just thinking about you!"

Cathy kept talking while Georgia took multiple dips of the key into the little bag. Cathy was a big, pretty, cheerful girl. I knew she lived in the Chelsea projects with a large family, seven or eight brothers and sisters. She wore her hair in a fringe around her head.

Georgia was a tiny, skinny girl. Her face was pretty but mean. She had on a big vintage Persian lamb coat and wore her brown hair swept up on top of her head, and way too much makeup. It was true she was homeless. She was supposed to be in foster care but she kept running away.

"Hey, Claire," she said, her voice sarcastic and thick.

I didn't say anything and gave her a look.

What happened between me and Georgia had happened long before, but it wasn't over. There was a boy, that was true, but friendships never fall apart over boys. We had no expectations for boys; boys were innocent bystanders in the wars of girls.

I hated Georgia. Just looking at her made something burn inside me.

I thought of Chloe. Of how she seemed to want people to hate her.

Meanwhile, Tracy was trying to get Cathy to focus.

"I haven't seen Chloe in forever," Cathy was saying, her voice rushed and breathless. "I mean, for a while we were hanging out all the time, you know? Georgia, you remember Chloe, right?"

With effort Georgia tore her eyes off me and looked at Cathy.

She'd had more to drink than her friend; her eyes were bleary and red and she wasn't nearly as wired. She seemed instead like she might fall asleep.

"Yeah," she said, her voice slightly slurred. "I know her. Fucking bitch."

"Why fucking bitch?" Tracy asked.

"'Cause of what she did to Cathy," Georgia said. "How she treated her. Fucking whore."

"So what did happen?" Tracy asked. I could tell her patience was wearing thin.

"Oh my God," Cathy said. "I can't even   I mean, I can barely talk about it. Still. It was like she cut me, you know. Like she cut me right where she knew it would hurt."

"She actually cut you," Tracy prompted. "Or—?"

"No, not *actually*," Cathy said. "What she did was, she fucked this guy I liked. Well, I don't know if they actually, you know. And I mean, not just liked. He was the one—I mean the only one. Okay. Okay. It was Hank Nielson. You guys know him, right?"

We both nodded. We knew him.

"Right," Cathy said. "I've known him since we were, like, twelve. We went to this summer camp together, this camp for bad kids, and I totally fell for him. And we were friends, but I don't think he knew. Maybe he knew. I don't think he knew."

"But Chloe knew?" Tracy interjected.

"Oh my God," Cathy said. "She totally knew. Fuck. I mean, I talked about him all the time. She *beyond* knew. So this one night we're all at Blanche's, and Hank was there. So he sits with us and everything's fine, and we're drinking and drinking. And then suddenly, it's like, Chloe is flirting with him. I mean at first I thought I was imagining it—"

"You weren't imagining it," Georgia cut in. "I was there. Saw the whole thing. Chloe totally threw herself at him. It was totally fucked up."

"Totally fucked up!" Cathy said. "We went to the bathroom together and I was like, what the fuck are you doing? And at first she was all like, what are you talking about? All like, I'm not doing anything. But then it got worse and worse. She was all, like, telling him how much she liked his band, and she'd never even seen his band. And all, like, touching him and shit. Like, she kept putting her hand on his shoulder and shit. So then we go to the bathroom again and I'm all, what the fuck? And she's all, you're not doing anything with him anyway. You know, like he's fair game now. I mean, he's my friend, a really good friend, so I've always been, you know, not wanting to fuck that up, but that doesn't mean—"

She looked at me and Tracy for validation. We both nodded. This was a clear violation of the rules.

"So what did you do?" Tracy asked.

"I went home," Cathy said. She looked sad, like she was living it all over again. "And the next day there's like five long messages from Chloe on my answering machine when I get home from school. I'm so sorry, please forgive me, all this shit. And then I hear from, like, a million other people that they went home together that night. And a few days later I heard it from Hank himself. They fooled around. A lot. They totally fooled around and maybe even fucked that night."

"Wow," Tracy said.

"So, Chloe," I said. "Chloe said that he was fair game . . ."

"Right right right," Cathy said. "She was saying all this crazy shit, like he's just a guy, why was I getting so upset, I was being stupid. And I looked at her—and it was like . . . like her voice was all different but also her face. Her face was like—like it was disappearing. Like it wasn't Chloe at all. Or like the other person, the Chloe I knew, *that* was never Chloe at all. Does that make any sense?"

Tracy looked at me and we both nodded. It made sense.

Cathy had nothing else useful to say, although that certainly didn't stop her from talking. Finally we got ready to leave.

"Screw you, cunt," Georgia muttered as we were walking out, her voice slurred and drunk. "Just screw you."

I went over to her and bent down next to her chair so we were on the same level. She flinched a little.

I reached up and took a piece of her hair in my hand. Everyone had grown quiet around us, reactions dulled and intoxicated.

"Don't fucking touch me," Georgia slurred, tensing. "Don't you fucking—"

I pulled hard on her hair. She stumbled toward me with an open hand but she was fast and easy to evade, and in a quick second we were rolling around on the filthy floor, hands in each other's hair and my nails on her face, until Tracy and Cathy jumped in and pulled us apart.

33

San Francisco

THE NEXT DAY I called Josh, Paul's friend who I'd spent the night with after the funeral.

"Claire," he said. "I've been meaning to call you."

"Why?" I said.

"I don't know," he said. "I thought we could get a drink or something."

I wanted to say *why* again but I didn't.

"Sure," I said. "Can I ask you something? Something about Paul?"

"Yeah, of course," he said, but his voice held back.

"I'm not asking this out of judgment. But I need to know. It's like a doctor. Total confidence. You just have to tell the truth, okay?"

"Are you really like a doctor?" he asked.

"Absolutely," I said. "It's practically the same thing."

I was nothing like a doctor.

"Yeah," he said. "Okay. I mean, it depends on the question, I guess."

"I think you just answered it," I said.

"Fuck," he said.

"Who was she?" I asked.

"Man," he said. "Claire. Come on. It was nothing. It was so

nothing. It was like, once or twice. Paul loved Lydia. You know that."

I sat on top of my kitchen counter and emptied out what was left of my cocaine and cut it with a business card from Jon's store in Marin. I started to roll up a five for a straw but felt cheap and instead found one of the crisp new hundreds I'd tried to bribe Bix with.

"Claire? Are you there?"

I sniffed a line through a rolled hundred.

"Once or twice with one person?" I said. "Or with one or two different women?"

He didn't answer. That meant *both*.

"The whole time?" I said.

"Oh, God no," he said. "No, not until the last year or so. And I don't think any of it was serious, at all. Just, you know."

"Just what?"

He sighed. "You know. Him and Lydia were fighting a lot."

I didn't know that.

"Did they fight about anything in particular?" I asked. "Or just fight?"

"I don't know. I think it started over real things and then it was just fighting."

"Do you know who any of the girls were?"

"Dude, you can't go and, like, interrogate her. I've known her forever. She is an old, old friend."

"I promise," I said. "No interrogations. The three of us grab a cup of coffee. She doesn't even have to tell me her name."

"Would you tell Lydia?" he asked.

"Of course not," I said.

I figured she probably already knew.

That night I felt restless. I drove to the Tenderloin and bought some more coke from a girl I knew named Rhonda. She was high and not doing so well when I found her, teetering on her high heels in the rain.

"It's gettin' tough for girls like us," Rhonda said. We stood in the rain. Our transaction was completed but you can't leave these

141

things until you're dismissed. That just isn't how buying drugs works. "No one knows how to feel anything anymore. No one knows anymore. Ain't no one care. People have, like, *experiences.* Everything just another *experience.* They do things, but they don't feel it. It just all goes right through them. Like they a ghost. Like we all ghosts."

"They sure are," I said. "*We* sure are."

"You ain't one of those girls," Rhonda said. "Those feel-nothing people. You feel every little thing right down your bones. You feel everything, just like me."

"I'm working on that," I said, cool rain on my face. "I don't want—"

"Uh-uh," Rhonda said. "You ain't gonna change. Girls like us don't change. We just keep going till they get every last drop out of us. Then they pretend they miss us when we gone."

34

SIXTY-TWO DAYS AFTER Paul died, I drove up north to check on the miniature horses and to see Lydia at Paul's house, now her house, on Bohemian Highway in Sonoma County.

East Sonoma County is famous for its wine. West Sonoma County isn't famous at all. It's somewhat well known, though, for its fog, its redwoods, the wide and ever-flooding Russian River, and being the home of the Bohemian Grove, the large parcel of the county owned by the Bohemian Club. The Bohemian Club was an all-male club that started in San Francisco as a private club for artists and writers of the upper class and demimonde. Now its members included presidents, ex-presidents, and a litany of shadowy men like Henry Kissinger and Alan Greenspan, men I knew I was supposed to think were important but didn't. They met at Bohemian Grove for two weeks every year, and no one knew exactly what they did there. Conspiracy theorists claimed the club drank blood and worshiped Satan, or at least had unauthorized discussions about the federal reserve and tax schedules. Defenders claimed it was just a fun outing of a very selective club. The Bohemians themselves weren't talking.

Paul's house was adjacent to the Bohemian Grove property, at the end of a long private road in the town of Occidental. Although the land around it was owned by the Bohemian Club, their actual camp was at least ten miles away, and there was no path or road between the two, just thick redwood forest.

By the time I got up to the house, it was dark out. I'd spent the afternoon at the Spot of Mystery. No news on the miniature horses. Jake had his very best men on the job, which may not have been the same as someone else's best men, but what can you do. Lydia greeted me from the porch. She wore a pretty white dress and her hair was long and freshly colored black. She had dark circles under her eyes, and her hands shook badly, but she looked better than she could have.

Life goes on. Nothing is permanent.

The air smelled like redwoods, a woodsy, piney, smoky smell.

"Come in," she said. "I'm glad you're here."

I couldn't tell if she was glad or not. Her mouth was curled into something kind of sardonic and kind of like a smile.

"Paul told me," Lydia said as she showed me around, "sometimes at night, when they would come here in the summer, if the wind was right they could hear the music from Bohemian Grove. You'd be surprised at who's in it—all these old hippies like Steve Miller and Jimmy Buffett."

The house was in a private clearing of a few acres in the woods. It was a craftsman-inspired "cottage" from the thirties, with a stone base and wood and plaster above, sloping eaves and a big porch. A stone chimney made it look like a witch's house.

"Paul said he and Emily tried to sneak through the woods a couple times. But these guys in suits would always find them and escort them back to the border."

Lydia frowned. She knew about Emily.

"Anyway," she went on. "Thanks for coming."

"Yeah," I said. "It's going to be fun."

But something in me turned and I had a sour taste in my mouth and suddenly I wasn't sure about that.

It was late and we decided to get dinner. We drove to a fancy-ish place in Guerneville where they knew Lydia. Lydia told me about trying to get the utilities and bills switched into her name. She seemed absent and a little off—I wasn't sure if she was exactly talking to me, or to whoever happened to be sitting across from her.

"It's like no one ever died before," she said. "It's like you call the phone company or the gas people and they're completely unprepared to deal with a customer dying. As if it doesn't happen to everyone."

I had less to drink than Lydia so I drove us home, back down Bohemian Highway.

"You want to come in?" Lydia asked. "Maybe watch a movie or something? Spend the night?"

I glanced over at her in the blue dark light. She looked lonely and sounded a little desperate. Must hurt to be alone if you're not used to it.

"Sure," I said. "Sounds fun."

We were almost at Lydia's long driveway when suddenly something was in front of the car and I slammed on the brakes.

A giant black vulture stood in the road in front of the car, lit up against the blacktop by my white headlights. I looked around. On the right side of the road a gang of five more vultures, presumably its family, were eating a deer. A doe. The doe had likely been killed by a car; she was on her side, glassy eyes staring toward the road, mouth open. The vultures worked on the deer's soft center body, leaving the bony head and legs for last.

Lydia stared at the scene like she'd seen a ghost. He face turned pale and her mouth formed a perfect O.

"Oh," Lydia said. "Oh, I—"

I looked at her in the rearview mirror. Her face was turned toward me but her eyes were going the other way, toward the window. Her mouth was open the tiniest bit and her eyebrows were drawn together.

Suddenly the vulture jumped up on the hood of the car, talons scraping on the metal. Its face was red and wrinkled, ugly and angry. It stood on the hood for a second and then spread its wings as well as it could.

Then it jumped up as if to fly and slammed into the windshield, shaking the glass in its setting.

Lydia screamed.

The bird wobbled and pulled its wide wings in, stunned. It stumbled and then spread its wings again. One black wing slammed against the windshield. A smear of blood smudged the glass. The bird made a sound like a hiss or a growl, high-pitched but from deep in its throat.

Lydia stared at it, transfixed.

"Oh my God." Lydia said. She looked like she was going to cry.

The vulture opened and closed its injured wings a few times. It didn't leave.

"Please," Lydia said, voice shaking. "Please."

I looked at her. She looked terrified, broken.

The vulture stood on the hood of the car, tending to its injured wings, confused and scared. I tapped the horn lightly.

After a mean look it hopped off the hood and landed, unbalanced, on the blacktop, lit by the bright white headlights. It made another hissing, grunting sound and then half walked, half flapped off toward the woods. Once it was out of the headlights I lost track of it. The rest of the vultures kept working on the deer, undisturbed.

I drove us home.

Lydia stared straight ahead the rest of the drive to the house. When I stopped the car she got out and went inside without a word. She went in the bedroom and shut the door. A few minutes later I heard the bath running from the attached bathroom.

After a while Lydia came out of the bedroom, hair wet, body wrapped in a big white robe. She smiled a feeble little widow's smile.

"Sorry," she said. "That totally freaked me out."

"Oh, hey, yeah," I said. "Don't worry about it. That was weird."

"Yeah," she said. "Doesn't that mean something? Like isn't there some thing where you see a certain bird and it means something? Like to Indians?"

"I don't know," I said. "Maybe." But I did know: There are lots of things like that, Indian and otherwise.

Lydia frowned but tried to shake it off. There was a cabinet full of DVDs and Lydia opened a bottle of wine and put on *Born to Kill.* I got the drift that this was what she did every night, alone or with company: an old movie and a bottle of wine. She curled up on the big sofa next to me. About halfway through the movie she dozed off. In her sleep Lydia grasped and groped and squirmed, like she had the night Paul died. She began to mutter and make little sounds—grunts and squeaks.

After midnight, *Born to Kill* over, I woke her up with a nudge. Lydia, drowsy in a way that made me guess she'd taken a pill or two, pointed me toward a guest room and then went to bed. I wouldn't have known, if Lydia hadn't told me earlier, that it had been Paul's room when he was a kid. His family used to come here often, at least four times a year, when Paul and Emily were little. In the eighties, when Paul and Emily were teenagers, their father died. Then their mother picked them up and moved them back east, to be closer to her own family. Paul had moved back to California for college a few years later and stayed ever since. As an adult, he'd had the house lightly redone, moving out the children's furniture and turning his and Emily's old rooms into guest bedrooms. When he stayed here, with Lydia or anyone else, he stayed in the master bedroom. After all, he was now the master of the house.

The day before Josh had called and asked if I wanted to meet his friend who had dated Paul. I did, but not right before I saw Lydia. Carrying around the knowledge that Paul had cheated wasn't so bad; like I said, I figured Lydia knew. If she asked me about it I would tell her the truth, but I wouldn't bring it up.

But meeting the woman was different. I asked Josh if we could do it next week and he said yes. Wednesday at four we'd meet at a coffee shop in Berkeley.

I lay in bed and thought about the woman. The woman Paul had slept with. Or had an affair with or spent too much time with or whatever they'd done together. There were as many ways to cheat as there were marriages.

I couldn't sleep. I thought I knew who it might be—the woman Paul had cheated with. I'd seen Paul talk to her at a show one night. You can tell. I kept thinking about Paul and the woman from the show. It was another band playing—Lydia's band? No, a friend of Paul's. Josh? Not Josh. I couldn't remember. The Swiss Music Hall. The girl was in a white vintage dress from the sixties with a boat neck and a full skirt and a trim waist. Who was playing? They had a stand-up bass and a snare drum. The girl in the white dress was dancing by herself, skirt spinning like a dervish. A tattoo of a tree on her calf. Birds on her arms. Her hair was short and white, a lot like mine. I'd come to the club with someone else. On my way to the bathroom I'd seen Paul and the girl in a corner, whispering. Paul was leaning on the wall next to her, standing too close. Nothing illegal, but you could tell. I figured he'd fight it off. I guess not.

In bed in Sonoma I stood up and turned the lights back on and rummaged in my purse until I found a stale half-joint tucked into a book of matches from the Shanghai Low. I lit the joint and looked out the window at the velvety black nothing outside. With the fog outside, the house could have been a ship, an island.

After I finished the joint I went back to bed and closed my eyes. The girl in the white dress spun on the dance floor, in front of the band. On her face was a smile that looked like bliss. I watched her from the balcony. Andray stood next to me and we leaned on the railing, watching her.

"She ain't your problem," Andray said. "Your problem is getting right with your case."

"You always act like you know me so well," I said.

"'Cause I do," he said. "You wearin' your heart on your sleeve, Claire DeWitt."

I looked down at my arm, stained with a big smear of blood.

"You think your problem is her," he said. "Your problem is *her.*"

He pointed toward the dance floor and I saw the girl in the white dress, still spinning, dancing alone. But it wasn't her anymore. It was Lydia. She was crying and screaming, furious. She choked on her tears and howled.

"If you know me so well," I said to Andray, "why won't you talk to me?"

"That exactly why, Claire DeWitt," he said.

The next morning was foggy and cold. A hawk circled overhead. Some poor little mouse or snake was gonna get it soon. You were reminded pretty quick around here that nature was a losing game.

"It clears up by noon," Lydia said.

We sat on the porch and drank coffee. A family of deer came

out from the woods to eat in the clearing. A mother and two children. We watched them for a while, vanishing in and out of the fog like creatures from a fairy tale.

"Hey," I said. "Do you remember that band? I think we saw them at the Swiss Music Hall a few times. They have a stand-up bass? And I think a snare drum?"

"Oh, I think that's the Salingers. Female singer?"

"I think so," I said.

"Yeah, I think he uses a little cocktail drum. Same thing. When did we see them together?"

"That time," I said. "That time when . . . Wait. Maybe it wasn't you. Maybe it was Tabitha."

"I think so," Lydia said. "I don't think it was me. They're really good. Paul was good friends with the guitar player, Nita. Come on. Let's go get breakfast before you go."

She seemed a little more cheerful today, a little less bitter. I imagined the long lonely day stretching ahead of her.

"Sure," I said. "Sounds fun."

The sky cleared up just like Lydia said it would and we went for a drive south. The roads were filled with slow-moving tourists, and Lydia was quick with the horn. In between each town were thick woods and clear, open pastures.

In Petaluma, a town that was almost a tiny city, with a densely plotted Victorian downtown, we parked and walked around a bit and got a big Mexican breakfast of eggs and beans and tortillas. Lydia bought a few things in an antique store; a lamp in the shape of a Geisha, a metal nutcracker in the shape of a squirrel. I bought a vintage fingerprinting kit—some good dust left and an excellent magnifying glass.

When we were almost back at her house I said, "I know you don't like to talk about this stuff. But the list of guitars you gave me, guitars that had been stolen—one was wrong. The Favilla. Paul actually sold it back to Jon, up in Marin, before—well, *before.*"

Lydia wrinkled her forehead. "Oh," she said. "Well, that explains where that is."

"Well, yeah," I said. "But there were five empty stands in the house when the police found Paul. And we know of four that are missing. So I'm wondering. Was there an empty stand? Or is there another missing guitar?"

Lydia looked confused.

"God," she said. "I have no idea."

I let it go. Her memory for details had never been good, and as she moved forward, putting Paul's death behind her—or trying to—it was all getting hazier.

When we got back to her house she invited me in again.

"You want a tea?" she asked. "One for the road?"

I could tell she didn't want to be alone, but I had things to do. Things to do like go home and wash the death off me. Maybe I wasn't so different from everyone else.

When I left Lydia I didn't go straight down 101 into the city; instead, I veered off at the 580 and drove to Oakland. I pulled off the highway and drove to the woods and parked at the first entrance.

The ground was soft with redwood needles, which smelled strong where I stepped on them. I hiked up to the top of the mountain and down the other side. Then I took a kind of rabbit trail off the main path, deep into the woods. Spruce and oak and then redwoods again as I went downhill, which made for easier walking, just soft oxalis and ferns and a few orchids and mushrooms underfoot.

I walked around for a while but I couldn't find the Red Detective. Maybe he'd moved, or maybe I'd gotten lost. I didn't feel like going home. Instead I went to a bar I knew in Oakland. When a man asked me if he could buy me a drink I said yes, and when we went home together he smelled like lavender and soap. When I woke up in the morning he was gone. I made a cup of tea, looked through the medicine cabinet, took what I wanted, and left.

35

SEVENTY-FOUR DAYS AFTER Paul died, I started again. I called Claude and asked him to come over. We sat in my living room. I had two big overstuffed red sofas I'd found on the street in Pacific Heights, and Claude sat in one sofa and I sat in another. I gave him new instructions. We had three potentially fruitful roads to explore: the poker chip, the missing guitar, and the keys. He would keep trying to research the poker chip, and he would go through Paul's credit card bills, eBay sales, photographs, and anything else he could think of to find the missing guitar. There was nothing to do about the keys.

When he left I called Carolyn, the friend of Lydia's I'd called from the police station the day after Paul died. Carolyn met me in a café on Solano Avenue in Albany. She lived nearby in El Cerrito. I asked her some questions like they would ask on TV: Did Paul have any enemies? No. Did he have a drug problem? Anyone want him gone? Not that she knew of. Shocking.

After a few more minutes of warmups I started the show.

"Between Lydia and Paul," I asked, "was there anything? I mean, I know they were an amazing couple. But I'm just wondering—were there any issues? Any issues at all? Just, you know, normal stuff."

Carolyn made a face. "To be honest," she said. "They were, things were not—well, not so good. They were definitely having a rough patch."

"Really?" I said. "What was that all about?"

"To be honest," she said again, "it had been going on for a while. Like, the first year or two was really good. The beginning. Then, you know. Fighting and fighting and fighting. Just about dumb stuff. Jealous stuff."

"Why didn't they break up?" I asked, concern furrowing my brow.

"Oh, they still loved each other," Carolyn said. "They were trying to work it out."

"Trying how?"

A look passed over Carolyn's face as she debated with herself for a few seconds.

"Well," she said, reaching a decision. "Telling you—I guess it's like telling a doctor, right?"

"Absolutely," I said.

"Okay, so," Carolyn said. She thought she hated telling me this. But she loved it. Loved releasing it and passing it on to someone else. I couldn't blame her. "Paul had been seeing someone else. I don't know who. I wouldn't say serious, but I wouldn't say not serious. And the girl, he gave her up to try to patch things up with Lydia."

I nodded nonjudgmentally, fake sympathy on my lips, concern in my eyes. It was a fragile moment and I didn't want to spoil it. Besides, I was pretending I was like a doctor.

"When did it start?" I asked.

"Well, jeez." Carolyn made a face. "It started with Lydia. She cheated on him. With this guy. When Paul found out, that was when—when things took a turn. When they became less nice. And then, you know, he had an affair, which was not a big deal, I think, and then this other one."

"Two?"

"That's all I know about," she said.

"And Lydia?" I asked.

She shrugged. "I wasn't exactly supportive of the first," she said. "So, I don't think so, but she wouldn't have told me. I don't really go for that kind of thing. I mean, you want to have an open relationship, I'm all for it, but the lying and the sneaking—I'm not into that. I don't think it's right. Paul wasn't perfect but he was a nice guy. So, there might have been others, I don't know. She only told me about the first one."

"Who was that?"

"This guy Eric. He puts on those horror movies at the Castro?"

I nodded. I knew who he was.

She shook her head, blond curls and red lips shaking.

"The whole thing is so sad," she said. "They could have made each other so happy. They could have had this great life. I mean, that big kind of love, that's what everyone's looking for, you know? But, I don't know. It was like they took a wrong turn somewhere and they were just, like—I don't know. I don't know what I'm talking about. I'm sure it wasn't as bad as I'm making it sound."

"But what?" I asked.

She frowned. "The thing about Lydia is . . . I mean, she's like my best friend, and I love her. But it's like—"

She made a face.

"Like what?" I asked.

"Like she has—*had*—this great husband, super-successful career, the house, everything. But somehow it was never enough. There's something in her—the things that are supposed to satisfy you—they never satisfy Lydia. Not really. And after a while, you start to wonder if anything could ever really satisfy her at all."

36

THAT AFTERNOON I WENT home and found Claude in my apartment. Which is not strange. He works there. He was sitting at the big wooden table frowning over a big fat book. *Modern Poker Chip Collecting.*

He looked sad.

"The poker chip," I said.

He looked sadder. I'd wanted to give him a little time to find it on his own, but that didn't seem to be working.

"I can't," he began. "I mean, I don't—"

"Okay," I said. "You looked for a mark?"

"I found a mark," he said. "And I looked in the books. Ace Novelty in Tennessee."

"That's good," I said. "You're doing great."

Claude wrinkled his brow. "No," he said. "I'm not. Because that's as far as I got."

"Well, Ace is one of the big boys," I said. "Where do they distribute?"

"Everywhere," Claude said. "Plus, they sell direct online. So pretty much anyone in the world could have bought those chips."

"I see," I said.

"So what do we do?" Claude asked.

I sighed.

"We're going to the poker chip man," I said. "And you, pal, are coming with me."

Claude laughed nervously. "You say that like it's a threat."

"It is," I said.

Claude looked anxious.

"Lydia and Paul were cheating on each other," I said.

Claude wrinkled his forehead. He mostly kept his personal life to himself but I figured he didn't have a vast body of experience in the sex/love/emotions realm of life.

"So what does that mean for us?" he asked.

"It means," I said. I thought about it. "It means," I finally said, "that a lot of people got hurt. And that we might have more suspects than we thought."

The poker chip man lived near the peak of Russian Hill, in a big apartment that from what I'd heard his grandfather had bought during the Depression. If the poker chip guy had any money, he fooled me.

There was no point in making an appointment because he would break it. Instead we rang his doorbell at two o'clock on a Friday afternoon. In my wallet I had a few hundred dollars in cash and in my right hand I had a box. In the box was a pie.

You never knew what the poker chip man would want. You could guess, but you never knew.

"What do we do if he's not here?" Claude asked.

"We come back," I told him. "Until he is."

There was no answer. I rang the bell again. And again and again. On the fifth buzz a male voice croaked through the intercom:

"What."

"I have pie," I said. "Coconut cream."

Claude looked at me. I shrugged. It may work or it may not.

The buzzer let out a long ratchety buzz. We went in.

"It's *you*," the poker chip man said when he opened the door. His face fell. "I thought—"

"I have pie," I reassured him again.

He raised an eyebrow. We'd reached a deal.

The poker chip man was somewhere between fifty and seventy years old, white, six feet tall or more. He was dressed in a tweed jacket worn at the seams and trousers and suede shoes and looked a little like Vincent Price. He was given to dramatic Price-ish facial expressions, which enhanced the resemblance. If you saw him walking down the street you might think he was a Berkeley English professor or you might think he was an alcoholic who used to be a professor. But he was neither. He wore a magnifying glass on a cord around his neck.

The apartment was big: three bedrooms, dining room, living room, impossibly luxurious extra no-reason-at-all room, two big bathrooms, and an eat-in kitchen. Most of the space was filled with books. Books were stacked ceiling-high on the floor and every available surface. I'd been coming to see the poker chip man for ten years and the space between the stacks had grown smaller and smaller each year. Next year there would just be paths between the stacks. You always wonder how people and their apartments get like that, and it was interesting to see the process in action.

The other occupant was poker chips. Most were in glass jars of every imaginable size and provenance—industrial-size pickles, peanut butter, brass polish, and more. Some were in steel coffee cans, some were in plastic or paper bags, and some were just loose. There were thousands.

First, the man went for the pie. He sat down at a table in the kitchen, pushed aside jars of poker chips, and fished out a fork from the sink. Then he opened the box and looked at me, as if waiting for an answer.

"House of Pies," I said. "Albany."

The man looked back at the pie. He took a bite, chewed slowly, and apparently deemed it worthy.

Then he ate the pie. The entire thing. Claude watched him eat, fascinated and horrified. The poker chip man didn't seem to mind. It took about half an hour, maybe less. I checked my email on my phone and then sat on the floor in one of the pathways and flipped through back issues of *Poker Chip Fancier* magazine. I was reading the obituary of a man who'd designed chips for the Sahara and Caesar's (Geoffrey van Der Crook, born in Indianapolis, survived by a daughter who would not carry on his legacy but instead had foolishly become an orthopedic surgeon) when I heard Claude speak.

"Uh, Claire," he said. "Claire, I think he . . ."

I looked up. The poker chip man was done with his pie and he held out his hand. I came over to the table. Claude and I sat and watched him.

"Give it to him," I told Claude.

Claude dug the chip out of his pocket and put it in the poker chip man's hand. The man looked at it for a moment or two, then wrapped his hand around it and closed his eyes. Then he opened them and started studying it with his magnifying glass. Then he smelled the poker chip. He smelled it again and then lightly sniffed a few more times.

"Menthol," he said, a little condescension in his voice, as if it were obvious. "No sun fading," he went on. "Never seen the light of day. See this?" he pointed to something I couldn't see. "A dent from a fingernail. People do it when they get anxious. But this dent is deep."

"So either a very healthy person, or—"

He cut me off. Maybe we were vamping a little for Claude. "A fake nail," he said. "Which is about a thousand times more likely."

"I know that," I snapped.

Suddenly the man licked the poker chip. He made a face: *Not half bad*. I held out my hand and he handed it over and I did the same.

"Nice," I said. "Cocaine," I explained to Claude. "And cocoa butter."

"And," the man said. "A little bit of Florida Water."

African American people were about 70 percent more likely to smoke menthol cigarettes than any other race. White people use cocaine more than any other race, but the cocoa butter and Florida Water are used almost exclusively by African Americans and Latinos. And Oakland had the highest African American population in the Bay area, more than double San Francisco's.

"So, Oakland?" I guessed.

The man raised an eyebrow: *Maybe*. He looked more carefully.

"You're sure it's Bay Area?" the man asked.

"Not sure of anything," I said. "But that's what I'm hoping."

He nodded and closed his eyes again. His lips moved, quietly, while his eyes spun under their lids. He murmured softly, syllabic sounds that sounded like a language but weren't: *gore gore, scorp, pista, pista.* His murmurs became louder and more like words: *No, no, no. Yes, yes, yes.* Finally, after five or six minutes, he spoke:

"The Fan Club," he said, eyes still closed, face still in visionary rapture. For a split second, he was beautiful. "Downtown Oakland. March 5, 2010. Blackjack."

He opened his eyes and looked up at the ceiling, beauty gone.

"A losing bet," he said. His eyes rolled down and he looked right at Claude. "Never bet on seventeen."

"No," Claude said quickly, frightened. "I won't."

I stood up. Claude looked from the man to me and back again, confused. I went over and took the chip out of his hand and replaced it with a hundred-dollar bill.

"Always a pleasure," I said.

The man didn't say anything. His face went back to its normal dour look, and I knew he was wishing he'd saved some pie.

"Next time," I said, "I'll bring two."

He looked at me and nodded. We had a deal.

37

Brooklyn

I F WE'D HAD A CAR, it would have taken seven or eight minutes to get from our neighborhood to Broadway and Kent. Walking, it would have taken thirty to forty minutes. On the subway it took forty-five minutes. We stood up and went to the door, watching the train inch into the station.

"It's like they're pushing it," Tracy said. "Like there's some guy back there pushing the train into the station."

"Except he fell asleep," I said. "And now his infant daughter is pushing it."

"But then she died," Tracy said. "And now it's her ghost."

"But she's not pushing," I said. "She blowing. She's blowing a gentle, delightful breeze onto the back of the train."

Finally the train stopped with a loud, metallic *thump*.

We still had a fifteen-minute walk. By the time we found what we were looking for, we were frozen and miserable.

"I fucking hate winter," Tracy said.

"Me too," I said. "And I fucking hate this city."

"Me too. I want to move to California."

"I want to move to Florida."

"Las Vegas."

"Arizona. Is that warm?"

"I think so. I think it's like the desert."

Finally we got there, a big industrial building that took up a city block. The door was unlocked and we entered into a dark, empty lobby. Through another door we heard a sound; guitars, or something like them. The door was a big sliding number and to open it you pulled a counterweight on a chain. We both pulled together and slowly the door creaked open.

On the other side was a giant empty space. It was dimly lit and you couldn't see where it ended or exactly where the ceiling was. The only area you could clearly make out was a circle near the center, where a makeshift stage had been set up and a half-dozen or so people milled about, lit by an industrial light overhead.

"I just realized I've been here before," Tracy said. "It looked different. It was a Thursday night. There was like a club in here. Chloe took me. A band was playing. There was a bar over there —"

She pointed to the far rear wall.

"And these girls who were like go-go dancers over there —" She pointed to the left. I could almost see the night she described; I'd been to a dozen like it.

"Who was playing?" I asked.

"CC and those guys. Vanishing Center."

"Chloe wanted to see them on her day off?" I asked.

Tracy bent her head to one side. "At the time it seemed like it was just a party where they happened to be playing."

We walked toward the stage.

"That's them," Tracy said.

As we got closer I saw she was right. It was Vanishing Center. Behind them was a canvas banner with their logo: a coffin with the words TIME'S UP inside.

No one noticed us as we walked up to them. Vanishing Center was setting up on stage, without CC.

It looked like a fight might break out. Stiv Black, the bass player, was arguing with Johnny Needle, the guitar player, about setting up the stage.

"Listen, shithead, I told you a million times, I don't want any cords along the front of the stage."

"So fucking move them."

"You put them there, you move them, dickhead."

First we went up to Ace Apocalypse.

"Hey," I said. "We're —"

"Hey, no chicks," Ace said, looking at the band. "I fucking told you. And they're like twelve."

"We're not with them," Tracy said. "We're looking for Chloe. She works for you. Have you seen her?"

"Holy shit," he said. He looked at us for the first time. "Chloe?"

"Chloe," Tracy said. "When was the last time you saw her?"

"Thursday," Ace said. He frowned. "Last Thursday. Who are you?"

"Friends of hers," I said. "We're looking for her. No one's seen her since Thursday night."

"Me either," he said. "Shit. I hope she's okay. She was fucking up lately, but she was fantastic. Best assistant I ever had."

"Fucking up how?" I asked.

"How lately?" Tracy said.

"Past few weeks," Ace said. The band kept arguing on stage behind him. "Maybe months. Usual bullshit. It's like every assistant gets the same instruction manual. Showing up late. Showing up too hungover to do anything. Once, she fell asleep on set. Or nodded out or whatever—I don't know what she does."

Ace didn't know anything else. We walked to the stage, where the band was still arguing.

"Hey," Tracy said to Stiv Black. "I need to ask you something."

He ignored her and went back to arguing about the cords.

"I told you a million times, I don't need to be falling on my fucking face during a show."

"I need to ask you something," Tracy tried again. "Uh, hey—"

"You don't?" Johnny said. They all notoriously fell off the stage at least once in each show.

They both cracked up.

"*Hey*!" Tracy said. "I need to ask you a *question*."

Both men stopped and looked at the tiny girl in front of the stage.

Before she lost their attention she got out a picture of Chloe and held it out toward them. "I'm looking for this girl. I need to know if you've seen her."

"What are you?" Stiv said. "Some kind of a fucking detective?"

The two men laughed. From behind I heard Ace laugh along with them.

161

"Yeah," I said. "We're some kind of fucking detectives."

"Oh, *detectives,*" I heard behind me.

Tracy and I both turned around.

CC had come in sometime while we were arguing. He stood behind us. He wore a frayed, stained green velvet suit with no shirt and combat boots held together with silver and black duct tape.

Tracy took her picture of Chloe and held it out to CC.

"We need to know when you last saw this girl," she said. "You know her. She works with Ace sometimes. Her name is Chloe."

CC ignored us. He stepped around us and pulled himself onto the stage.

Tracy showed the picture to Johnny and Stiv. They crouched down to look. They smelled dirty, like a bar in the morning.

"Yeah," Stiv said. "I've seen that girl. But not, like, today."

"When?" I asked. "When was the last time you saw her?"

"I don't know," Stiv said. "She's just some girl. It's not like I was keeping track. You see her, Johnny?"

Johnny shrugged. Then he blinked, and looked away. "I know I seen her before. But that's all I know."

"No one's seen her for like four days," I said. "There could be foul play."

CC took off his green jacket and tossed it on the floor. A musky smell came off him with the jacket. I took the picture from Tracy.

"Hey," I said to CC. "All I'm asking you to do is look at a picture."

"I don't want to look at your stupid fucking picture, little girl," he said. From somewhere else in the building I heard another band start; angry drums, screeching guitar. "Go away. You're annoying."

Stiv plugged in his bass and checked his tuning. The guitar player did the same.

"All I'm asking you—" I said to CC.

But he cut me off. He reached into his back pocket and I saw a quick flash of silver. Like a magic trick, he suddenly had a razor-blade in his hand.

"I don't care," he said. "You can ask and ask and ask and I will never answer."

162

I felt something turn over in my stomach and suddenly I felt a kind of panicky, fearful desire. A feeling like something had been lost forever, like I'd forgotten about something living that needed me, and I was flooded with shame and regret and sickness and I knew.

I *knew*.

The feeling is always different but always unmistakable, some times wonderful and sometimes painful, but you always know it so well, like an old friend or your worst memory or your own shadow.

CC knew Chloe. CC was a clue. CC was *the* clue.

I looked at Tracy and our eyes met I saw that she felt it too. A chill crawled up my spine. Before my eyes I saw a quick flash from the dream I'd had the other night, Chloe with her face blacked out, caving in . . .

"You knew her," I said to CC. "You *know* her."

"Maybe," CC said. "Maybe not." He took the razorblade and made a small incision in his wrist, heading up to his shoulder, as shallow as a hair. A crimson streak followed behind the razor.

"Shit," Ace said, "I'm missing it." Ace grabbed his camera, a Minolta Super 8, and started to shoot. CC pulled the razor across his chest and down his other arm, slowly.

"Maybe she doesn't like you," CC said. "Ever think of that?"

I turned away. Suddenly it seemed too hot in the room.

"Sure," Tracy said. "But there's people she does like who haven't seen her either."

CC put his fingers to his incision to push out more blood. He pulled the blood down to cover as much skin as it could.

"Go away, little girls," he said. "*I* don't like you."

He flicked his fingers, flicking blood toward us. I jumped back.

"Go away," he said. "Unless you want everything I've got. I'm contagious."

Everyone laughed. I stepped forward.

"You know where she is," I said.

"Go away," CC said again. "You're boring. No one cares about you."

"I know that," I said before I could stop myself. "But I'm going to find Chloe."

"Ace!" CC called. "Do you want to kick these little bitches out or do I get to do it?"

"Try, you fucking piece of—" Tracy began, but Ace was already on his way to us. Firmly, without unnecessary violence, he put a hand on each of us and pushed us toward the door.

"Believe me," he whispered. "Just leave. I'll call her roommate if I see Chloe, okay?" He had dark stubble and smelled like a man.

"And if I catch you hanging out front waiting for him," Ace whispered as he pushed us out the door, "I'll kick your little asses myself."

38

WE ADMITTED DEFEAT and took the M back to the Lower East Side. We started at a bar on the corner of First and First. Tracy had a plan and it was a good one. We knew the bartender a little, a guy named Greg who used to drink and play in punk bands and now just drank. He was young — not yet twenty-five — but his life seemed laid out for him, a highway he would speed down to bad relationships and street life and an early death.

Tracy and I got shots of tequila from Greg and bought one for him.

"Oh my God," Tracy said, as we'd arranged. "I saw Vanishing Center at International Bar last night. Just, like, hanging out drinking. I kept trying to get CC's attention, but he barely noticed me."

"Ew," I said, according to script. "He's gross! You like him?"

"I think he's cute!" Tracy protested. "You know him, don't you, Greg?"

"Yeah," Greg said, a little proud of his association.

"Can I have another shot?" she asked. "Where does he live?"

An hour later we were slightly drunk and knew a lot more about CC. He'd been evicted from his apartment two weeks ago. Which was a squat. I didn't know you could be evicted from a squat. Soon we were at the squat, talking to a guy with a tall mohawk, wearing red plaid pants and a leather jacket and no shirt. It was on

Seventh between C and D. The guy with the mohawk smelled like he had never taken a bath and was kind of cute anyway. Or maybe because of it. The building was an old tenement, not in substantially worse shape than some of the other tenements in the neighborhood, except there didn't seem to be any doors, anywhere, and the walls were covered in graffiti.

"I mean, Jesus," Mohawk Guy said. His chest under the jacket was white and smooth. "You can imagine what it takes to get kicked out of here."

"Yeah," Tracy said. "What *did* it take?"

We were sitting on dirty sofas in a kind of living room in a kind of apartment. When we knocked on the door a beautiful, filthy girl a year or two older than us let us in. When we said we were asking about CC, she rolled her eyes and called for the man with the mohawk. She called him Boss Man.

"The first thing was, he shit on the floor," the Mohawk Guy said. "I mean, we don't have many rules here, but that's one I'm okay with. I mean, the toilets are backed up a lot, but, you know, shit in the trash can or something. Jesus."

"I know," Tracy said. "Jesus."

Tracy had the amazing ability to drag anyone into conversation, to make anyone feel as if she was on their side and in complete sympathy with their experience. Like she too had experienced the shitting on the floor versus using the trash can dilemma.

"And then," Mohawk said, "there was the whole thing with the razorblade." His hands were big and the ends of his fingers were square. His hands looked older than his chest.

"Right," Tracy said. "What exactly happened with that?"

"All I'm saying," Mohawk Guy said, "is blood is *not* cool. I mean, you don't know who's got what around here, you know? You want to play with knives, fine. Not on people's beds, man."

"Wow," Tracy said.

"Wow," I agreed.

"I know," Mohawk Guy said.

"So you have no idea where he is now?" I asked.

"Sorry," Mohawk guy said. "I mean, I seen him around from time to time, but I pretty much try to avoid him. He's bad news.

Hey. So my band is playing at Hell on Sunday. If you guys aren't doing anything."

We knew Hell. It was an S&M club on the west side where punk bands played on the off nights.

"That's so cool," Tracy said, and I couldn't tell if she was still in character or really thought it was cool.

We took a flyer for his show and thanked him for his time and left. We walked back up to Sophie's and got a beer.

"So," Tracy said. "We're back to nothing."

"Basically," I said.

"Fundamentally," Tracy said. "Essentially."

"Nothing."

"Less than nothing."

"Nothing with nothing subtracted."

"I gotta pee."

I drank my beer while Tracy went to the bathroom. When she came back she was holding a piece of paper in her hands and smiling.

"What?" I said.

She showed me the piece of paper. It was a flyer.

"It was on the floor," she said.

THE DELINQUENTS ★ THE MURDER VICTIMS

JUNKIE WHORE ★ VANISHING CENTER

TOMPKINS SQUARE PARK FRIDAY . . .

It was Friday. The show was tonight.

"Look," she said. "We found CC."

I smiled. "Wow," I said. "We really are the greatest detectives in the world, aren't we?"

39

San Francisco

THAT NIGHT I WENT to the Fan Club with Tabitha. She met me at my place and I drove us to Oakland. Tabitha was wearing a long dress from the seventies that was dirty around the hem from the city streets. Supposedly she was a writer, but really she watched movies and did drugs all day. She'd written a few books that were required reading in college courses —a book on film noir, a book on detective fiction—and the royalties kept her afloat. It seemed like she kept getting advances for new books but never wrote one. Maybe it was just one advance for one book that she'd stretched out for years.

The Fan Club was just outside of downtown Oakland, in a neighborhood where the police wouldn't mind an after-hours club too much. It was a typical gambling joint: dark, bad music— in this case bad hip-hop and R&B—and full of people who work nights: prostitutes, waiters and waitresses, bartenders, strippers, shift workers, filmmakers. There was a bar and gambling tables —poker, roulette, and craps—and that was about it.

The ladies' room was like an addict's fantasy of a ladies' room. Stalls with toilets that had actual tanks, with solid white tops, which you likely could have snorted clean to good effect. The sinks were freestanding types, but along another wall a kind of shelf at shoulder height provided the perfect venue for even more cocaine, which two ladies were taking of advantage of as we entered.

The two women, one white and one black, were past thirty and my guess was they were working girls on a date, their man or men busy in the main room. Or, more likely, in the men's room. Whoever they were, they had high heels and a lot of makeup and leather jackets and hair that had taken hours and a lot of money. The black woman had a gold cap over her front tooth with a five-pointed star cut out.

Tabitha wasn't shy.

"Where'd you get that?" she asked right away. She was asking about the coke, not the tooth. "Do you think you could introduce us? Is that Albert's? Is he here?"

There was a reason I'd invited Tabitha. The white girl held out a rolled-up twenty to her.

"Go on," she said. "You can get the next one."

Tabitha smiled and helped herself to a long, deep snort. She passed the ersatz straw to the black girl, who held it out to me. I took a fair enough serving.

"Oh my God," Tabitha said. "This is really, really good."

"You know Albert?" one woman said.

Tabitha nodded. "But this isn't his," she said. "This is way better."

"I'll introduce you," the other women said. Sisters under the skin. "You know Julio?"

"In San Mateo?" Tabitha said. "He's still around?"

They talked cocaine for a while—common acquaintants, after-hours clubs, quality and cuts. Then Tabitha brought the conversation around to our mission.

"We're actually here because we're detectives," Tabitha said. I bristled a little at the *we*. "Not cops. Private eyes. My friend here is investigating a murder case."

The women's eyes widened.

"Like *Forty-Eight Hours Mystery*?" the white woman said.

"Exactly like that," I said, and tried to sound serious and sane like someone on *Forty-Eight Hours Mystery*.

"Or that other one," the black woman said. "*The First Forty-Eight*."

I nodded and tried again to look like someone on a TV show who wasn't the villain. Or the victim. Or the disturbed witness who you believed only because she didn't seem competent enough to come up with a lie.

"You really a detective?" the black girl said.

"For real," I said. "That's what I do."

"Isn't taking drugs on a case, like, invalidating?" the white girl said. "Won't that be, like, inadmissible and shit?"

"Well, psychologically, maybe," I said. "It could complicate things. But legally, I can kind of do whatever I want. I don't work for the courts or anything."

"Wow," the white girl said. "So, you're investigating a murder?"

"I sure am," I said. "Actually, we have reason to believe the victim was here . . ." *The victim, the victim,* I told myself, *no one I know, just a victim.* I paused for dramatic effect ". . . with the murderer."

The girls each shook a little and almost jumped. Then they both giggled.

"Look," I said, reaching into my bag. "I've actually got a picture of him—"

I took out a picture of Paul that I had found online. He and Lydia holding hands on the street in Los Angeles, circumstances unknown. They looked happy. They looked like two people in love who could possibly stay that way forever. I'd picked it because he was smiling, and you could see his face clearly. He looked like the Paul I knew. Had known.

"Oh," the black woman said. "Oh, oh, oh. I know her. I mean, I seen her. Poor little thing—she got killed?"

I felt something turn in me, something shift gears. Tabitha noticed and looked at me sideways.

"No," I said. "Him. The guy."

"Well, I seen *her,*" the black woman said. "Bought some yay off me, her and her skinny little boyfriend. Cute, but not like that guy." She pointed a long nail at my phone. "Not a man like him. A boy."

I felt a shiver up my spine. I didn't know what it meant. But I knew it didn't mean anything good.

The white woman shrugged and went back to her cocaine,

170

Tabitha along with her. The black woman looked at me long and hard and I realized she was the smartest person I'd met that day.

"You really a detective?" she said.

"Yeah," I said. "Really."

She looked at me again. "My brother's up in Quentin. Also murder. Couldn't find no one else to blame it on so they put it on him."

"He didn't do it?" I asked.

The woman gave me a long, tight look. "My brother a fucked-up kid. He did a lot of shit. But not that. I know it for a fact. I know where he was, what he was doing, all that."

I took out a pen and wrote my phone number on a napkin and gave it to her.

"Call me," I said. "Maybe I can help."

The woman looked at me.

"Yeah, okay," she said, wary but wanting to hope. "I just might do that."

The conversation drifted. Tabitha was having a good time with the girls; I wandered away and came back a few times. I talked to a few other people: no one else knew Lydia or Paul. The end of the night rolled around, our last chance to go home before the cold stare of daylight.

I said goodbye to the girls. The white girl gave me a kiss. The black girl didn't.

We looked at each other.

"You ain't lying about my brother, are you?" she said. "You gonna help us?"

From my purse I got out a little magnifying glass. Then I took the woman's hand and looked at it under the glass. Her skin was a little rough and hot and damp.

I used the magnifying glass to read her fingerprints. Her Curl of Sin was strong and pronounced. Her Moon of Pride was deeply grooved. She'd been born under a bad sign, I saw that right away. Nothing but bad luck for her. But her Line of Insight was also strong, and her Gypsy's Swirl was exceptionally placed.

If she said her brother was innocent, I believed her.

"No," I said. "I'm not lying. Call me in a few weeks, get everything you have together, and we'll talk. If I can't help I'll find someone who can. I know some lawyers."

She held back a smile that was too good to be true. I had five hundred bucks in my purse and I took out two and gave it to her for an eighth of an ounce of cocaine.

"Gimme three and I'll give you a quarter," she said.

I took out another hundred and handed it to her. She smiled when she handed me the bag.

"That's some good shit, girl," she said.

When we left the club I drove us back to the city and dropped Tabitha off and went home. I took a few more stolen sleeping pills and lay in bed until I fell asleep, my mind still chattering and raw.

When I woke up the next day my jaw felt like I'd been chewing on a lamppost all night. I spent the day watching *Monk* reruns, angry at my hangover, angry at myself, angry at the world. My thoughts tasted bitter and sounded like a cheap drum machine.

That night I called Claude and told him what I'd found out. The poker chip had led us to a club that had led us to a boyfriend. Lydia had a boyfriend.

I didn't blame her for not telling me. I'm sure it didn't seem like there was much point, now.

"Okay," Claude said. "So how do I find him?"

"You just do," I said. "To begin with, we know they met at some point. So look at the places Lydia was likely to meet men. Start there."

Claude frowned. "Where do women meet men?" he said, as if it were a mysterious question.

"Wherever they see each other," I said.

40

Brooklyn

BY NINE O'CLOCK in Tompkins Square Park it was clear things would come to a bad end. To start, the show was illegal; they'd gotten no permits or permission from the city to use the small band shell in the park. The police came up on stage to boos and hisses and screams. After a few minutes of talk with the musicians the cops agreed to let the show go on as long as they were done by midnight. The audience cheered.

"This'll be fun," Tracy said sarcastically.

"It'll be the most fun ever," I said.

"Just think," Tracy said, lighting a cigarette. "We could be in school."

"Well, that does make it seem fun," I admitted. "But I'd kind of like not to be so close to the dogs."

We were standing near the K-9 unit. A dozen officers had German shepherds on leashes. The officers looked pissed.

We wandered away from the dogs and walked around the perimeter of the crowd. The air smelled like cigarettes and pot and homeless people. Like everything in the Lower East Side concentrated into one big bloom. The crowd was squatters and homeless people from the park and kids like us and cops. All people with too much energy and nothing useful to do with it.

Junkie Whore, the first band, took the stage. They didn't really look like whores—they were all men in their twenties with bad tattoos and dirty clothes—but they did look like junkies.

"We need to get to the stage," Tracy said.

I agreed. If CC was here, he would likely be by the stage with the other musicians. We were at the edge of the crowd, but as soon as the band started to play people started slam-dancing, and it was already reaching back to us. A boy shorter than me knocked into us. I shoved him back into the crowd.

"Let's go around," I said. "Probably we can get to the stage more easily from the back."

Tracy agreed and we walked around the perimeter toward the stage. More people knocked into us. We shoved them back into the crowd. We made our way to the back of the stage, but no one was there.

"Claire."

I looked around. It was Fabian, a boy I knew who went to Bronx Science. He was kind of sort of homeless—he had a home but didn't like it very much—and so he spent most of his time hanging out down here in the park.

"Fabian," Tracy said, after hellos. "You know Vanishing Center, right?"

"Kind of," Fabian said.

"Are they here yet?" Tracy asked.

"Yeah," Fabian said. "They're in their van down on Avenue B."

Tracy and I looked at each other and smiled. Tracy looked at Fabian and suddenly she was pretty.

"Fabian," she said in her pretty voice. "I am such a big fan. I'm kind of, like, obsessed. Could you pleeeease show us their van?"

The van, a nondescript white Dodge, was parked on Avenue B across the street from the park. Fabian pointed it out while we were still on Seventh Street.

"I think the guys might be in there now," Fabian said.

Tracy broke into a run first, and I followed. I don't know how we knew, but we knew.

Chloe was in that van. We couldn't see her or smell her or feel her. Those senses are overrated.

I knew because I felt her in our bones. Because she was my

victim, and I was her detective. And when fate ties two people together, those ties aren't given up lightly, if ever.

We heard the motor start as soon as we turned the corner onto Avenue B. By the time we'd crossed the street the van was moving. There was no way we were going to catch it, but I kept running anyway. I wanted to see.

CC was driving. In the passenger seat was Chloe.

It was less than a second. Her eyes caught mine and a look passed her face — fear, loss, confusion.

CC reached over and pulled her away from the window.

The van turned a corner and was gone. Gone.

Tracy was across the street. I jogged over to meet her.

"I saw her."

"I know. Me too."

Fabian came to meet us.

"What just happened?" Fabian said, confused.

Tracy rolled her eyes at me. Then she smiled and became pretty again.

"Oh my God!" she said. "CC! I can't believe I missed him! Where does he usually go after a show? I mean, does he just hang out, or—"

"I don't know," Fabian said. "But sometimes he likes to go to Hell."

41

WEDNESDAY AT FOUR I met Josh and the girl, Paul's girl, at a coffee shop in Oakland. The girl and Josh were there when I arrived. It wasn't the girl from the Swiss Music Hall—the girl in the white dress. It was a woman I knew. Her name was Sheila and she lived in Berkeley. She owned a bar on San Pablo Avenue where bands played, including, I bet, Paul's band. I was sober and bright-eyed after three cups of tea and a real breakfast. I was turning over a new leaf, flying right and solving the case. Starting *right now*.

Sheila turned to Josh and rolled her eyes and said, "You didn't tell me it was *Claire!*"

"I didn't know you knew her!" Josh said.

"Like the one fucking detective I've ever met," Sheila said. "And you couldn't have mentioned that?"

"If you knew a detective," Josh said, "you could have mentioned *that*, you know?"

I sat down. "It coulda been worse," I said. "Believe it or not, there's people worse than me."

"It isn't that," Sheila said. "I'm just so embarrassed. I thought this would be, like, anonymous."

"I won't tell anyone," I said. "Not unless it's gonna make or break the case. In which case I will. Okay?"

"You won't tell his wife?" Sheila asked. She looked regretful. Like she knew she'd done something wrong.

"No," I said. "Not unless I absolutely have to, and I'm sure we're all in agreement that solving Paul's murder is more important that sparing you an awkward moment. So come on. Spill."

Sheila gave up the drama and spilled.

"God, I'm so embarrassed," she said again. "I met him at the bar. I knew Paul was married. I didn't know Lydia but I knew who she was. We flirted, but, you know, it was totally innocent. Well, it started innocent. He left and it was fine. But then, total coincidence, I ran into him a few days later. At Moe's. The bookstore."

"What was he getting?" I asked.

She frowned, trying to remember.

"I don't know," she said. "Does it matter?"

"Yes," I said. "Everything matters. It's not such a hard question."

She nodded assent: not such a hard question. "What'd you get?" I asked.

"I was buying a cookbook and a photography book. Chez Panisse and Man Ray."

"Did you sleep together?" I asked.

"Oh, no," she said defensively. "Not for a while. We ended up walking around Berkeley a little bit after the bookstore. He was this totally charming guy. So interesting, and he seemed so interested in me, what I did and what I thought about things. I don't know. Then I ran into him again, but it wasn't by accident — he came by the bar a few days later. His wife was on tour. He made it sound like things were pretty shitty. And we were getting along so great. Not that that makes it okay," she added quickly. Defensively.

I looked at her. "You know, it's not the end of the fucking world. People do it all the time."

"Yeah," she said. "Well, *I* don't. And it's just. Him and his wife, they didn't have that much time together. If I'd known." She stopped and frowned. "It's just hard to talk about. I mean, I liked him. A lot. He totally — well, I don't think he meant to hurt me. But he did."

I wondered what Paul saw in her. She was a pretty girl, but nothing about her seemed so interesting to me. She couldn't hold a candle to Lydia, that was for sure. I was about 99.9 percent sure she'd never killed a mouse, let alone a human. She wasn't on my list of suspects.

"Did he like you?" I asked.

Josh cringed a little but Sheila answered honestly: "No, not really. At first he seemed to, but after we saw each other a few times he lost interest."

I figured Sheila seemed nice. Easy. Uncomplicated. That could be attractive. And I figured Paul got bored with her real fast.

"Tell me something about Paul," I said.

"There was something dark in him," she said. "I don't think any girl would have changed that. I guess I thought I could make him happy. Didn't take long to see I was wrong about *that*. I don't think any girl could do that. I think there was something inside him that no girl was ever gonna touch, not me or Lydia or anyone else."

She cocked her head to the side, thought for a minute, and then corrected herself.

"I guess if he met a girl like him," she said. "A girl as weird and dark as he was. I guess if he ever met a girl like that, it could have worked."

42

THAT NIGHT THE SALINGERS were playing at the Hemlock Tavern. I went by myself to see them. Less than a dozen people came. They played old country songs, Hank Williams and the Carter family. When the singer sang it was like something in her had been split open. Like she was singing from a part of her most people didn't even know they had. Like she'd found a direct pipeline to her soul. About four people stood up front watching the band. One couple tried to swing dance but it wasn't the right music for that and they couldn't get a rhythm going. In the back some college kids yelled at each other, laughing. No one listened. She didn't stop singing.

After their set I headed to the stage, where they were breaking down and putting away their equipment. *Girl, boy, girl, boy*—I decided girl, and went up to Nita, the guitar player.

"Hi," I said. Then I realized something and I said, "I think we've met before."

"Oh my God," she said, recognizing me too. "You're that girl."

"That girl?" I said.

"That girl," she said. "That girl that Paul was in love with."

I excused myself and went to the bathroom and did two fat lines of cocaine off the top of the toilet. I looked through my bag for something more and found a Tylenol 3 I'd taken from the guy I slept with in Oakland and took two.

I waited at the bar for Nita as she finished loading up her equipment into someone's van. She was about my age but looked hardened, leathery. At the bar she got a Red Stripe and I joined her.

"That time in Chinatown," she said. I remembered. It had been a while since I'd seen Paul. We hadn't spoken since I'd gone to Peru. I walked by the vegan restaurant one night and heard someone call my name. It was Paul, having tea with Nita. I went in and sat down and had tea and a slice of carrot cake with them.

"When you left, Paul said that he'd been crazy about you. That you were like the one who got away."

I shrugged. Exes always looked attractive late at night.

"I was surprised when he married Lydia," she said. "Really surprised. I always thought he would, I don't know. That you guys . . ."

Her voice stumbled off as she realized she was saying something stupid. I asked her about the blonde in the white dress.

"Oh," she said. "That's Lucy. She's a friend of Pete's girlfriend. I know Paul thought she was attractive. You could tell. But cheating on Lydia—you think so?"

"I don't know," I lied. I didn't see any reason to burst her bubble. "It's more just that she might know something."

"I knew him pretty well," Nita said. "I don't think anything happened." She took a big inhale and let the air out slowly. "I don't know. He was different this past year. He seemed depressed." She frowned. "He was smarter than most people know," she said. "Musicians, you know, people don't expect much. But he read all the time, he knew all this weird shit. But he wanted to play, you know? Not read books all day. And for a long time, he did it. But then . . ."

"But then what?" I asked.

Nita shrugged. "I don't know. Life caught up with him, I guess. He was fighting with Lydia a lot. I think he knew things were falling apart."

"Why?" I asked.

"I don't know," she said again. "It's easy to blame her. She always wanted more from him, you know. That kind of girlfriend. The kind who gets offended so fucking easily."

From the look on her face I figured Nita'd had a lot of those girlfriends.

"But Paul wasn't perfect either," she went on. "He loved her, and he even liked her a lot, but he never really—he never seemed *crazy* about her. I mean, I think he was devoted to her, and really wanted to work things out. But something wasn't there. That extra something. Like when he saw her walk into the room—like when he saw her he was happy, you know, but it was never like *wow*. It was never that way men look when they still really love their wives. That thing in their eyes.

"And his career was going okay, but, you know, the usual bullshit. I mean, he was at that state where he was too busy to do everything he wanted but not big enough for a good manager or assistant or anything like that. He seemed, I don't know. Just getting older, I guess. Like all of us. I mean, that's the thing about this life. Playing music. You put all your eggs in one basket, you really devote yourself to something, and that basket—I mean, you don't even have to drop it. It just gets old. It gets worn out. I'm kinda seeing now that no one ends up with a lot of eggs." She made a bitter little laugh. "You sit up at night and you count people who would do you favors if you needed the money bad enough, but things don't really work like that anymore. It's all big corporations, and no one's paying you to sit in on a session 'cause you're an old friend, you know? You end up hoping someone had their first kiss to a song you wrote or took acid for the first time at one of your shows and then when they strike it, you know, strike it rich or even middle-class, they'll invite you to come play at their fucking town fair. Their corporate retreats. That's what I'm doing next week." She drank some more beer and frowned. "Dental technology conference in Encino. There's your egg. There's what's left of your basket."

Silette, bitter and old, wrote in a letter to Jay Gleason: "The detective won't know what he's capable of until he encounters a mystery that pierces his own heart. However, I tell you, it isn't worth it to know. I'd rather be the sorry fucking detective that I was before, and have my daughter back."

43

I FOUND LUCY, THE girl in the white dress, on Facebook by befriending Pete from the Salingers and then his girlfriend, Kim, and through her, Lucy. I did this as Wanda DeVille, a tattoo artist in Williamsburg, Brooklyn. Slight adjustments were made to Wanda's details as needed. She was one of about ten on-line ghosts I'd invented and maintained. Wanda had 4,289 friends, and she'd been on Facebook nearly since it began.

Lucy was thirty-two. She played bass in a band that was kind of successful. They were on a major label and their albums sold some copies. On YouTube I found a video.

There she was. The girl in the white dress. But now she was wearing a blue dress and playing bass on top of a hill. I looked at the tattoos on her arms. Bluebirds—no, blue jays. Birds who screeched and scared away other birds. Surrounding each blue jay was a wreath of roses, thorns and all.

There was a contact form on her website. In the subject line I wrote: *Paul Casablancas.* I told her I was a PI investigating his death and would like to meet. Anyone who liked blue jays and thorns wasn't all bad.

She wrote back in seven minutes.

Hey, she wrote. *I would LOVE to talk to you.*

She gave me the address for a vintage clothing store on Hayes Street and said she'd be working there every day this week if I wanted to come by.

I did.

• • •

San Francisco was a city a little in love with itself, and sometimes its inflated self-esteem rubbed off on its citizens. Eric Von Springer, née Eric Horowitz, was famous, at least in San Francisco, for being handsome and wearing vintage suits and having a waxed mustache and smoking little Indian bidis and doing interesting things. Once a year he put on a show of vintage horror movies at the Castro. He produced a music festival at Adventure Park in Berkeley every summer. He had a small company that released DVDs of silent films.

I met Eric at his place in Albany, north of Berkeley, a little Deco bungalow filled with monster toys and film canisters and movie posters. He smoked a bidi and wore a hat I couldn't quite classify and a trim gray suit. I'd told him I was looking into Paul's murder. We'd met before a few times but briefly: once after a movie at the Red Vic and then again at a party in Noe Valley and then some other night, some other time.

"So you were friends with Paul, right?" Eric asked. We sat in his living room. "I used to go out with his friend Lindsey. You know Lindsey, right?" he said. "From the Trunk Murderesses?"

"Yeah," I said. "Aren't you friends with Ray Broderick, too?"

"Oh, yeah. He's in Sweden now. You know Cooper, right?"

"Cooper Daily?"

"Cooper Jones? That guy who does the book fair."

"Oh yeah, right," I said. "He always has good stuff. I got these cool vintage criminology books from him last year."

We looked at each other for a minute.

"And you know Lydia Nunez," I said.

He tried to look innocent. I gave him a give-it-a-rest look. He groaned and shook his head.

"Jesus," he said. "Does everyone know?"

"Nah," I said. "I'm a detective. I know lots of stuff other people don't know."

"Jesus," he said again. He lit another bidi. "Well, I guess there's no point in lying about it now. What do you want to know?"

"The basics," I said. "You can start from the beginning."

He let out a big heavy sigh. "Okay. So, Lydia and me, we've known each other, like, forever. And, you know, I've pretty much had a thing for her the entire time. Something about her—I swear, I have had a thing for this woman since, like, the nineties.

183

You know, she's smart, beautiful, the whole package. But I was with someone, then she was with someone, and I never thought she was that into me anyway. We flirted, but that was kind of her thing, and I think that was as far as it went with her. But I liked her. A lot. I mean, I gladly would have ended many relationships to be with her."

Eric seemed like a man who liked women.

"Anyway," he said, bringing himself back to the timeline. "So, I have all these feelings, and Lydia gets married. Which is okay because probably nothing was going to happen anyway, right? So, I resign myself to this, this married thing, and it's cool. Then one night, we were showing *Cemetery Man* at this place in Oakland, and she's there with her friend Carolyn. So we watch the movie, the projector keeps breaking down, whatever. Afterward, I go to talk to her, and Lydia is, you know . . . I don't know if she was exactly flirting, but there's something there. So we go to this bar in downtown Oakland, this dive I know. And, shit." He sighed. "I am really not into breaking people's marriage vows." He sighed again. "And believe me, I got what I deserved."

He lit another bidi and shook his head, looking at something invisible in between him and the wall. He blew smoke at the invisible thing.

"So it didn't last?" I asked.

He shook his head slowly. "It did not last," he said to the wall. "We got together that night, and the next morning—" He twisted his mouth to the side and paused for a long time. "I woke up and she was on the phone with Paul. Screaming. Fighting. I mean, you know. I don't think it's like she had *no* feelings for me. I think she —I don't know. Fuck it."

I didn't have to be a detective to tell he still thought about it. A lot.

"So what was her deal?" I asked. "What was she doing?"

He shrugged. There was a bitter little frown on his face. "I don't know. Maybe I do. I mean, look, I've been with a lot of women. I think I kind of get women." I thought he kind of got women too. "And Lydia, until we slept together, I didn't get that she —she's one of those women who thrives on the attention, you know? On being chased. I think she loves those scenarios where some guy, some guy like me, will go to the fucking end of the earth to get her. But she's not that interested in the next part of the story. The happily ever after. That's like the *longueur* in the story to her."

"What's a long—longue—" I tried to ask.

"*Longueur*," Eric said again, with a slight French accent. "It's like the long boring part in a story no one wants to read."

He looked at me.

"Didn't you and Paul used to . . ."

I nodded. "Yeah. A long time ago."

"You know, if you and him had stayed together, none of this—" He stopped himself and looked at me, shamefaced.

"Oh, God, I'm sorry," he said. "I didn't mean to say that. I'm so sorry."

"No," I said. "No, of course. No worries. Can I use your bathroom?"

He pointed the way. In the bathroom was a framed poster of Bela Lugosi as Dracula. I turned on the faucet and then took a bag of cocaine from my purse and used my house key to do one bump, and then another. I looked in Eric's medicine cabinet and hit gold: a nearly full script of thirty Percocets. Eric Von Springer, née Horowitz, thank God for your oral surgery. Thank the angels for your bad teeth and diseased gums. I couldn't remember how many milligrams were good, so I started with one pill and then on second thought took another, and then stuck the rest of the bottle in my purse.

I felt my head buzz and I lay down on the cool white tile floor. It smelled like pine. I wondered how anyone's bathroom floor could be so clean. Maybe they cleaned it. My mind raced.

Eric wouldn't kill anyone over a woman. He liked Lydia, but he liked a lot of us. I couldn't imagine that any single one was irreplaceable to him.

Eric knocked on the door. "Claire? Um, sorry. Are you okay in there?"

I thought about how much cocaine it would take to overdose. I thought about the last time I ate, which may have been the day before sometime. The white tile was cold and the whiteness made me want more drugs. I wondered if I could get some without sitting up, and I thought yes, probably. I reached for my purse and with a little shifting of my shoulders, it worked.

"Claire? Claire, are you in there?"

I sniffed one bump more and after it rushed through my sinuses my heart fluttered in my chest, skipping a beat or two. It felt good. It felt exciting. Like it could change me. Improve me.

If I'd stayed with Paul, maybe he would have died anyway. Maybe I would have killed him. But slowly, and a little bit at a time, and we'd both still be around to watch me do it.

Eventually Eric broke into the bathroom and kicked me out and then I spent the rest of that day and most of the night driving around the city. With each day that passed something ugly was growing in me. I watched it grow. I fed it cocaine. I loved it and held on to it, kept it alive. Something had died, but maybe what had replaced it would be better. Maybe this was how people lived, normal people who weren't me.

Samsāra was one name for the wheel of life and death, the stupidity we wander through, lost, until we find enlightenment and get to join with the divine. All the shit that hurts so much. The big things like death and loss and pain and also just the everyday grind of eating and sleeping and wanting and wanting and wanting—that was samsāra. You were supposed to want to get out of it. You were supposed to look for the exit, the golden ticket that could take you to the chocolate factory. Escape from New York. This way to the egress.

I took a corner too sharp. I pulled over to take a break and do another bump. After I felt it hit my sinuses, icy and shaking, I remembered that I'd already done too much, and decided not to do anymore. I felt my membranes burn and a little trickle of hot blood drip from my nose.

Some people took the bodhisattva vow. The vow that, even if enlightened, they would continue to incarnate wherever they were needed the most—earth, hell, purgatory, wherever. Constance had taken the vow. People acted like bodhisattvas were all so fucking selfless, but I figured half of them just liked it better here. Heaven for climate, hell for company.

186

I remembered I'd forgotten to eat again.

I figured half the bodhisattvas liked it better here and the other half were scared to leave, so they pretended to care about the rest of us. They didn't give a shit. They were just scared to go. Just as scared as everyone else of giving up their worst self. The self they knew the best.

Which I figured was pretty much what had happened with Lydia and Paul.

44

THE PERSON I IMAGINED as Lucy—the person I'd seen in the video—was probably very close to who Lucy used to be. I imagined a woman who smiled often. A woman who would dance by herself to a song no one else loved.

That was before Paul died.

Now, even the way she sat on a high stool behind a cash register was angry—one leg swinging over the other, shoulders pulling in to surround her heart. She was behind the counter in her friend's vintage clothing store, surrounded by piles of beaded sweaters and spangly purses.

I drank a kombucha that I hoped would settle my stomach. After a few hours of tossing and turning the night before, I'd gotten up and made myself eat some toast for breakfast. Then I did some more coke and threw up.

"Lydia was completely fucking cheating on him," she said, leg kicking the counter in front of her. "Some guy she shared a rehearsal space with. Or maybe their bands rehearsed in the same place. Something like that."

The room spun a little, and for a very fast second I wondered if we were on a boat. The room settled and it passed.

"So Paul knew?" I asked.

"Paul totally knew," she said. "And that guy was *not* the first."

"Who was the first?" I asked.

"I don't know," she said. "But it had been going on for a while."

"What was it like," I asked. "I mean. Their relationship. Was there something particular, some one problem, or—"

"You know what it was?" Lucy said, pointing at nothing, angry. "They would rather be miserable. I swear to God. You know, it was, honestly, it was kind of fucking sickening after a while. Breaking up, getting back together. Treating each other like that."

"Like what?" I asked.

Lucy gave me a mistrustful look and I wondered if she might be a little crazy. I knew I was not entirely lucid myself.

"You know," she said, "couples who just drag each other down like that. Down and down and down."

That was a pretty good description of talking to Lucy. She was a black hole, pulling everything and everyone in with her as she collapsed.

"Supposedly they had this big love," she said. "Gigantic. Like the song. Supposedly they were this perfect fucking couple. Well, nothing is so perfect. Not like *that*."

"No," I said. "It's not. Did Paul—I mean, other than you, I mean—"

"You mean did he sleep with other girls?" bitter, angry Lucy finished for me. "I have no idea. Not while we were seeing each other. He broke it off just a few weeks before he died. Wanted to try to work things out with *her*. *That* worked out great."

I looked around the room. Maybe I saw a mouse run behind a rack of dresses and maybe I didn't.

"I hate this job," she said all of a sudden. "My song is on all these fucking charts and somehow I still have a day job. I never thought I'd be doing this again. My old label sold half as many records and I made twice as much money. Biggest mistake of my life."

"Is there something you would hate less?" I asked.

She shook her head. "I just want to be done with this shit." Her eyes were bright, not in a good way, and I wondered again if she was a little crazy. "This whole never-quite-making-a-living shit. This whole touring nine months of the year and then coming back to this shit two months later. It used to be worth it. Now everyone keeps telling us to put our shit out ourselves and sell it on the Internet. I don't want to do that. I don't want to do any of it."

She hugged herself.

"When you're young it all seems, you know, so cool. Touring and dressing up and makeup and sleeping with whoever you want. And now I'm thirty-four and, you know, I'm broke, and someone I really, really cared about is dead, and I fucking hate my band, and someone I cared about, someone I thought I had a future with—"

She stopped talking and blinked, as if she'd just realized that she'd been saying those words out loud. She shook her head and shrugged, ending a conversation with herself.

I asked her if she wanted to grab a drink. I didn't like her but Paul had cared about her.

She shook her head.

"I gotta watch the store. Besides," she said. "I've been drinking too much already. As you won't be surprised to hear." She laughed.

"Any friend of Paul's," I said. "You know. If you ever want to talk or anything. Or just get a drink or whatever."

She looked at me. "Who are you?" she said. "Are you, like, some kind of a fucking shrink or something?"

"No," I said. The room spun a little again. Maybe I saw a squirrel run across the room and maybe I didn't. "I just—"

"I don't give a shit if you were friends with Paul," she said, getting louder. "You weren't such good friends, anyway. He never mentioned you. He never said 'My friend Claire this' or 'My friend Claire that.' Why are you even here?"

"Because," I said. "I need to know who killed Paul."

"Who cares?" Lucy said, almost yelling now. "Jesus. You think that matters? It was a robbery. Who cares?"

"I do," I said.

"What's the fucking difference?" the woman yelled. I knew I knew her name, but I couldn't bring it to mind. "Who fucking cares?" I didn't remember what she was yelling about anymore. Everything was starting to go red and then black around the edges. "He's not coming back. Nothing's bringing him back. Who cares who shot him? You think you're some kind of fucking detective? Like the countess did it in the drawing room with the poker? I got news for you, lady: No one cares, it doesn't fucking matter, and in the end he'll be just as dead."

I left just before I fainted. The fresh, foggy air revived me. I took a few deep breaths. I was okay. I stumbled to a hamburger stand around the corner and got a hamburger and ate half and felt better.

It it was Lydia who was dead, I would have pegged Lucy in a heartbeat. But she'd seen Paul as her salvation. I couldn't see her shooting him. And if she had, she'd spill something at the scene or leave her wallet or shoot herself. She was that kind of messy girl.

I checked my phone. There was an email from the lama. *Have u heard from Andray?* I hadn't.

And there was an email from Sheila, the other woman Paul had dated.

I remembered the book. A Little Book on the Human Shadow, *by Robert Bly.*

Silette wrote: "The detective who pretends not to see the truth is committing something much worse than a mortal sin, which can only ruin her own soul—she is committing all of us to lifetimes of pain. The truth is not just something we bring to light to amuse ourselves; the truth is the *axis mundi,* the dead center of the earth. When it is out of place nothing is right; everyone is in the wrong place; no light can penetrate. Happiness evades us and we spread pain and misery wherever we go. The detective above all others has an obligation to recognize the truth and stand by it; the detective above all, the detective above all."

45

Brooklyn

THE NEXT DAY for no particular reason we took the train to the end of the line to Coney Island. The train was elevated and outdoors, and you could see Coney Island miles before you reached it, see the new Cyclone and the old cyclone and the long-closed parachute drop. Under a sheet of snow they looked mysterious and lonely, like the statues at Easter Island or the pyramids in Egypt.

At Stillwell Avenue the train shuddered and shook to a halt and we got off. Our first stop was the bar built into the cavernous mouth of the train station. It was dark and filthy. At the bar two old white men, the last of a dying breed, drank whiskey and beer. They didn't laugh. They didn't talk. Tracy and I each got a shot of tequila.

After shots we walked across the street to Nathan's. It was empty except for a group of girls from the projects and a few boys loitering around them, standing at one of the aluminum tables. Tracy and I kept our eyes straight ahead.

"White bitch."

"Go back to Manhattan."

We got hot dogs and fries to go and ate them on the frigid boardwalk, looking out at the gray and dirty ocean, shivering.

"Is this real?" Tracy said. She frowned. "Would you tell me?" she said. "Would you tell me if it wasn't?"

I nodded. "I would," I said. "I promise."

But after that we went to the big bar on the boardwalk and got more tequila shots and beer, and I went to the bathroom and I looked in the mirror and looked and looked but I didn't see a thing I recognized. Who was that girl? Was she real?

If she was real, why didn't she have anything to say? Why didn't she do something?

I hated her. I took out my lipstick and crossed out her face in the mirror, scribbling over it until she was covered in red, until she didn't exist anymore. Someone banged on the door.

"Fuck off," I yelled.

On the train back a man looked at Tracy. Men looked at Tracy all the time. Men looked at all of us all the time. We were trying to talk about the case but he was distracting her. He was young, in his twenties, handsome, and wore a suit and tie. Lord only knew what he was doing in Brooklyn.

"So if Chloe is with CC—" she began, but broke off. She bent the Cynthia Silverton digest she was holding back and forth in her hand.

"Jesus," she said. "What is that guy's problem?"

"I don't know," I said. "So. We know CC likes—"

But Tracy wasn't listening to me. She was staring at the man. The train was quiet, other than the squeak and roar of the metal wheels against the track. A few people were reading. A few people were staring at nothing. At the end of the car two boys were writing on the rear window. BDC—Brooklyn Danger Crew. I didn't recognize them but I recognized their tags.

Tracy looked at the man. At first he smiled at her. She didn't smile. Then he looked straight ahead. Tracy still looked at him. Then he started to squirm a little.

Suddenly Tracy spoke.

"What the fuck are you looking at?"

The man tried to ignore her.

"What!" she screamed. "*These?*" She grabbed her breasts.

The man turned red and looked down, around, straight ahead, anywhere except at Tracy.

"What do you want?" she screamed. "Is this what you want?"

As we pulled into the next station she threw her book at the man. He swerved and ducked but the book caught him anyway, just above the eye. He picked it up and threw it back at her. It hit me painlessly on top of my head. A small smudge of blood rose where a sharp corner had hit him. The man looked hurt and confused, like a wild animal who'd been shot by an automatic weapon he couldn't see or understand.

The doors opened and the man ran off the train.

Tracy's face was red and damp. Her lungs heaved up and down. I thought she was going to cry. Instead she turned to me and said, "I should have killed him."

"Yeah," I said. "Really."

"He should be dead."

"Absolutely," I agreed. "He should be dead now. He's lucky it was you instead of someone else."

She nodded. "He was lucky," she said. "Because he should have died."

That night we decided to go to Hell. We were supposed to meet Kelly at my house at eight, but she showed up at nine with a bruise across her left cheek and a foul mood. Kelly's father had left when her mother, Lorraine, got pregnant and according to Lorraine this was Kelly's fault, and she never let her forget it. Now she was convinced Kelly would make the same mistake and ruin her own life as Kelly had ruined Lorraine's. They had always fought. But Kelly's new boyfriend set off something deep and ugly in Lorraine. Lorraine was thin but strong. I imagined she'd cornered Kelly somewhere in their dingy little two-bedroom railroad apartment. Kelly couldn't win a fight with her mother but she was nimble and young and could escape easily. Which was probably exactly why Lorraine hated her.

She would stay with me until things cooled down with Lorraine, which they would in a few days. Lenore, who didn't seem to have a maternal bone in her body for me, was strangely gentle with Kelly. Lenore's own father had hit her, and for all her faults she never laid a hand on me. Eventually Lorraine would track Kelly down and deliver an apology, backhanded like her slaps: *You know I'm sorry, but . . . I shouldn't have hit you so hard, but . . .*

My room was almost as big as Tracy's apartment, if twenty degrees colder, so we got ready to go out there. Tracy took little nips from a pint of vodka as we got dressed. I didn't know what had happened in the two hours since I'd seen her, but she'd gotten into a bad mood. Or maybe a sad one: she wasn't bitchy, like her usual bad moods, so much as quiet. I kept catching her staring off into space, like she was somewhere else. When we were doing makeup Kelly went to the bathroom and got cornered by Lenore —"Baby, your momma did that to you? Jesus, what happened?"

Tracy stared at herself in the mirror. I was pretty sure she wasn't seeing anything, though.

"Hey," I said.

She pulled herself back in from wherever she'd been. For a split second it seemed like she'd actually left her body. Like she was really gone. I shivered.

"What's up?" I said. "You okay?"

"Yeah," she said, quick and defensive. "I'm fine."

"Did something happen?" I asked. "Like with your dad or something?"

She picked up a lipstick and slowly rubbed it on her lips.

"Yeah," she said. "Someone wouldn't mind their own fucking business, and I had to smack them."

I felt my stomach drop and my shoulders tense. When Tracy wanted to be mean, she was a genius at it. Fights with her were little bloodbaths that ended quick and left permanent scars.

Our eyes met in the mirror and she had that mean look, when you couldn't tell if she was going to be funny or cruel.

But then she cracked up laughing.

"Everything's cool," she said. "I was just thinking about how I'm never going to meet a guy I would even consider having sex with. I mean, it's just impossible. I don't think there's a single boy in New York City who isn't disgusting, crazy, or even more disgusting."

"Oh come on," I said. "There's CC."

"Ewww!"

Now we both laughed. But our eyes met and suddenly we weren't laughing and we were both thinking the same thing. *Chloe did it.*

Did she? Really?

195

Again I felt like I was in a dark woods.

Or that Chloe was in the woods—lost, confused, terrified. And the only way to find her was to follow her there.

Kelly didn't come with us to the club. Just before we went out she called Jonah and they got into a fight.

"We have to *go*," Tracy said into Kelly's free ear. "We're on a *case*."

"Leave her alone," Lenore said from the door. I hadn't known she was listening. She was standing in the doorway holding a long, skinny cigarette. "She can stay here. You girls go do your little detective thing."

Kelly mouthed a thank-you to my mother as if Lenore was the friend and Tracy and I were the interrogating, fun-ruining adults. She turned her back on us and went back to her call.

We left without her.

46

San Francisco

THAT NIGHT I DROVE around the city in my little Mercedes. My car felt like a cocoon. I didn't know what I was looking for. When it got late enough I dropped by the Fan Club. The black girl I'd met wasn't there, but it was easy enough to buy a bag off someone else, for not as good of a price. I bought it from a tall skinny man with sunglasses on. "I should at least get a kiss," he said, after pretending he was giving me a bargain. I kissed him but afterward I felt exactly the same, not even ashamed, which made it worthless.

At dawn I ended up in the Oakland hills. The Red Detective looked at me and said, "How's your missing girl coming along?"

"There is no missing girl," I said for the hundredth time. "It's murder."

"You let me know when you find that missing girl," he said. "And have fun with the lama tomorrow."

"The lama?" I said.

He nodded. I checked my phone. There was an email from the lama: *Come down and visit tomorrow if u can. It's been 2 long. Kids r putting on a play u will like.*

When I got home it was the next morning. I fell into a fitful, cocaine-troubled sleep and dreamed about Paul again. It was a story from one of the Cynthia Silverton books, the Case of the Suspicious Sideshow Performer. In the story Cynthia wrestled with Herman, the suspicious and swarthy tattooed man, for the knife that would prove he'd cut the trapeze artist's safety net after all. But in my dream it was me, and I was wrestling with Paul.

I won the fight, faking him out with a kick to the ribs from the left while I ducked and grabbed the knife from the right. Just like Cynthia always won, just like I always won. Just like all us detectives always win, at least the small wars. We wouldn't be detectives if we didn't.

But in my dream I took the knife and handed it back to Paul. I didn't want it. I didn't want to fight and I didn't want to win. He had that smile he got when I did something that made him happy, that smile that made me feel like all things were possible, like previously locked doors had been thrown open wide—which was often at first and then less often and then never.

Once, when we hadn't been dating long, I'd met him at a Mexican restaurant on Twenty-Fourth Street. I was forty-five minutes late. A case. Always a case. When I came in Paul looked so happy to see me, with such an astonished smile. And I said *What's up?* And he kissed me and said *I thought you weren't coming. I thought I wouldn't see you again.*

In my dream he reached out to take the knife, unsure, happy, proud, smiling that same astonished smile.

Go on, I said. *I trust you.*

Which I'd never said to him, or anyone, in my life.

47

THE NEXT DAY I DROVE down to Santa Cruz. Highway 880 shifted into the slow, winding mountains of Highway 17 and fog began to roll in off the water. I got off in Scott's Valley and headed up the mountain. That morning I slept late and didn't do any drugs. But then I got stuck on the highway and started to feel like I might fall asleep or faint or otherwise check out, so I did the tiniest bump. And then one or two more.

The fog was thicker here and it looked like it would rain, but it wouldn't. By the time I reached the top of the mountain the sky was clear and blue, and when you tried to remember the fog it seemed like you were making it up.

At the gate of the Dorje Temple I stopped the car and pushed the buzzer.

A female voice with a thick Bhutanese accent answered through the intercom: "Who is it?"

Just my luck.

"Claire DeWitt," I said. "I'm here to see the lama."

"Oh no!" the woman said. "You shouldn't be here."

"I don't know about *should*," I said. "But I am."

"Why don't you just go away," the woman pleaded. "Just leave us alone."

Just then I saw the lama walking down the road with two boys.

"Hey!" I called out to him. "Hey!"

He looked at me and squinted.

"Claire DeWitt," he said. He stopped and looked at me, smiling. Then he noticed I was on the other side of the gate. He told the boys to go back to the garden and came over and talked into the intercom through the gate.

"It's okay," he said to the woman on the other end. "She can come in. I'll keep an eye on her."

Silence. The gate buzzed and swung open.

"Go park by the orchard," the lama said. "I'll be in the garden."

I parked by an apple tree and walked over to the garden. The temple itself wasn't much, but the grounds went on for acres and the living quarters, cheaply and quickly constructed, were ever-expanding. A few pre-fab houses were supplemented with trailers, yurts, and tents.

I walked over to the garden. The lama was watching a young woman, about twenty-one, teach a bunch of teenagers how to prepare a garden bed.

"Worms are your friends!" the teacher said. "Fungi are your allies!"

The teenagers putting up the garden, about ten of them, were dirty and smelled bad. Some of them wore ragged clothes and had hand-done tattoos across their hands and arms, some across their faces. They all did as the teacher asked, digging up the earth with little spades, keeping their eyes open for worms and mushrooms. One girl couldn't stop talking, but she still did the work.

The lama saw me coming and came to meet me.

"Claire," he said. "My biggest failure."

"You never get tired of that line, do you?" I asked.

He shook his head, smiling. "Not really. I kind of love it. I feel really good when I say it. It makes me feel important. Tea?"

"Sure," I said.

We walked toward the main house. At the door we ran into Jenny.

She looked an accusation at the lama.

"Jenny," he said. "You have a long memory. People change."

"Not her," Jenny said in her thick accent. "She stays exactly the same."

I shrugged. She was probably right.

"Jesus Christ, enough already," the lama said. "Claire, whatever it was you did to Jenny, can you please just apologize already?"

"No," I said.

Jenny sneered.

"Jenny?" the lama said.

Jenny snorted.

Jenny was a devout Buddhist. When she was younger she'd been a human rights lawyer who specialized in children's issues. Fifteen years ago she'd come to work here, when the lama was just getting this place started. She'd devoted her life to taking care of the men, women, and children here.

My first time at Dorje Temple, she'd walked in on me having sex with a young monk-in-training in the toolshed and had called me a whore.

Neither of us was apologizing anytime soon.

Constance had sent me here to study with the lama nearly twelve years ago. They kicked me out after two weeks. But the people Constance introduced never gave up on each other, not entirely. We might take breaks, but we never threw each other away. Not even in the Kali Yuga.

In the kitchen the lama made us tea and we took our cups to a deck out back, where we sat in cheap plastic chairs at an old glass-topped table. Behind us the mountains rose up, jagged and solid.

We drank our tea in silence for a few minutes.

It wasn't that I minded the arbitrary label of "whore" so much as the intent behind it. Although I guess you weren't supposed to worry about that if you were a Buddhist. You were just supposed to deal with things as they were.

"How's Terrell?" I asked.

"I can't really tell you much," the lama said. "You know that. I'm his religious advisor. But he's okay. And I would tell you if I thought he was in danger."

The lama had a prison ministry where he spent some time pen-paling with prisoners around the country who were interested in Buddhism or just needed someone to talk to and had no one but a stranger in Santa Cruz to listen. When I knew Terrell, the kid from New Orleans, was going to be put away one way or the other, I called the lama. The lama sent him letters, talked to him by phone once or twice or a month, sent him care packages, and just generally did what he could to make his life at the institution more pleasant. He was too good of a kid to rot away in a Baton Rouge treatment facility—not technically a prison but a home for whatever the polite name for the criminally insane was these days. Of course, a lot of kids were too good for whatever prison they'd been stuck in, but Terrell was the only one I'd put there.

The lama got us another cup of tea and sat back down. I wondered if I went to the bathroom if it would be obvious what I was doing in there—more drugs—and if it was, if that mattered.

"Did he say anything about Andray?" I asked.

"You did your job," the lama said. "Terrell is doing his job. Andray has his own job to do. He's doing okay."

"You talk to him?" I asked. Apparently everyone talked to everyone, except me.

"Yeah," the lama said. "We talk once in a while."

"He alive?" I asked.

"He's not making the safest choices," the lama said. "But he's doing okay."

Stupid fucking lama. I realized my hand was pressed against my temple like people do when they can't deal with something, when they're about to say *I just can't deal with this right now.*

"Claire," he said. "If you had let Terrell go, he wouldn't be getting the help he needs now. And he is getting better. He has possibilities now," the lama said. It sounded like he was trying to convince himself. "He can see a future. He didn't have that before. He didn't think he'd make it to twenty-one, and he probably wouldn't have. Now he's looking forward to whatever comes next. You saved his life, Claire."

I wasn't sure about that. I put my hand on my temple again. *I just can't deal with this right now.*

"You think you took him away from Andray," the lama said. "And left Andray with nothing."

I didn't say anything. My head throbbed and I rubbed my temple.

"Maybe you did," he said. "I don't know. I do know that Andray is getting better. I talked to him a few times. He's an incredibly smart kid. You start talking to him about, you know, the precepts or whatever and he just gets it, right away. And he's finally left New Orleans."

"Really?" I said. "When? Where?"

My hand pressed against my temple.

"A few months ago," the lama said. "Shit. I wasn't supposed to tell anyone that. But I see that you're worried. He went on the road with his friend Trey. They're hopping trains and seeing the sights."

"So where is he now?" I asked.

The lama shrugged. "Last I heard he was in Kansas City."

I frowned. I thought of Andray in Kansas City, nearly as dangerous in its own way as New Orleans.

"You know," the lama said, "when you met Andray, you fulfilled a contract that had been made many lifetimes ago. You met each other for a reason."

"So you think it's all planned?" I said. "This was already decided, lifetimes ago?"

"Maybe," the lama said. "I don't really think so. *Planned* is the wrong word. Karma can't be negotiated. But it does take interesting twists and turns. It's like you're given a series of words and it's up to you what kind of story you fit them into."

I didn't say anything. I thought about other people's lives I'd ruined. Pretty much everyone I'd met, it seemed at the moment.

"People think love is, you know, this spiritual thing," the lama said. "This *feeling*. But that's not my thing. In my book, love is a physical act. Love is not ethereal. Love is sticking by someone when they're in the nuthouse. Love is when you keep calling someone even when they don't call you back. Love is dirty and solid. Love is, you know, earth and shit and blood and hair."

A bell rang. The lama smiled.

"Come and see the play," the lama said. "The kids are putting it on. It'll be fun, and they love having an audience."

The "stage" was a raised grassy knoll near the woods; behind it someone had strung a clothesline and hung sheets painted with a gray city skyline. About ten kids were in the play and about twenty adults and older children sat in the audience. The kids were smaller versions of the kids I'd seen in the garden. They didn't have the ratty clothes or the tattoos, but they had the same look in their eyes — scarred, damaged, but impossibly, somehow, open.

One kid, a boy about ten, took the stage.

"Thank you for coming," the boy boomed to the crowd. Everyone cheered. "Today we are pleased to put on a production of *42nd Street* by the Dorje Temple players."

Everyone in the audience cheered and clapped and stamped their feet.

The first group of girls came out in ragtag dresses and did a little dance. Everyone cheered. A different boy came out and started yelling at the girls.

"You call that a show!" he yelled. The girls tried to hide their giggles. "I want you to dance like you've never danced before!"

The girls did a different dance. This time the boys joined them. After the play I went over to the kids and told them how good they'd been. I told them it was the best play I'd ever seen, which was true, but they were already jaded and not one of them believed me. One little girl with white hair looked at me like I was saying it just to hurt her. The lama was busy with the kids and I left. But when I had my car started and in gear, the lama jumped in front of it to stop me. I put the car back in park and rolled down my window. He came over to speak to me.

"Claire," he said. "You know you're welcome here, anytime. Not just to visit. You want to chip in, even come stay for a while — our door is always open here. I mean, any friend of Constance's. And the kids could always use another hand around here. Jenny, you know, she'd be cool."

"Thanks," I said. I put the car in gear again but the lama had a look on his face so I kept my foot on the brake.

"You know," he said. "I wasn't a Buddhist before I met Constance."

"Really?" I said.

He shook his head. "I thought I was a detective," he said. "I was confused. She hooked me up with this lama in L.A. and that kind of, you know, set everything in motion. So, you know, like I said. Any friend of hers."

"Me too," I said, and I drove away before we each had a chance to see how much we'd embarrassed ourselves.

I drove down into town to get a cup of coffee for the ride home. The girl making the coffee was about twenty-five and her arms and legs were already covered in tattoos. I told her I didn't understand young people. What was going to happen when she turned thirty and wanted something new? She read the tattoos on my arms; a fingerprint, a magnifying glass. QUESTION AUTHORITY EVERYTHING. BELIEVE NOTHING. I dropped my jacket off my shoulders and she read LIVE FREE OR DIE across the top of my back.

"You know what they say about freedom," she said, and I thought she was going to quote the Janis Joplin song but instead she said: "It's the only thing worth living for."

I could think of other things but I didn't argue with her. I wouldn't have believed it at twenty-five. She got off work and we walked down Pacific Street together, me with my coffee, and then down to the wharf. On the wharf we watched the sea lions for a while and then I bought her lunch at Stagnaro's. She'd never been there before and I could tell she thought it was sort of fancy. After lunch we walked up toward town. At the top of the hill she kissed me.

I kissed her back. She wanted to go back to her place, a room in a share on the flats, but I got a hotel room instead. I'm too old to face roommates in the morning. The next morning I left quickly and quietly, while she was still sleeping, and hoped I would never see her again.

48

CLAUDE FOUND OUT where Lydia rehearsed. He got it from the drummer's Twitter feed. It was a place people rented out by the hour in Bernal Heights. We could have just asked her, of course, but it didn't seem like a good idea to include her in this particular line of investigation. Claude, testing his skills, had narrowed it down to three bands—three bands that possibly contained Lydia's action on the side.

"So there's, like, twenty bands that rehearse there. And she doesn't date girls, right?" he said, hesitant. We were in my apartment, sitting on the big sofas and drinking a pot of white peony tea I'd made us.

"Pretty sure not," I said.

"And I figure, she likes a certain type of guy, right?"

"Excellent," I said.

"So I eliminated about half of them based on gender and looks and musical taste. I mean, I don't think she'd date someone in, like, something hippie-ish, right?"

"Aces," I said. I was proud of Claude, deducing away while I drove around at night doing nothing.

"I also eliminated hip-hop, jazz fusion, a yoga thing, and this band that was just kind of screaming. Sound good?"

"Sounds perfect," I said.

"So we're left with three bands with potential mates for Lydia. The first is a kind of punk band called Scorpio Rising, young for her but in the realm of potentiality, I think. The second is a—"

"Stop," I said. "Stop right there."

He looked a question at me, insecurity on his face.

"You didn't do anything wrong," I said. "It's the opposite. You've done everything right. But now you're presenting me with three, when I think, in your heart, there's one."

He made a face like he didn't know what I was talking about.

"One," I said. "You have three. But you know it's one. Our life depends on this, Claude. The ship is sinking and you are picking a lifeboat. There is a gun pointed at your head and one chamber is loaded."

He frowned.

"Just tell me," I said. "I won't be mad if you're wrong. But I will be mad if you lie."

"I don't know," he said. "Really." But then he got a look on his face I'd never seen before and he said: "Scorpio Rising."

"Are you sure?" I said. "Remember, the gun is pointed at us. One bullet. You got it right?"

He looked at me and I saw something in him change.

"I'm sure," he said. "It's the Scorpio Rising."

I knew he was right. In the middle of the night last night, in the hotel in Santa Cruz, I'd gotten up to go to the bathroom. When I came back I saw something I hadn't noticed before: a scorpion tattoo curled into the lower back of the girl I'd just slept with.

Claude and I looked at Scorpio Rising's Facebook page. They were attractive and unoriginal, young men with good looks and marketable anger. They were playing in Oakland tomorrow night. I would be there.

Eighty-eight days after Paul died I did what I'd been doing almost every night lately: driving around the city, stopping for a drink a few times, finishing up yesterday's coke, and buying more from a guy I knew in the Mission. Adam. He folded his drugs up in pages from *National Geographic*. "The Condor's Last Flight." "Man's Search for Gold." "The Magic Muds of Iberia." Adam was a million years old and lived in a dingy little place on Valencia that he'd had since time began. He sold me an eight ball for a good price — he remembered me from the Case of the Liminal Landlord, which was why he could live in that apartment forever. Some people remember but most don't. Most people will tell you every day that you are wrong. Most people will look at you as if every case is your first. Most people will forget that you know. That sometimes, not always, you know what's real.

Even you, yourself, will at times forget this. Until the truth is so painful to bury in your chest that it escapes and spills onto the floor, bloody and red, and you have nothing left to hide.

Tracy called, I remembered, driving up the Embarcadero. It was ten. No, midnight. Two. Three. I floated past the Ferry Building, skimmed under the bridge, turned around, and went back toward Chinatown and didn't remember why.

No, not Tracy. Kelly. I checked my voice mail.

Mumble mumble call me about this Cynthia Silverton thing mumble mumble.

I drove out to Oakland and rang Bix's doorbell. He didn't answer. I rang again and then a few more times. He came to the door with a baseball bat, like a suburban dad whose daughter had come home with a Hell's Angel.

He didn't drop the bat when he saw me. Just sighed.

"Come on," I said. "Just let me look."

"It's three o'clock," he said.

"It's not like you were doing anything," I said. "Come on. I'll pay you."

I opened my wallet. It was empty.

"Next time," I said. "I'll pay you next time."

He stood at ease and let the bat droop down to the floor.

"This is not the best time," he said.

"If we wait for the best time," I explained, "things rarely get done."

"I have a friend over," he said.

"You could sell me the comics," I said. "Or even just lend them to me. Then I'd never come over again."

He sighed again.

"I know," I said. "You'd miss me."

"No," he said. "I really wouldn't."

208

He sighed a third time. Three's a charm.

"Come in," he said. "You're going to have to read in the bedroom. I need some privacy."

"Are you sure *you* wouldn't like the bedroom?" I asked as we climbed the stairs.

"We're not there yet," he said.

He let us into his place. A pretty girl in a yellow dress was sitting on the sofa. She wore black cat-eye glasses and tennis shoes. She looked at me like I was Bix's mom.

"Hi," I said. "I'm Aunt Claire."

She gave me a confused smile and a little half-wave. "Hey," she said.

Bix set me up in his bedroom with the books. I lay on his bed, which he'd made carefully, hoping to get lucky with the girl in the yellow dress, and picked a book at random. Book number 13. I remembered this one. I skipped the comic and went right to the Cynthia Silverton Mystery. Alongside the story was an ad for a PI School in Nevada. *Hey, kids, how would you like to make a living as a REAL detective?*

I thought I'd like that very much.

"How do we solve mysteries?" Cynthia said to Professor Gold. "If all that science is for squares—well, how *do* we get people to confess? How *can* we solve mysteries?"

I heard music coming from the other room, something classical. As I read I could practically see it play out in my head: Professor Gold, smug with his pipe and his wisdom, Cynthia in her robin's-egg blue summer dress, sitting in Cynthia's spotless midcentury living room in Falling Rapids. A fire burned in the fireplace. A cool early-summer evening.

"Good question!" the professor said with a sly smile. "This is where a professional detective can really distinguish herself, Cynthia. You know what it means to make an offering, right? A sacrifice that we make for others?"

"You mean like how on my altar I offer incense and water to the *tertons* who've come before us?" Cynthia asked, sipping her illegally obtained martini.

Professor Gold stood up and headed toward the fireplace. He knocked his pipe against the stone, letting out the ashes.

"Exactly," he said. "But there's other kinds of offerings too. Not just incense or water. When you give of yourself, when you —but no, Cynthia. I'll let you put it together!"

Cynthia smiled an anxious smile. Was she up for the challenge?

"Well . . ." Cynthia began, hesitating. "I could. I mean." She frowned. This was tougher than it seemed! "I could offer them money," she mused. "But they can steal *that* whenever they want. I could offer them myself, but, as you know, I'm saving myself for Dick! Boy, Professor Gold, I give up!"

The professor smiled at Cynthia, his favorite student. He reached into the pocket of his blazer and pulled out a little pocketknife, handle made of deer antler. He opened the knife and cut open his chest. He started under his neck and cut down, not at the center but on his left, until his flesh hung open down to the bottom of his ribs. Then, pushing aside the bones, he reached in and took out his heart. Holding his heart in both hands, he held it out to Cynthia. Blood dripped onto the carpet.

Cynthia laughed and squealed with delight. "I get it now!" she said. "Oh, thank you, Professor Gold, I get it now—I really do!"

49

Brooklyn

ELL WAS ON THE FAR West Side in the twenties. The block was a busy hooker stroll. The streetwalkers in Brooklyn wore dated blue jeans and parkas and looked like homeless women, which many of them were. The fancy hookers in Manhattan looked like hookers in movies, with big hair and makeup and high heels and short shorts. Some just wore lingerie, teddies and merry widows and garter belts, stomping their feet to stay warm.

The cab let out us out across the street. In the car next to us I saw a man and a woman doing something rhythmic and urgent, something neither of them seemed to be enjoying.

Hell was dark. The music was loud and it smelled like stale liquor and spunk. Along the wall people tied each other up and hit each other. I tried not to look. We wandered around. In another room people rode other people like horses or ponies. One woman rode a man in a black patent outfit, a shiny little black horse. We lingered and watched for a minute. If we hadn't been on a case it might have been funny.

It didn't bother me until we got to the room with the needles. The room with blood.

The music throbbed. I felt something on me, something on my arm, my hair. Before I could turn around I heard Tracy say, "Get your fucking hands off her. Don't you touch her."

"Sorry," I heard a rough male voice say. Everything started to go black around the edges.

The man was gone and I was sitting on a chair. Someone pushed a glass of cool water against my lips.

"Drink this," Tracy said. "You'll feel better."

I drank it and I did feel better. I saw Tracy in front of me. We were in the ladies' room, sitting in front of the mirrors. Everything became clear again. Under the throb of the music I heard moaning. I turned around. Two sets of high heels shifted in one of the stalls.

"What happened?" I asked. "Did we find her?"

Tracy shook her head. "There must be another room," she said. "A VIP room, something like that."

A woman washing her hands — why bother? — at the sinks overheard us. She turned around. She wore a patent-leather corset that left her huge breasts uncovered, matching shorts, and high patent boots. She was in her forties and her hair was long and dark. Something was strange about her, and it took me a minute to place it: she was sober.

"I don't know who you're looking for," she said. "But there *is* a private room. Lenny's office. He's the owner. It's like a party room — he only lets his friends in, people he knows, and they can do things there they can't do here. Does that help?"

She smiled a sunny smile. I couldn't quite look at her, at her impossibly old breasts, at the gold rings through her nipples, at her bright smile. But Tracy looked right at her eyes and said, "Thank you so much. That's a huge help. We're looking for a friend of ours, actually — maybe you know her."

Tracy pulled out her picture of Chloe and showed it to the woman. The woman looked and shook her head.

"I don't," she said. "But she sure looks like Lenny's type. I'd try his office."

The woman gave us directions to the office: behind the bar, up the stairs, door at the end of the hall. But before we left the bathroom she stopped and looked at us and said, "Most people here are pretty nice. If they weren't, I'd take you to the doorman and get you kicked out. But Lenny — I see that you're not normal kids. I see that. But he can be tricky, okay? I like to party pretty hard. But he's not someone I party with. Not anymore. You hear me?"

We looked at each other and nodded. We heard her. What we'd seen so far had not exactly cheered us.

"Okay," she said as she left. "Play safe, kids."

We found Lenny's office exactly where the woman said it would be, at the top of the stairs and down a dark corridor. When we reached the door I felt a chill. I looked at Tracy and I knew she felt it too.

Chloe was behind that door. I knew it. I felt the cord that bound us, detective and missing girl, hum with tension. There was no turning back, no undoing the cord or untying the knot. For lifetimes, I knew, Chloe and I were bound, whether I found her this time, or last time, or the next time. She would always be the missing girl and I would always be the detective. And I would be missing and she, the detective, would find me. We were bound together, but we had choices; we could live in heaven together or in hell. Either way we'd be stuck with each other, and the ripples from our choices would change every last word ever said.

Which was why I was scared to open the door.

Tracy reached past me and grabbed the door and pulled it open, like ripping off a bandage.

No one noticed us at first. It was a dingy, dark little bar office like the office of any bar in the world. Like there was one back room and in every bar was a door that somehow opened up to it. At a battered desk sat a man I figured was Lenny, the owner, in sunglasses. In the middle of the room were two women doing—well, I wasn't exactly sure what they were doing. But one, skinny and pale, was on her hands and knees on the dirty floor. Above her was another woman, standing on her knees, using some kind of—what was she doing?

I took in the rest of the room. A few scattered chairs. A desk and a beaten sofa. Maybe eight people all together, most of them chattering with that particular grating cocaine-induced pitch. On a small coffee table near the sofa were a few lines of coke cut for whoever wanted them.

As my eyes adjusted to the light I saw that one of the men on the sofa was CC. He wore the same green velvet suit with no shirt. He sniffed and rubbed his nose and watched the two women in the middle of the room.

I turned back to the two women and finally I realized what the woman on her knees was holding. It was a knife. She was cutting the woman on all fours beneath her. In the dark room I hadn't seem the blood right away. She was writing a word on her back, right above her ass, with the knife. So far she'd gotten to BITC.

Then I realized. The girl getting cut was Chloe.

Chloe saw us and froze like a wild animal. After a minute she sat up and looked at us. Everyone followed her eyes. The woman with the knife stopped cutting. She was a brunette, thin but curvier then Chloe, and she looked like she was enjoying what she was doing. Chloe stood up, stumbling a few times on her way.

Chloe was rail thin and her ribs poked out from under her top. Her hips protruded sharply around the tiny thong and garter belt she wore, both cheap and already a bit ratty.

"*You*," she said, accusingly, as if she'd half been expecting us. As if we'd already fought about all of this and she'd won. "What the fuck are *you* doing here?"

She laughed. It became clear she was bombed, maybe drunk or more likely on heroin.

"You guys wanna get in?" Chloe waved Tracy over to the spot she had just abdicated in the middle of the room. "You wanna go next?"

I stood still, frozen. A million thoughts ran through my head. But none was true; each was only an evasion, a distraction, my own reaction to what I was seeing.

"We—" Tracy began. But her voice faltered.

"We came—" I started.

"To find you," Tracy said, her voice thin and weak. "We were looking for you."

"Find me?" Chloe said. She laughed without smiling. She and CC looked at each other and they both laughed. Chloe wobbled a little on her feet, teetering on her heels. She half walked, half tripped onto the sofa. CC caught her and they laughed.

"Find me?" she said again. "Right. I forgot. You guys have your little girl detective thing. That book or whatever." She turned to CC. "They're into some book," she explained. "Some book about solving mysteries. They think they're detectives or some shit like that."

"I got something you can find," Lenny quipped. "It's in my pocket."

Everyone laughed again.

Chloe gave us a look that would have made anyone squirm.

Anyone except Tracy.

"Reena said," she began. "Reena asked us to find you."

Chloe made a face like she'd tasted something bad.

"That bitch," she said. "I just, you know." For a split second she looked like she might cry, but it passed as quickly as it came. "Fuck her. Asshole. Working all the time. Fucking priss. Fucking little Miss Perfect."

"She was worried," Tracy said, regaining her voice. "Worried about you."

"Yeah, well, as you can see," Chloe said bitterly, "I don't need any rescuing. So, you know, unless you want to get a drink and hang out . . ."

Everyone laughed again.

"Are you really detectives?" one of the other men said. "You really solve mysteries?"

I tried to say *Yes, yes, we do.* But I opened my mouth and nothing came out.

"Nice seeing you," Chloe said, sobering up, her voice like an icicle. She waved a hand at us. "Bye-bye, girls."

Blood ran down her arm from an earlier cut. A smear of blood was on her hip.

"You can come with us," I said with all the effort I could find. "If you want. We can take you home, right now."

My voice sounded small and tinny, even to me. Everyone laughed again.

"Go screw yourself," Chloe said. She looked away, at the wall. "Just go fuck yourselves."

Tracy opened her mouth and closed it again.

No one looked at us, and everyone went back to their private conversations, their drugs, their personal dramas. Chloe closed her eyes and put a hand over them, as if she was scared of seeing us again when she opened them.

Tracy and I looked at each other. Neither of us had anything to say.

"Just go to hell," Chloe murmured.

"They're already here," CC said.

50

BIX WOKE ME UP at two the next day. I looked at the comic book. The Cynthia Silverton story in here was entirely different—it was the one where Cynthia's crazy aunt Eleanor comes to visit and her girl-servant gets murdered. Bix had a pot of green tea on a little tray. That was a thoughtful way for a man to kick you out in the morning. We sat in the living room and drank tea. The girl was gone.

"I have shit to do," he said. "Sorry."

"Thanks for the tea."

"You're welcome. Got any plans for the day?"

"Not really," I said. "I gotta be back in Oakland tonight for a show."

"Who you seeing?" Bix asked.

"This guy who I think might have murdered someone," I said. "This guy I knew. I used to go out with him. That's who he murdered."

"Oh," Bix said, wrinkling his brow. "Sorry."

"Yeah," I said. "Thanks."

I sipped my tea and waited for the pity to sink in. It did.

"If you want," Bix said. "You could read some more comics. I mean, I don't know about all day, but a few hours."

"Really?" I asked. "Are you sure?"

"Sure," Bix said, relenting. "Why not?"

When all this was over I'd give Bix Manipulation Resistance 101. For now, I stuck around and read the comics.

I read for a few hours. Reading the Cynthia Silverton digests was like falling into a black hole of memories.

At six I took Bix out to an early dinner at his favorite restaurant, a vegan soul food place in downtown Oakland. We talked about the girl he was dating.

"If you like her that much," I said, "just do what it takes to keep her, okay?"

"Well, it's not that easy," he said.

"It is," I said. "It really is."

Bix frowned. I excused myself and went to the bathroom and did a long line of coke off the top of the toilet.

Would it really have been that easy? Was anything ever that easy? It seemed so now. Now that everyone I loved was gone, it seemed like it would have been so easy to keep them.

Someone banged on the door. I ignored them.

"Claire? Uh, Claire? Are you okay?"

Because he wasn't ready. Because better things were waiting for him. Because I thought if I set him free, he would fly off to some better nest, where someone better than me would love him, where someone better than me would stay with him.

Someone banged on the door again and I didn't answer and then it was the police and they were breaking the door down. I paid my bill and was escorted out with a stern warning and a brief lecture. Bix was gone.

Because we'd all been handed heaven on a silver platter, and instead we'd kicked it away and asked for hell.

I parked my car in front of a dirty little club on the border of Oakland's downtown and Chinatown. I dug the little bag out of my purse and used a credit card (Discover; name of Juanita Velasquez; enrolled in Delta Skymiles and Comfort Rewards; no criminal record) to scoop out a little more coke. It smelled awful, like nail polish remover. I wondered how anything could taste that bad. Cow tranquilizer. Canine antibiotics. Baby monkey cough suppressant.

Scorpio Rising weren't very good. The opening act was atrocious, which made Scorpio Rising much better than they might have been. That still didn't say much. A kind of rehashed punk deal. Maybe it was supposed to be ironic in some way I didn't get. It was likely there was a lot I didn't get, both in general and especially that night.

But despite not being good, they were good. The crowd loved them. People were having fun. They were beautiful young men, and as the night went on they took off their jackets and then their shirts. The singer sprayed beer out from his mouth to the crowd. The drummer threw his sticks at the audience. Everyone was so young, it seemed amazing they were allowed out of the house by themselves. But when I was their age I'd already been on my own for years.

The first guitar player and singer were better looking than the others, and well aware of it. I didn't see Lydia going for that type. Too slutty, too unsubtle. The drummer pounded away, angry and methodical. He didn't smile. No. The bass player never stopped smiling—he was a little younger than the others, and stuck out his tongue at the audience a few times. He couldn't stop laughing. Also no.

That left the other guitar player. He was likely just under thirty. He played a black imitation Les Paul. He had that thing girls liked in guitar players—concentration, absorption, dedication. I didn't know if women liked it because it implied the man could pay that same attention to her, or because it meant the man was capable of ignoring her so completely that she could believe the worst about herself.

The guitar player was good-looking enough, and sexy, but no heartthrob. He looked dirty. He had dark hair that he'd slicked back but kept falling in his face. He wore a wifebeater shirt that showed off homemade tattoos: streets or jail. Or maybe kids paid five hundred bucks an hour for tattoos like that now. But from the way he held himself I guessed streets. I noticed he kept his back to the wall, and his shoulders and brow stayed tense.

Toward the end of the set the singer introduced the band. They'd all adopted the last name Scorpio. Cute.

" . . . And on rhythm guitar—"

The drummer tapped out a drumroll.

"—Rob Scorpio."

Getting backstage was not a big production. You just walked over and went backstage. I was the oldest person in the club by a hundred years. The band was drinking beer, hyper and high from the stage, comparing notes on the show, laughing excitedly.

Everyone except for Rob Scorpio.

I saw a door against the back wall. DO NOT OPEN. ALARM WILL SOUND.

I walked past the band, unnoticed, and pushed the door. Silence. Outside was Rob Scorpio, smoking a cigarette. He wasn't smiling.

"Do you have another one?" I asked. "I left mine in the car because you can't smoke anywhere here. But here we are and I think you can smoke."

He nodded and held out his pack. Natural Native No-Additives Only-Gives-You-Good-Cancer Lites. I took one and he lit me up.

"Thanks." I leaned against the wall a few feet away. "Hey, are you Rob?"

He raised a slow, sad eyebrow at me. His desire to be someone he was not was painfully clear. That and something more—something so heavy on him, he couldn't lift his eyes to meet mine.

The guitar player in the drawing room with the gun.

My heart raced and adrenaline cleared my head, sobering me up.

"I think you know my friend," I said. "Lydia. Lydia Nunez?"

He looked a little to the left of my eyes.

"No," he said.

"I think you do," I said. "I think—"

"I don't," he said. He looked at me and threw his bottle on the street, vaguely in my direction. It didn't break but instead landed with an unsatisfying *thunk*. Then he turned and went back inside.

I picked up the bottle. The singer came out to start loading gear into their van. He looked at me.

"There's a sip left!" I said. I took my beer bottle and went back to my car.

In my car I drank the last sip of beer and put the bottle in my purse and did a little coke, feeling sleep crushing in, and checked my phone and waited.

When Rob and the drummer came out an hour or two later I would follow them back to wherever Rob Scorpio lived. My plan failed. I started up too close behind them and they saw me. The singer, who was driving, slammed on the breaks and two Scorpios came out of the van, one holding a bat. I threw the car into reverse and sped away. Apparently bats were the weapon of choice in Oakland.

Back at home I carefully took Rob Scorpio's beer bottle out of my bag and set it up on my desk. Then I took out the Cynthia Silverton comic I'd borrowed from Bix. I fully planned on returning it. Someday. From a drawer I got out a fingerprinting kit.

I went to my file cabinet and took out Lydia's fingerprints. I didn't take fingerprints of everyone I met, but if it seemed like I would know them a while I asked for a set. Some people didn't like it, but then you had to wonder what they were hiding.

Lydia's heart center was scarred, a little line right in the middle of her thumb. Her Whorl of Love was overdeveloped, unsurprisingly. But her Arc of Compassion was strong. That did surprise me.

Carefully, slowly. I used a sheet of sticky paper to lift Rob Scorpio's fingerprints off the beer bottle. I printed them onto a card and labeled them with his name and the date.

Poor kid. Everywhere you looked, broken lines, scarred swirls. No fully-shaped Destiny Whorl. Nothing of his own. But if he wanted to he could turn it around. Prominent Wheel of Forte.

I had the prints I'd collected from the house. Most were useless but a few were solid enough for comparison.

I looked at the piles of prints. Matching them up was supposed to be meditative. Part of the process. It seemed like a big fucking drag.

I emailed the prints with instructions to Claude. Then I called Andray.

"Hey," I said. "I was just wondering if you're okay. And, you know, Mick. Just wondering if you'd seen him or whatever. I don't know if he's in therapy or anything like that. I don't know. I think I mentioned this before, but my caseload here is nuts. It's, like, really crazy. If you ever wanted a job or anything."

I rubbed my nose and a smear of blood came away.

I got off the phone and then somehow I was at the Shanghai Low. I went into the office with the bartender, Sam.

"Is this that stuff cut with the cow tranquilizer?"

He took a long, shivering snort. He wasn't shy. When the bar closed we went to a closed Chinese restaurant across the street, which the restaurant workers made into an informal after-hours bar at night. A cook Sam knew from Imperial Palace bought us a round and then we bought him one. Paul took me here once. He'd lived in San Francisco longer than me and knew secret spots, privileged corners.

The sun came up but no one saw it through the fog until the morning guys came in to get the restaurant ready for the day and kicked the night shift out. In front of the restaurant Sam tried to kiss me.

"Are you kidding?" I said. The inside of my mouth tasted like dirty cardboard and my teeth felt like sandpaper.

When I got home it was noon. Claude was in my place. I was grinding my teeth and my eyes were wide but I was ready for bed.

"Hey," he said, used to a range of states of disarray in his employer. "I checked all those prints."

"And?" I asked.

"And this guy," Claude said. "He was in the house."

"Where?" My teeth were trying to wear each other down, grinding each other into oblivion.

Claude looked at me. "The refrigerator," he said.

"Fuck," I said again. The refrigerator was an intimate place in a house. A casual visitor rarely touched it. I realized I hadn't blinked in about nine hours. I blinked, feeling my lids drag against dry corneas, and took off my jacket and my shoes.

"He was there," I told Claude. "We need to find him."

"He could have been there anytime," Claude said as I walked into the bedroom. I took off my jeans and sat in bed, pulling the blankets around me.

"He was there," I said.

"How do you know?" Claude asked.

"Because we trust one thing," I said, wondering if a small black cat was running around the apartment or if I was seeing things. "And only one thing, ever, and never forget this okay? There's only one thing that you can trust. You know what it is, right? Tell me you know what it is. Tell me you get it. Because if not, I don't know what I'm doing here."

"The clues," Claude said. "We trust the clues."

"Yes," I said. Worlds were born and spun and crashed before my eyes. "Yes. Yes."

"And you," Claude said. "I trust you."

"No," I said. "Don't. Never trust me, or anyone else. We're all assholes. Especially me. Only the clues."

And again I remembered:

Remember. The Case of the End of the World.

51

Brooklyn

I SLEPT UNTIL NOON the next day. My parents were out. I
made coffee and smoked a cigarette and called Tracy.
"We forgot about school," I said.

"Oops," she said.

At about two she came over and we watched *Hawaii 5-O* and
then *Columbo*. We wore the same clothes we wore last night and
we smelled like Hell, like blood and disinfectant and stale beer. I
made us coffee with big shots of amaretto from my parents' liquor
cabinet, and Tracy made grilled cheese sandwiches. She made really good grilled cheese. After sandwiches we went back to the TV.
We watched *Sally Jesse Raphael* and *Three's Company* and *Hart to
Hart*. Mrs. Hart was kidnapped. Again. Max and Mr. Hart found
her. Big fucking surprise, Max. Try our case and see how you
like it.

In the evening we walked up to Brooklyn Heights. On Hicks
Street we got wonton soup and lemon chicken and mai tais at
SuSu's YumYum. The walls were covered in scratchy red velvet
and we sat in red and black chairs.

"I wish we could live here," Tracy said. She meant the design,
which was already pleasingly retro. But I think she also meant
the quiet and the kindness and the never-ending supply of food.
Tracy's father meant well, but the kitchen was usually empty.

"My dad got laid off again," she said when we were almost

done eating. She looked down at her plate, the remains of lemon chicken and fried rice.

We both knew what would happen: He'd start drinking earlier and earlier, more and more, until he was drunk all day, every day. Then he'd realize what he'd done, sober up, apologize to Tracy, and start looking for a job again. Then he'd start drinking again.

"That sucks," I said. "You can always stay with me."

"Thanks. But then, you know. I worry if he's eating. He falls. You know."

From SuSu's we went to a bar we liked across the street that had a padded door with a porthole-like round window like bars in old movies. After mai tais we figured we should stick to beer and got big pints of Genny at the bar. We smoked cigarettes and put Frank Sinatra songs on the jukebox. At the bar a few old men argued about sports or politics or whatever old men argue about.

"I don't understand," I said, once I was finally drunk enough to talk about Chloe. "I mean—"

But I didn't know what I wanted to say.

"I know," Trace said. "I mean—"

But she didn't know what to say either.

At midnight we went home. We kissed good night on the cheek, but it felt cold. At home I took off my dress and put on a big Ramones T-shirt over my tights and got into bed and drank amaretto from a stolen bottle I kept underneath. I put on the TV. *Unsolved Mysteries* was on.

I couldn't sleep. I thought about Chloe. About how Chloe had been the one person. About how solving mysteries had been the one thing. How Chloe didn't want us and the mystery, her mystery, didn't want us to solve it.

It felt like the inside of my body was a desert. A dead place.

I got out my notebook and wrote: *Someday this will make me a great detective. Someday this will make me a great detective.*

But it didn't seem true anymore. If you were really devoted to the truth you had to admit that there wasn't much of a point to it all. Not without the one thing that had made sense, at least a little. Not without solving mysteries.

Under my pillow I had four codeine pills from when I'd broken a tooth on the Case of the Broken-Into Bodega. When I saw the dentist I told him I didn't want any painkillers—they made me feel funny—and it worked: he gave me fifteen pills. The first one had been heaven; the next ten had each been progressively less wonderful, tolerance already building.

I took the four I had left and washed them down with the rest of the bottle of sweet liqueur.

When I fell asleep I dreamed I was dead.

I was in a black, barren lot. It could have been a city that burned down or a forest that died.

I lay on the dirt like a doll, broken and forgotten, shattered glass glittering around me. My eyes were closed, my lips were pale and blue.

Days passed. Ages passed. I was dead for years. I was dead for centuries.

Slowly, barely there, I felt something push my arm. It pushed again and again.

I wondered if it would hurt me.

It did. It pushed hard and then harder.

Pain never ended, apparently. So that was the big reveal, after all that.

I felt something scrape on my hand and I realized it was teeth, or a hard mouth, gently biting on my hand, my arm, not breaking the skin.

I felt the hard mouth on my neck, brushing the skin. The mouth searched and found the neck of my dress, and grabbed it.

The thing with the hard mouth pulled on my dress, and dragged me away.

The thing dragged me for hours. Maybe years. My eyes were closed but I felt my dead body roll over sharp rocks, broken glass.

Finally, we stopped. The thing let go of my dress.

All of a sudden I felt a hot breath and the strangest sensation on my face, something rough and wet, like damp sandpaper, rubbing over and over again. The rough wet thing reached my eyes. It poked gently at my eyelids, pushing again and again until my eyes were open.

226

I could see. Above me was a huge black bird with a red feather-less head, cleaning my face. The bird leaned back.

I sat up. I was alive.

We were in a forest. Moss carpeted the ground. Ferns bloomed underneath giant trees with rough red bark.

We looked at each other. The bird had tiny black eyes that saw everything.

It bent down low. It smelled like dirt and dead things. Its feathers were black-brown and dull.

It whispered in my ear.

"This is not the price you have to pay. This is not your punishment for loving something."

Suddenly it hit me, hard, across the face.

It hit me again.

I opened my eyes. My vulture was gone. Lenore was standing above me, slapping me.

After I opened my eyes, she stopped.

"Jesus, baby," she said. "You scared the hell out of me."

I looked at her.

"You didn't wake up," she said. She looked scared. "Your phone was ringing and ringing and you didn't wake up."

I had my own phone line; Kelly had somehow jury-rigged it, cutting into someone else's line. Sometimes I listened to the Puerto Rican family whose line it was. The wife was having an affair. No one knew except the youngest son.

"What's wrong with you?" Lenore said. "What happened? Are you sick?"

I shook my head, heavy and thick. "Nothing," I said. "Just sleepy."

She looked at me. "You sure?" she said. "You sure you didn't take anything?"

"Of course not," I said, still groggy and half-asleep. "What would I take?"

She sat at the edge of the bed.

"You know I worry about you sometimes," she said. She put a hand on my knee.

"You don't have to worry about me," I said, confused. But the words came automatically. "I'm okay."

"Really?" she said. She looked worried.

"Of course," I said. "But I better see who called. It might be our case. Maybe Tracy found something."

"That detective game you guys play," she said. "At least I know when you're playing that, you're safe. Right?" She said it with a little desperation in her voice. *Right?*

I nodded.

Suddenly she reached over and pulled me into an awkward hug.

"You know I love you, right, kid?" she said. "I mean, I know I'm not the best mother in the world. But you know I love you, right?"

I hugged her back. "Of course, Mom. I know that."

She pulled away and smiled. "Okay. Go call your friend back. It's late, but you're on vacation, right?"

She left. But on the way out she stopped and looked at me. Her gaze was sharp and stung a little where it hit me.

"What?" I said.

"Nothing," she said sharply. "You look like shit. Go call your friend."

She left. I stood up, head spinning a little, and called Tracy.

"I had a dream," she said. "A dream about Chloe. We have to go see Chloe."

"Did you solve the case?" I asked.

"I don't know," she said, "but I can think we can solve it to-night."

And all of a sudden, I was alive again.

I went to the bathroom and made myself throw up the rest of the pills.

Tracy met me on the front steps of my house. It was two thirty a.m. The block was quiet. From far away we heard solitary motors, sirens, a long low whistle. We walked to the train station. We lit cigarettes and couldn't tell the difference between our frozen breath and our smoke. I was still fuzzy and slow from the pills, but I was quickly coming alive. As we walked, with every step life became more real.

I looked at Tracy and I knew that she, like me, felt absolutely, entirely real. The coldness of the air, the smell of the subway station, the feel of cold painted metal on our hands as we lifted ourselves up to jump the turnstiles—every sense was sharp and every input was distinct and clear.

No one else was waiting for the G and no one else was on the train and no one else got on. But it felt as vibrant and busy as rush hour. That girl from last night was another person, long gone.

"What was it?" I asked. "Your dream?"

Tracy frowned. "Something about Chloe," she answered. "We have to get her out of there."

"If we have to drag her," I said.

"Yes," Tracy said. "Even if we have to drag her."

I knew we would get Chloe where she was supposed to be. We would go back tomorrow if we had to. Every night. But we would get her where she was supposed to be.

"The detective is cursed," Silette wrote in 1959. "Solving mysteries is the only time he will be truly alive. The rest of his life will be a distant blur, good only insomuch as he can use the things he sees there in his work."

CC and Chloe were sitting on the couch in the office in Hell. In the corner, a man we'd never seen before was doing fat lines off the desk. But it was obvious CC and Chloe hadn't been doing any coke. She was nodding off on CC's shoulder. In the middle of the room, where Chloe had been doing her little act yesterday, a boy about our age was trying to get something going with another young boy. Both boys wore jeans and no shirts and had short blonde hair. The first smacked the second halfheartedly across the ass.

"Harder," the second boy whined. "Come *on*."

"Shut up," the first boy said. "You're so lame. No one's even watching."

Chloe woke up when we came in.

"*You* again," she said. "What the fuck do you want?"

Tracy didn't answer. Instead she went over to the sofa, sat next to Chloe, and began to whisper in her ear.

At first Chloe scowled and pulled away from Tracy.

"Fuck *off*," Chloe said.

Chloe cursed Tracy a few more times. She stood up to leave but

Tracy held her down, an easy job even for tiny Trace. Chloe was literally nearly skin and bones, her abdomen concave.

I didn't know what Tracy was saying. Maybe she would tell me or maybe she wouldn't. Tracy liked secrets.

Chloe started to squirm a little in her seat, to turn away from Tracy like a baby turning away from food it didn't want but needed. But Tracy kept talking and kept her hands on Chloe, pinning her down, and didn't let go. After a minute Chloe's face became smoother, quieter. More like the face I remembered.

Then Chloe started to cry.

"No no no," I heard Tracy whisper. "You didn't know. It's okay. It's all okay."

Chloe said something but I didn't hear what, and they whispered to each other for another minute. Chloe looked at Tracy as if Tracy was telling her the answer to a question she'd had all her life.

I realized not one person in this room other than Tracy or me cared if Chloe lived or died. And that she had put herself here deliberately and intentionally, in this city of the dead, where no one would ever love her.

Chloe started to sob, and clutched Tracy.

"It's okay," Tracy said. "We're all going to be okay."

Tracy stood up and Chloe stood up with her. I took off my coat and put it over her and together we walked out of the room through the club and out to Eighth Avenue.

First we went back to Chloe and Reena's apartment. Chloe didn't stop crying. Not in the cab, not when we pulled up, not while she waited outside while Tracy talked to Reena. Later I would find out that Tracy had told Reena that Chloe couldn't see her right now. Reena understood. She was just glad Chloe was all right. She stayed in her bedroom with the door closed as Chloe, still crying, went into her room and packed a few bags.

"I have an aunt," Chloe said. "In L.A. I want to stay with her."

"You sure she'll take you?" Tracy asked. "You don't want to call first?"

"She'll take me," Chloe said defensively. "She said if I was ever in trouble I could stay with her. She loves me. I know she does."

She said it as if we wouldn't believe her. As if no one could believe it.

She was still crying as she finished packing and still crying as we took the train up to Port Authority and still crying as we all pooled every penny we had and bought Chloe a bus ticket to L.A., plus twenty dollars for food on the five day trip.

The sun came up as we sat in Port Authority. Homeless people took most of the benches. Pimps and their bright-eyed protégés kept a sharp eye out for new arrivals.

Nothing good ever happened in bus stations. Not until now.

At eight Chloe's bus started seating. She hugged us each, hard, still crying.

"Thank you so much," she said through her tears. "Thank you forever and ever."

Chloe got on the bus, still crying. Tracy and I got on the A train and took it to the F to the G to home.

It was nearly ten by the time we got off the train in Brooklyn. The sun was bright and the cold had abated a bit. A year later, Tracy disappeared, never to be seen again, and a year after that I left Brooklyn forever, leaving Kelly alone with the mess we'd made of our lives. But for now Tracy was smiling, which was rare. Her cheeks glowed and she looked more alive, somehow. More like she belonged here. She had solved her mysteries.

"What should we do today?" Tracy said, blinking in the bright sun.

"I don't know," I said. "Might as well go to school."

And that was the Case of the End of the World.

52

San Francisco

THE NEXT DAY I woke up late into the dark evening, with the sad, confused feeling sleeping through the day always brings. Claude was gone. I made some tea and then some more tea and then said fuck it and made some coffee.

The Case of the End of the World. Neither Chloe nor Tracy ever told me what Tracy dreamed, or what she told Chloe.

I figured it couldn't hurt to ask one more time.

It's easy to find someone who's making no particular effort to hide. Chloe Roman had a Facebook page, from which I found out she wrote poetry and she lived in Los Angeles. From there it was just an hour or so, most of it spent on hold, to find out that she had no landline but had a cell phone, billing address in Los Angeles county.

I recognized her voice right away.

"It's Claire," I said. "Claire DeWitt. From Brooklyn."

"Oh my God," she said. "Oh my God. Claire. Hi. Wow. How are you?"

"I'm good," I lied. "How are you?"

We talked for a few minutes. I told her I was a private eye living in San Francisco. She knew that already; she'd searched me out online a few times. She told me she was a writer now. She wrote movies and TV shows for money and poetry for fun and was working on a memoir about growing up in New York City with her famous, negligent parents.

"I've been looking," she said. "I've been looking online. I read all about you and I found a little about Kelly. But I couldn't find anything about Tracy. Is it true they never found anything? *Nothing?*"

"That's actually why I'm calling," I said. "I don't know if you remember. That night, that night when Tracy came and got you. I was wondering—she had a dream. Did she tell you about it? About the dream?"

"Dream?" Chloe said. "You mean your dream?"

I felt my head spin.

"My dream?" I said. "No, what happened was—" I stopped myself. "Chloe. What did happen that night?"

"Well," Chloe said, "you guys had come the night before and, you know—Jesus, I'm so sorry. I wasn't very nice."

"It's okay," I said. "I haven't always been so nice myself."

"And then the next night, you guys came back. You and Tracy."

"And what did we do?" I asked.

"Well, you came over to me," Chloe said. "I'll never forget. You came over—"

"You mean, 'you' *me*? Or 'you' both of us?"

"*You* you," Chloe said. "Singular. You, Claire. Tracy waited by the door. You, Claire, came over and sat on that couch next to me. And you put your hand on my knee, and your hand was so warm. And I was, like, trying to get away—you know, I couldn't stand the thought that anyone cared about me that much—it just made me sick. Sick, like I could die. You know."

I felt the room spin around me and I lay down on the floor. I put my cheek against the cold floor and tried to ground myself to earth, but I felt like I was floating away. I did know. Sick like I could die.

"I tried to get away but you wouldn't let me," Chloe went on. "And you started to tell me about this dream you'd had."

"What did I say?" I asked Chloe.

"Well," she said, "you told me you had this dream. And I was all, you know, why would I give a shit? But you wouldn't stop, you started telling me about this dream. This dream about a peacock. Well, you said 'peacock,' but I think you really meant peahen, because it was a girl. But anyway, that this peacock wanted to find God. Because God was so pissed off at people and he'd turned the lights off. So it was like the dark ages, you know? Like how some people call this the Kali Yuga? Like that. Everyone was fighting and killing each other and it was just generally like hell. Like shit. You know, like things are.

"So this peacock, she decides she's going to get the lights turned back on. And, you know, she was this vain, stupid bird, or so everyone thought. I mean, she was a peacock. Everyone was, like, laughing at her and throwing things at her. You know, she was the patron saint of whores. She was a girl. But no one else could fly that high. No one else even tried."

I rummaged through my purse and found a Percocet. I put it in my mouth and chewed it and swallowed. I remembered whispering in Chloe's ear, my voice still so young, but I knew what I was saying was true. I was entirely certain that I was alive, and that I belonged on this earth: "People thought she was just a stupid girl. Just this stupid, slutty girl no one cared about and nobody loved."

I heard Chloe make a sound and I wondered if she was crying. My hands were shaking and I took out another pill, but then put it back.

"But she did it," Chloe said. "The peacock. She flew and she flew and she found him. She met God. And she told God how much she loved us, how we really weren't so bad after all, about how, you know, we'd fucked up everything so bad, but we could do better. It might take a few lifetimes, it wouldn't happen right then, but we could get better. She saw the best in us, even though we'd ruined everything. Even though we'd screwed up and ruined it all. And he was so impressed, he changed his mind. He turned the light back on. He didn't think she was just some stupid girl. He thought she saved the whole world."

One arm around Chloe, pulling her close, warmth growing where we touched, Chloe shivering, smelling salted, metallic blood from her cuts. I was wiping tears off my face.

"But when she came back down," Chloe told me, telling me the story I had told her, "she wasn't a peacock anymore. The sun had burned her feathers black, and blistered her crown red, and now she was a vulture, the wisest animal on earth, the animal who knows all the secrets."

Whispering to Chloe, her squirming to get away.

"It's okay," I whispered in her ear, "you didn't know. Soon we get to be vultures again. We don't have to pretend we don't know everything anymore. We just have to grow up a little first, that's all."

"Claire? Claire, are you there?"

"Sorry," I said. "I'm here. I just—I remembered it differently. That's all."

"Yeah," Chloe said. "It was such a strange thing to say, but somehow it made sense. I mean, it made everything make sense. All of it. Like a poem."

We didn't say anything for a minute. My hands were shaking.

"Claire?" Chloe said again. "Are you there?"

"I'm here," I said. I was too here. More here than I ever wanted to be. Chloe told me about her kids, her husband, her writing. Her life sounded pretty good.

"It's all because of you guys," she said. "All the good things that happened—they were all because of you and Tracy. Because you came and got me. Because you didn't give up."

"No," I said. "They were because of you. Because *you* didn't give up."

"No," she said. She started to cry. "I have two beautiful children, they're like these little fucking miracles, they're so normal and not crazy. Because of you. Because of what you said."

I remembered now: waking up in the night, calling Tracy, still sick from the pills. *We have to get her out of there. I had this dream.*

"And Tracy," she said. "I never talked to her again. Not after the last time."

"Well none of us—" I began and then I stopped myself. The Percocet kicked in. I felt as close to nothing as possible. But something stuck in my throat.

"The last time?" I asked Chloe. "When was the last time you talked to Tracy?"

"After I'd been in L.A. for a while," she said. "She found me. She found my aunt's number and called me."

A chill crept up the back of my neck.

"When?"

"Maybe a year after I moved out here," she said. "Maybe a little more."

Tracy had disappeared on January 11, 1987. Chloe had gotten on the bus to Los Angeles January 14, 1986.

"So it's true no one ever found out anything about Tracy?" Chloe asked. "Not even you?"

"Yeah," I said. "It's true. But I'm starting to have an idea."

Chloe asked for details, but I didn't want to tell her. It was just an idea.

But it was a pretty fucking good one.

We got off the phone with promises to get together and keep in touch. Maybe we would.

But for now, we hung up and I lay on the floor for a while.

Maybe out of everything I thought I knew, there was nothing I was more wrong about than my own life story.

When I got off the phone there was a message from Claude. I felt a little dizzy and weak. I drank a glass of orange juice and took a shower and did a line of coke before I called him back.

"Hey," I said. "Hi. I mean, it's me. What's up?"

Claude paused. I felt a drop of blood trickle from my nose, and I wiped it away with my hand.

"Are you okay?" Claude asked.

"Of course," I said. "I'm fine. What's up?"

"I think I found the guitar," he said. "I went through all of Paul's money stuff and I found it. The missing guitar. It's a Wandre. The one that was stolen. He bought it two years ago, and I'm pretty sure it was never sold or traded. It's just gone. Does that help?"

"Yes," I said, and told Claude I would call him back. In my mind I pushed aside Chloe and Tracy and Claude. Instead I did another bump of coke and opened my computer and read about Wandres. They were not common. Paul's would get a nice piece of money if the thief sold it to the right person, but that right person would be hard to find. Almost no one knew what Wandres were.

And people who did know were passionate about them, making the one stolen from Paul hard to sell. An ordinary thief would have passed it up. Only one kind of person would have taken it —someone who wanted to keep it and play it.

Wandres had been built in Italy by Antony Pioli in the 1950s and '60s. They were strange guitars—odd shapes, off colors, metal necks, electronic bits Pioli developed himself. I couldn't pin down the exact story behind Pioli and his Wandres. One person said Pioli designed motorcycles and that was where he got his ideas. Another said he'd worked in an airplane factory, another that his father had been a luthier. None of that felt true. After a few hours online I found another story: In 1955, Antony Pioli was indeed the son of a luthier, a man who made boring, insipid guitars. Antony thought he'd rather do anything than work in his father's shop, which smelled to him like defeat and despair. Then one night Antony, well into his thirties but still living like a boy, came down with a terrible fever. The doctor came. Antony's fever was so high, the doctor packed him in ice and prayed. Antony screamed and shook and finally, close to dawn, his fever broke. And in a few days, when he was able to walk, he got up and made his first Wandre guitar, an amoeba-shaped heresy in brilliant reds and greens, saying the design had come to him in a dream the night he nearly died. No one thought it would play. No one believed it would work. They were wrong. He went on to build some of the best guitars the world had ever seen. Then, in 1970, just as suddenly as he'd begun, he stopped making guitars and never touched his workshop again. People said he'd fallen in love with the wrong woman. That his heart, once broken, turned bitter, and could never find the inspiration to build anything again. No one seemed to know what became of him after that.

I thought that story was true.

I asked Claude to send me the details of Paul's guitar and he did. The model was a Doris, supposedly named for the woman he loved.

I called Claude back.

"This is it," I said. "This is the clue."

"*A* clue," he asked, "or *the* clue?"

"*The* clue," I said. "The only clue. Whoever killed Paul wanted that guitar. I can't imagine it's why they killed him. But they couldn't resist it."

"So you think it was one of her boyfriends?" he asked. "Or one of his girlfriends?"

"I think," I said, "it was someone who loved somebody else very much."

53

THAT NIGHT I DID fat lines of cocaine off my kitchen counter and called Kelly.

"Hey," she mumbled.

"Hey," I said. "Remember Chloe Roman?"

"The Case of the End of the World," Kelly said.

I told her what Chloe had said—that she heard from Tracy after the case, possibly after either Kelly or I had last seen her.

"Shit," Kelly said. "Is she sure?"

"No," I said. "She's not."

Kelly didn't say anything.

"So what's up with the comics?" I asked. "Why are they so rare?"

"I don't know," she said. "But it's weird. It looks like they hardly made any, and out of what they did make, only a few lasted."

Kelly didn't say anything for a while. But I knew she wasn't done.

"I know at the time," she finally said, "at the time we didn't know what normal things were, so they seemed normal to us. But now, when you think about it, don't they seem strange to you? Doesn't it seem like they were written just for us? Like they weren't normal comics at all?"

"Yeah," I said. "I did think that."

"And didn't you ever think," she said, with a little accusation in her voice, a little anger, "about how weird it all was? About finding *Détection* in your parents' house, and the bookmobile, and the comics? About how it seemed like all these things came together, all these things conspired, to make us who we are? I mean, that's a pretty big fucking coincidence."

"Of course I've thought about it," I said. But I hadn't, not really. Fate hands us our cards and we play them.

"I mean," she said, "who the fuck are we? Did you ever think about that? Who the fuck are we?"

Kelly was done, and she hung up. I felt a shiver in my bones and I knew she wasn't wrong.

Who the fuck were we?

54

W E DIDN'T KNOW WHICH night Rob Scorpio rehearsed, or what time. Claude called the rehearsal
studio and they told him Scorpio Rising had a
standing date for Thursdays at eight thirty. But when we showed
up at eight thirty on Thursday, the Rabid Elves were rehearsing.
They said they'd switched with the Scorpio clan, giving them their
Friday ten p.m. slot. The Rabid Elves were pretty good and I suggested they change their name, but the singer, a tall, heavily tattooed Latina woman named Marie, told me to go fuck myself.
Agreed. Friday at ten we showed up to find Lucky Strike rehearsing, a surf band with white Strats and a Farfisa organ. They didn't
know anything about Scorpio Rising. They'd switched times with
"these guys who played rainsticks."

I didn't want to spook young Scorpio, so I didn't want to
ask any more questions. Instead I just had Claude surveil until
Rob showed up. We figured it was a weeknight (weeknights were
cheaper) and we figured it was late (Rob did not strike me as a
morning person). Claude staked out the rehearsal studio Monday
night, then Tuesday night, then Wednesday night. He had never
done intense observation before. I gave him the rundown. Drink
few liquids and carry empty bottles. Bring some audiobooks or
good music — you can't count on radio reception. Whatever helps
you focus is good — coffee, tea, cocaine, Adderall — and whatever
spaces you out is bad — heavy meals, opiates, marijuana.

Thursday came and went. Friday. Saturday. Sunday. Monday he switched to day.

On Tuesday night I went over all the evidence again, the whole file. It was thin and weak. Maybe my worst file ever. Even the Case of the Miniature Horses was thicker and more organized. I looked again at the Tearjerkers record, Lydia's first band. I put on the B-side this time, "Never Going Home." The band was loud and tight and polished and very good—it was no shock they'd become somewhat big after this.

I looked at the sleeve again. Produced by Kristie Sparkle. Two minutes on the Internet and I found the woman once known as Kristie Sparkle again, now Kat Dandelion, an herbalist in Marin County. On her Facebook page she wrote:

> *I am also known by the names Kristie Sparkle, Mistress Kitty, Kris K., Kristine Katalyst, and Kristen Bachman. I have been a music producer, a sex worker, a performer in a traveling circus, and a professional body piercer. I am now an herbalist in Marin County. I specialize in miracles.*

The drive over the Golden Gate Bridge never stops being beautiful. In every kind of weather on every kind of day it's a different kind of beautiful. On the other side of the bridge I veered off the highway onto Sir Francis Drake Boulevard, which I could never quite believe was a real road—I kept expecting a man in a hat and ascot to jump out and detour me back to the 101—and drove into the woods around the outskirts of Fairfax. Kat Dandelion's house was up a hill that might have been called a mountain in another state. A twig fence surrounded the lot and was just high enough to keep out the deer, one of whom was peeking over it to see the beds of herbs within.

Before I got out of my car I took a pair of dice from my purse. One was lapis and one was turquoise. I tossed them on the empty passenger seat.

Snake eyes. Not encouraging. I figured it earned me an extra bump. I'd done a few lines before I left the house and they were fading fast.

"They don't eat them," Kat said, coming out of the house to

242

greet me. She meant the deer and the herbs. "Too powerful. Only they don't remember that until they've tasted them all and trampled them half to death."

Kat was about fifty and wore a long white dress and a white turban with a gold pin in front. She led me into the house and we sat at a wood table in what had been built as a kitchen and was now an office/exam room. Herbs in glass jars lined the walls, labeled with their Latin names: *Camellia sinesis; Trifolium pratense; Amanita muscaria*. A long exam table lay empty.

We sat at the wood table. I became self-conscious of my inability to sit still, which made me fidget worse. Kat Dandelion didn't seem to mind.

"So," she said. "How can I serve you?"

"I lied when I made the appointment," I said. "I didn't really come to see you about herbs. I came to see you about Lydia Nunez."

She didn't seem surprised.

"Why did you lie?" she asked.

"I figured you might say no," I said. "I'll still pay you for your time. We made an appointment."

She reached out a hand to my wrist. She looked at my fingernails as she took my pulse.

"Only if you let me do something about this liver heat," she said.

"I'm already seeing someone," I said, as if we were all dating.

"Are you doing what he told you?" she asked.

"Not really," I said.

"It's into your lungs, too. Hot and dry."

She got up from the table and started pulling glass jars off the shelves.

"If I make you something that tastes bad," she said, "you won't drink it, will you?"

"Probably not," I said.

She nodded and looked at the herbs again.

"So ask me about Lydia," she said, with her back to me. "I heard her husband was killed."

"He was," I said. "That's why I'm here. I'm a private detective. They're also friends of mine. I mean were."

"You mean you're not friends anymore?" she said.

"No," I said. "I mean Paul's dead."

"I saw her not long before he died," she said.

"Really?"

She turned back around, more glass jars in her hands. She put them on the table. From a cupboard she got a plain paper bag.

"Really."

"Why?"

She looked at me. "I'm not going to tell you," she said.

She started shaking out herbs into the paper bag, mixing them with her hand. I remembered the dice. Snake eyes.

"It might help me solve the case," I said. "I'm trying to find out who killed Paul."

She stopped, holding a jar of herbs in midair for a long second before she started again.

"My job," she said, "is to create miracles. People come to me when they have no other hope. Possibilities are my department. Facts are yours."

On the side of the bag she wrote the herbs she'd put in. Mint, Chrysanthemum, Honeysuckle.

"I'm not that kind of detective," I said. "I just want to know who killed Paul."

"Will he be less dead," she asked, "if you find out?"

"Maybe," I said. "Maybe some part of him somewhere will be less dead."

I thought about saying *Maybe I will* but I thought about it and realized it wasn't true.

She folded the paper bag over and shook it up.

"Make a tea," she said. "You don't have to steep it too long, it's mostly flowers. There's some to cool your liver and some to ground you. You could use a rest." She handed me the tea and I took it. "And use this around your nose."

She handed me a small lip-balm type tube.

"It'll stop the bleeding," she said. Without thinking I reached a hand up to my nose. It came away streaked red.

"When you're ready to stop, let me know," she said. "I'm sorry I couldn't help you more with Lydia."

"You could," I said. "But you don't want to."

"Yes," she said. "That's true. I'm sorry I don't want to help you more."

I paid her for the appointment and the herbs and left.

I drove out to Point Reyes to check on the miniature horses.

"We've got a lot of leads," I told Ellwood James. "A lot of new evidence. But nothing firm."

Then I drove up to the Spot of Mystery. Jake was in his office. We went out to sit at the picnic tables.

"Got any leads?" I asked him.

"Not really," he said. "My guess is the guy has a mountain lion issue. Maybe a bobcat. Shoulda thought of that before he started shrinking horses."

The things we should have thought of could fill the ocean. Back in my car my heart was racing from the rail I'd done in the bathroom at the Spot of Mystery. I waited for my heart to slow down before I started my car. The sun was bright and warm in the parking lot, almost like summer, almost like something good.

55

ONE HUNDRED AND EIGHT DAYS after Paul died, Friday afternoon, at four thirty p.m., Claude called me: he'd spotted Rob. I was in my apartment getting dressed and starting my day and pretending I had something to do. I had nothing to do. I'd blown off all my other cases. I could barely make it to my car without stopping for air and my thoughts had lost distinct edges and bled into each other, cutting each other where they'd been broken and torn. I was dressed and doing lines off the kitchen counter while a video of Iggy Pop doing "Gimme Danger" played from my computer.

I had planned this whole cool surveillance situation where we would follow Rob back to his place and surprise him and I would be a calm professional detective and Claude my trusty assistant. But I was pissed off and high and not thinking especially clearly, and so instead I jumped in my car, drove to the studio, stopped my car in the middle of the street and jumped out and ran into the studio and grabbed Rob by the collar of his stupid leather jacket from behind—he was turned toward the drummer and bass player, tuning up—and pushed my gun against his cheek.

"Hi," I said. "It's Claire."

The rest of the band looked as if we weren't real and said nothing and did nothing. They watched with wide eyes as I left and took Rob with me.

· · ·

We took Rob to Claude's apartment in Berkeley. We didn't plan it that way, but it made sense. To Claude. I was high and my head was full of thorns and out of sense, so I deferred to his wisdom. Claude lived in a two-bedroom with a roommate, also a chipper and cheerful Berkeley scholar, who was making scrambled eggs when we arrived. Claude pushed him out the door with apologies.

Claude waited in the living room and I took Rob into Claude's spotless bedroom. I wanted Claude outside for two reasons: to stop Rob if he tried to leave, and because I thought I'd do better alone with the kid. I figured another man would put his defenses up more than a woman alone. It was just a hunch, but it was right.

Rob looked ready to cry by the time I pushed him into a chair at Claude's desk. A poster hung on the wall: GRADUATE STUDENT BOOK FAIR! DON'T MISS IT! Underneath that a picture postcard of Vladimir Nabokov sitting at a desk, looking at the camera like we were bothering him. Well, Vladimir, some of us have mysteries to solve.

"Tell me," I said. "Tell me about Lydia and Paul. And don't even dream of lying. Don't even think about it."

"I don't know why you're doing this to me," Rob said, scared and indignant and petulant. I hadn't let him talk in the car, and now the words spilled out, overeager excuses and lies. Now that I had him to myself I saw how young he was, how unformed. His hair was short like a little boy's. His face was unlined and unwise, eyes blank but trying for something more. "I hardly even knew Paul. I mean, yeah, I fell in love with his wife, and I know that's completely fucked up. But, you know, shit happens in life. He could have treated her better. Maybe none of this would have happened if he'd treated her better."

I looked at him. What a little nothing. What a little worm. Especially compared to Paul. Paul who was dead while this piece of shit lived.

I sat down on Claude's bed and let myself think about what I shouldn't. Paul. Paul who wasn't coming back, even when everyone knew who killed him. The musician in the living room with the gun. The detective in her apartment with the rolled-up fifty.

I'd never be able to tell him about how I solved his big murder. At least not anytime soon.

Rob stood up as if I were letting him go.

"No no," I said, standing up and pulling the gun back up and pointing it at Rob. "No more spacing out. Let's stay focused here."

I didn't know what to say. I didn't have any plan. I had trusted divine providence to provide me with the clues. Divine providence had failed. I didn't know what to say.

"I don't know what you want from me," he said, whiny and defensive. "I don't know anything about any of it."

Suddenly I knew this was real. Suddenly I knew I was alive and I knew exactly what to say. My head was clear and the drugs coursing through me sharpened into something cruel and cutting, something that would get this job done.

"No," I said. "That time is done."

Everything was entirely, completely real.

"The time for making up stories and acting like a boy is over," I said to Rob. "You got mixed up in some things you couldn't understand and you couldn't handle. And that's happened to all of us. But you can't go back and change that by lying about it now."

His eyes were wet but he tried to keep his face blank and strong.

"Now," I began again, "it's time to start acting like a man, and end this, so we can all move on."

He started to cry. I let him.

"I know you have Paul's Wandre," I said. "It's gonna be very easy to find now that I know about it. I already have your phone tapped." That was not true. "I have twenty-four-hour surveillance planned the second you walk out that door." That was also not true. "There is no way you can get away with this. None at all. It's over."

He looked everywhere but at me. Tears ran down his face and his nose started to run. No big handsome punk boy now. Were all men like this underneath? All women? Was there anyone left who went to the chair screaming their innocence, or cracking wise to the executioner? Or were we all so fucking guilty about everything, all the time, that when we finally murdered someone we were ready to confess a lifetime of sins?

248

"So tell me," I said. "And believe me, I'm the person to tell. You don't think I'm a very nice person and you're right about that. But I know the truth when I see it, and if you tell me the truth I'll believe you. I'll make sure everyone else does too."

He pulled his lips together tight and wrinkled his face and looked at the floor for a long minute. Without moving his head he looked up at me.

"I did it," he said. "I know it was wrong—Jesus. I didn't want it to happen. Any of it. He—he came in and he found us. Me and Lydia. Together. She had no idea. I mean, of course she knew he found us, but he just, he just, he turned around and left. Lydia knew he was pissed, but she didn't know the rest. It was later, later that night. We went out and Lydia, she went with her friend to the club and I went back to the house. I went back to the house and. And."

He looked at the wall. More tears. His mouth shook.

"That was good," I said. "But not good enough. Now tell me the truth."

He turned to me. "I'm telling you," he said, confused. "I'm telling you what happened."

"No," I said. "Tell me the truth."

"I told you," he said. "I did it."

"No, you didn't," I said. "Now tell me how Lydia killed Paul."

56

M Y MIND WAS STILL and all of my attention was focused on Rob Scorpio. I was entirely alive; I smelled
diesel fuel in the air and heard three sparrows outside. In the apartment next to Claude's someone was taking a
bath. I felt a heavy bass line from a car half a mile away in my chest.

"You're a good kid," I said to Rob, and I meant it. Maybe in
some other lifetime he'd get days off for good behavior. Maybe
even in this one. He hadn't killed Paul and we both knew it. I
didn't know anyone willing to take the rap for someone they
loved. Not in the Kali Yuga. But he was. "But, see, no one will
believe your story. Ever. It isn't true and we both know it. The
best thing you can do for her now is tell me the truth."

"Fuck," he said. He started to cry harder.

"You can't save her," I said. "I know you want to. I admire you
for trying, I really do. But it will not reflect well on her if the new
boyfriend tries to take the blame. It won't make her look very
nice."

I didn't know if that was true or not but it sounded good.

"You were at the house," I said. "*His* house. You were with
Lydia. So what happened? Paul came in?"

He sniffed and looked around for a miracle and didn't find one.
Maybe God would be dishing some out tomorrow, but he was all
out today, here in Berkeley.

"Yeah," he finally said, head down, voice barely above a whisper. "That's what happened."

"Yeah?" I said. I tried to sound gentle. It worked.

"He—he came in while I was there," Rob began. I could tell he was going to tell me everything. It was all over now. He swallowed and went on: "She thought—we thought—he'd be long gone, but his car broke down. Fucking alternator." He said it bitterly, as if it were the car's fault Paul was dead. The alternator broke down so Paul had to die. Nothing to be done about it. "So he walked in on us. We weren't—I mean, not literally. We were on the sofa and we were just kind of, kind of fooling around.

"So he comes in and, you know, it's crazy. Of course it's crazy. I mean, this guy just walked in on some other guy practically screwing his wife, I would freak out too. I mean, I understand that. But. I don't know. This rage, this fucking rage from both of them, it was nuts. It was like—Jesus, like they hated each other. I mean —Jesus, I know this sounds crazy."

"Nothing sounds crazy to me," I said.

His sobs slowed down and he shivered a little.

"It was like I knew," he said. Now there was something in his eyes, something real. "Somehow, the way they looked at each other, the way they were yelling. I had this thought, this horrible idea—we are not all leaving this room alive. And I started to freak out but I told myself, you know, just chill out. It's just a fight and yeah, it's upsetting, but just take it easy. We're all adults and we're going to sort this out."

"But that's not what happened," I said.

Rob shook his head. "They were screaming about, you know, everything. P—he was all, *I knew it, I knew you never loved me, you were always screwing around,* and she was all, *The funny thing is I did love you, you prick, before you ruined it all.* You know the things people say."

I nodded. I did know. All it took was one word, I saw now. One word to end it all. Or begin again.

"So they're yelling for a long time and I'm just sitting there. And like I said—I mean, I was just getting more and more anxious. Just kind of freaking out, because, I don't know. I guess . . ."

"Yes?" I prodded, gently.

"I didn't see it at the time. But now, I guess the way they were fighting was like how my parents used to fight, fight before they would *really* fight, like try to kill each other and stuff. And they almost did, a few times. Like once my mom was in a coma and they didn't even know if she was going to make it. They were actually waiting outside to arrest my dad for murder, but then she didn't die. But then she did die, from cancer. But it was like that, like that energy in the air."

Suddenly my face was wet and I realized I was crying too. I felt bad for the kid. I felt bad for all of us, for the whole fucking world. Our fucking hearts. No wonder they were so hard to come by these days. They were hiding from us, trying to preserve what little life they had left for someone who would appreciate them. Or at least not murder them.

"So they're fighting, and then somehow Lydia has my gun. Then I knew—I mean, I really knew. At least one of us wasn't getting out alive. So—"

"Wait a minute," I said. "You had a gun? And Lydia somehow suddenly had it? Did you give it to her?"

He shook his head. "I never would have done that. I grew up in the country, guns were a part of life. I mean, we used them in bad ways, like when my parents fought, but also we needed them for rattlesnakes and mountain lions and shit. You don't call nine-one-one out there. That's the only reason I had one. Just used to having it around, just used to feeling protected like that. And then, you know, living on the streets and stuff. I mean, I took good care of it. I never, like, abused it or anything. Almost no one even knew I had that thing."

I figured before that night he'd had two things he was proud of in his short, miserable life: his gun and his relationship with Lydia. Now both were ruined.

"But bringing a gun into, you know, into a home like that, into an argument, I never would have done that. Never." He stopped and looked at the floor. "I don't think so," he said.

"I don't think so either," I said. "But I don't understand. Then how'd Lydia get it?"

"Well," he said, a little shamefaced, as if he didn't want to admit it. "I had it in my pack. My backpack. I was staying in this squat in Oakland and—" He looked at me. "Okay. The real truth is, I think she took it earlier. I thought it was in my pack, see, because that's where I kept it, 'cause I was staying at this place in Oakland that wasn't very safe, so I was just keeping it with me. But honestly, I can't tell you the last time I saw it. She could have taken it just when Paul came in or she could have taken it, like, a week before."

"And you're sure it was your gun?" I asked.

"Oh, yeah," he said. "A Colt. I'd had that gun since I was a kid." He frowned.

"Do you know what happened to it?" I asked. "If we can find it, we can get it entered into evidence, and then maybe you can get it back someday."

He shook his head. "We tossed it in the bay."

"So let's go back," I said. "So they were fighting, and suddenly Lydia had your gun."

He nodded. "And *he*—" I noticed he couldn't say Paul's name. "When she got the gun, it was like . . . like all the anger just went out of him. All the fire. And he just got this look on his face, this mean look. Like, defeated, but *mean*. It was like—like Lydia, like me, like the whole world had just sucked all the nice out of him. Like there was just nothing good left. And Lydia's still screaming, you know, *You stupid son of a bitch, look what you made me do. I hate you, I fucking hate you.* And he's just sitting there."

Rob didn't say anything for a second.

"He knew what she was going to do, didn't he?" I said.

Rob nodded. "I think so. It was so—" He started to cry again. "I *do* think he knew. Like I knew. Like we all knew but her, you know: This is happening. It was like, Jesus Christ. Like we were on a train and we couldn't get off. Or *didn't* get off. Like we could have stopped, but—"

He didn't finish his sentence.

"So then?"

Rob wiped his nose with his hand. "So then. She's yelling and screaming, you know, waving the gun around, saying he's cheating on her, that he never loved her, all this stuff. And she screams and she screams until she runs out. Just empty.

"And then Paul, he just looks at her and he says, *I can't believe I thought I loved you.*"

We both knew what was coming next.

"That was it," he said. "Lydia pulled the trigger."

He shook his head like he still couldn't believe it.

"I got up and, you know, I tried to stop her. I mean, as soon as I saw she had my Colt, I tried—Jesus. It was just like it. Just like when . . ."

Again I felt bad for the kid. I didn't know how many times you were supposed to watch your mother and father kill each other in one lifetime. But his karma was his, and there was nothing I could do to change that.

"You know none of this is your fault, right?" I said, because I didn't know what else to say. "Lydia and Paul decided on this a long time ago. Long before any of us were born."

He looked at me. "You really believe that? Like reincarnation, and choosing your own life and all that shit?"

I looked him right in the eye. "Absolutely," I said. I had no idea if I believed it. "And I know this. You didn't come here just to be, you know, the guy with the gun. You have your own things to do. And when all this is over, you need to get back on track and do them, okay? Do you know what I mean?"

He nodded. He understood, or I hoped he did.

"You have your music," I said. I tried to think of something else he had. "And you're young," I said. He didn't say anything.

"So what happened next?" I asked. "After she shot him?" Now I couldn't say his name either, or hers. The words felt like dirt in my mouth, like old leaves and rot.

"She shot him," he said again, and I realized what a relief it was for him, to say it out loud, but also how excruciating. "She shot him, and, you know. I mean, I don't know if you've ever seen that, close range—"

I nodded.

"It's like this little explosion. And then it takes a second. I mean, at first it's just like a hole in his shirt. And then the blood."

"I know," I said, and I realized I was shivering. "I've seen it." I'd shot a man at close range, but somehow before that moment I had never actually imagined it happening to Paul. How scared he must have been, so alone . . .

I sat back down on the bed.

"His eyes were open—I think he lived for like a second or two. Or maybe he just looked alive. But it was a few seconds before the blood started, and Lydia, she just stood there. Just watched him die. It only took a few seconds, there was nothing to do. Then, I guess we both freaked out," he said. "I mean, Lydia—it was like she just couldn't fucking believe it. She was just *Oh my God, oh my God*. You know, just total horror. I mean, she was even calling his name, like he wasn't dead. I had to take her and get her out of there. She was all, like, trying to pick him up and shit. I was like, Girl, it's too late. You did it."

"So you got her out of the house," I said.

He nodded. "I grabbed her and we just ran, at first. I was pretty sure no one saw us, but it was a while before I was even thinking like that. I mean, we just ran."

"And on the way out," I said, "Lydia grabbed both sets of keys —hers and Paul's. She grabbed the keys and locked the door behind her, just like she always did."

Rob looked at me. "Yeah. How'd you know? She did take both sets of keys. I mean, it was just something she always did—lock the door behind her."

Habits die hard. Harder than people, apparently.

"A few days later I tossed them in the trash in Berkeley," he said. "Anyway, that night. *That* night. So we just ran out and I started thinking. We'd just committed a murder and we needed, like, an alibi and all that shit. Like on TV. And Lydia, she couldn't even think. So I made up this story—Lydia, it wasn't you. Someone else killed Paul. You're gonna go to the Make-Out Room, make sure some people see you there, and then when you go home, late, you're gonna find there's been a robbery. And the weird thing was, it was like she believed me. I just kept saying, 'Everything's gonna be okay. I'm gonna fix it all. It never happened.' And by the time she got home that night, I think she kinda believed it. I mean, at first she knew she was lying, but then I don't think she did. I think it was like she, you know, like in her mind she just covered up the whole thing."

"So you went back to the house," I said.

"No," he said. "First I got rid of the gun. Tossed it in the bay.

I mean, you watch a lot of cop shows and you figure out what to do. Get rid of the gun. Figure out an alibi. Lucky Lydia took those extra keys, because I used them to get back in the house and go down to the studio. I just—Jesus, that was the worst. I mean, he was there and I just pretended I didn't know. With the—anyway. So I got Lydia's car, went to the house, made sure no one was looking, grabbed some gear from the studio, and split."

"And you also locked the door behind you," I said.

"Yeah," he said, regretful. "It was completely fucking stupid. I should have left the door open and left the keys in the house. I thought of it like an hour later. But it was already too late."

"So what happened to the guitars?" I asked.

He made a face. "I ditched them," he said. "I drove out to this place in Oakland, this place I know, like an abandoned lot, and I just ripped them all apart. Just fucking smashed them all to pieces, then I burned them. Then a few days later I went by and cleaned up what was left and put it in the trash."

"Except the Wandre," I said.

He nodded.

"Where is it?" I said.

"At my friend's place," he said. "My friend who lives down in Santa Cruz. I told him I'd ripped it off from this rich couple in the Mission and asked him to hold on to it until things cooled down. It was so—it's just so fucking beautiful. Like a fucking work of art. When I was busting up the other ones I had it there and I couldn't. I just couldn't."

Is the thing we love always our downfall? Always our destruction?

I reached into my purse and he looked a little scared, like I was going to pull out something even worse than my gun. Instead I took out a pen and paper, stood up, and handed them to him.

"Your friend," I said. "Name and address."

He looked at me like I was kidding.

"I can't fucking believe this," he said. He started to cry again. He wrote down the name and address. I thought he was crying over the guilt of his involvement in taking a human life. I was wrong.

"I want to see her," he said in between sobs, face wet and red. "I miss her so much. Can't I just see her? I haven't seen her since that night. I didn't want anyone to see us together."

I looked outside. It was raining, and so foggy that I could hardly see across the street. I wondered if there was fog like this in the other yugas. Or just here, in the Kali Yuga, where the lights had been turned off and no one knew how to turn them back on.

I turned back toward Rob.

"Rob Scorpio," I said. "Today is the first day of the rest of your life."

He looked at me and sniffed. "What the hell does that mean?" he said, still crying.

First I hit Rob on his left cheek and then again, harder, knocking that fucking astonished look off his face and knocking him off the chair. He didn't fight back. I didn't know if he was scared or stunned or just guilty. While he was on the floor trying to get away from me I kicked him, hard, connecting with his thigh near his knee. He tried to get up but I punched him in the side of his head, as hard as I could, and he fell back down, blood running down his face.

Claude heard the commotion and came in to save him.

"What the fuck?" Rob said sobbing and bloody.

It was true that it wasn't his fault. But he could have stopped it and he didn't.

There were very few good things in this world, at least as far as I knew, and Paul had been one of them.

Before Claude got me away I got one more strong kick in and felt Rob's rib bone crack under my boot and it was the closest thing to good I'd felt since Paul died.

Claude called the cops and told them we had a witness and they came and arrested Rob. Huong and Ramirez took him away in handcuffs.

"Not bad, DeWitt," Huong admitted as she took Rob away. Ramirez said nothing.

Rob looked numb. Claude looked like he was in shock.

I went into Claude's bathroom. I heard the cops leave and I

heard Claude sit heavily at the kitchen table, stunned. He'd never done anything like this before. It was his first big dénouement. I looked through Claude's medicine cabinet. His roommate had a full bottle of Valium. I took two. And then a third. And then stuck the rest of the bottle in my pocket.

I felt like something was ending.

But it wasn't over yet.

57

THE TRIAL WOULDN'T start for a long time. The case was getting a lot of press and each side was building their argument. Rob confessed to the police as easily as he had to me. The police took him to Santa Cruz and they got the Wandre at his friend's house.

Not one person called me to say, *Good job, Claire. Nice work, Claire. You rock, Claire. Gee, Claire, how'd you solve* that *one?*

"If one is looking for a life of kindness," Silette wrote to Jay Gleason, "look elsewhere."

They arrested Lydia in the house on Bohemian Highway. Someone tipped off the press and there were pictures on the front page of the *San Francisco Chronicle* and the *Oakland Trib* and the *Santa Rosa Press-Democrat* and even the *LA Times*. In the *New York Times* Lydia made the front page of the National section.

That night I watched it on CNN. Someone filmed her being brought out of the house in handcuffs.

If I'd ever seen a more beautiful woman I couldn't remember it. She was the most glamorous thing in the world. She'd been heading out to dinner with Carolyn. She wore a black dress from the forties and a white silk flower in her black hair. On her finger she still wore her gold wedding ring.

I figured that still would be the picture they'd use when they put her in those big picture books—*Women Who Kill!* and

I didn't feel any better. Nothing was over. Nothing had begun.

One hundred and fifteen days after Paul died, I lay on the floor listening to one of Paul's records. I felt drained of everything good. I was out of cocaine. I'd used up all the Percocet days ago, and the purloined Valium had barely lasted a day.

Everything hurt. Every nerve in my body had a grievance.

Claude came over. He'd called a bunch of times and I hadn't answered, so he broke into my apartment. He had keys and he could come over anytime he wanted, but it felt like a break-in. He looked at me with what he pretended was concern. I knew it was disgust.

"Are you ever getting off the floor?" Claude asked, voice heavy with fake concern and pretend affection, as transparent as glass.

I tried sitting up and I felt the room spin. I knew the rest of the world was just as exhausted and spent as I was. I lay back down.

"Get me my purse," I said.

Claude got my purse. I looked through it and it was devoid of cash.

"Go to the safe," I said.

"You don't have a safe."

"Then get me the cookie jar," I said. On my counter was a big cookie jar shaped like a cookie with a sticky note on it that said MONEY. I figured if someone broke in I didn't want them messing everything up. I was almost sure I did have a safe but Claude didn't know about it.

Claude brought me the cookie jar. Inside was a few hundred bucks. I took out a handful of cash and handed it to Claude.

"Go get me some coke," I said.

Claude looked at me like I was crazy.

"No," he said.

I told him Adam's address, told him where to go and what to ask for and to say it was for me.

"You're fucking kidding me," he said.

"I don't kid," I said. "You know that."

"Or what?" he said. Claude had never spoken to me like that before. I was proud of him.

"Or you're fired," I said.

I looked at Claude and he looked like he was underwater. The whole room did. It was unbearable. I closed my eyes. That was not especially more bearable.

"You're fired," I said. "And then I shoot myself and it's your fault. So go get me my drugs."

He would hate me eventually. Might as well start now.

The record repeated itself. Paul howled. After Lydia was arrested no one bothered to change her locks and I'd gone to the house and taken what I wanted, which was this record and the Spot of Mystery cup from Paul's dresser. On the way home I'd broken the cup.

Claude was gone. While he was gone I lay on the floor with my eyes closed and thought about whether any of this was real. I was nearly certain I had let the real parts slip by and this was some kind of substitute.

"Don't ever make me do that again," Claude said. Apparently he was back. He tossed the bundle at me, little envelopes of "A Very Special Blue Jay" and "When Elephants Roam." I opened one of the envelopes and dumped it onto a hardcover book (*A Brief History of Indonesian Criminology*). From my purse I found a dollar bill, rolled it into a straw, and snorted up the cocaine. I felt my body come halfway back to life, my brain approach something like a waking state.

I sat up. Claude stared at me.

"You look like a ghost," he said. "I'm calling someone. I can't handle this. I don't know what to do."

"You call whoever you want," I said, or thought I said. "I'm pretty good like this."

I heard Claude on the phone and I tried to ignore him until I couldn't. He took the phone into the bathroom for privacy, to talk about me without my prying ears spoiling it. When he was in the bathroom I left.

Once I got downstairs I remembered I didn't know where I'd left my car. The garage; yes; I had a garage I used on Stockton. I went to the garage and the man didn't want to give me my car.

"You sure you okay to drive, Miss DeWitt?" the man said. He was young and sweet, Juan or Jose or something like that. Fucking Mexican club kids, showing us all up with their hard work and kindness.

"It's Miss DeMitt," I said, "and get me my fucking car."

He shook his head and gave up pretending not to hate me and got my car.

I got in my car and I called Tabitha and we met at the Shanghai Low. Claude and his evil phone calls hadn't reached her yet. Sam left his friend Chris in charge of the bar and we went in the back and did a few lines of Tabitha's coke. She said I didn't look good.

"Thanks," I said.

"Did you sleep last night?" she asked.

I hadn't slept since they'd arrested Lydia, not for more than a few hours at a time. Before I could answer, Sam said, "Do you guys want to go to this after-hours I know out by the beach?"

We did. It was a Russian bar/club where Sam knew the secret door knock and the name to drop and we were let in. Incredibly bad music played. The older Russians had bleached blond hair and gold chains; the younger ones had tattoos and wore Converse. Sam bought more coke from a Russian guy who was about fifty. He invited us into the back room and I wondered if every place on earth had a back room. Maybe there were back rooms in ancient Greece, back rooms in Papua New Guinea, all connected, one big dusty interconnected labyrinth where those of us who couldn't face the light of day hid with our cocaine and our self-loathing.

The back room of the Russian club was slightly cleaner and everything was in Russian. The Russian man cracked open a bottle of tequila and passed it around. He seemed to have endless amounts of cocaine; it was like a magic trick where he pulled rabbit after rabbit out of his pocket long after there shouldn't have been any rabbits left. The sun came up and even though they had the shades pulled little cracks of sun broke in and it made me angry. What right did it have? Who did it think it was? I could tell Sam felt the same way and after a few more minutes or hours of this outrage he said, "Come on, I know a better place."

We got in my car, me and Tabitha and Sam and some guy and some girl, and Sam drove my car in circles for a while, getting lost, and Tabitha gave him directions, so speedy and determined that

262

her words fell on top of each other, rocks tumbling down a hill, and the guy and the girl chewed on coffee stirrers and said nothing. "Do you want some?" the girl finally said. I said no. Thank God for tinted windows, for sunglasses, for my jacket, which I pulled over my face when the fog cleared and the sun got bright. My nerves felt raw, like their protective clothing had been ripped off and thrown away.

Finally Sam found the better place. It was an apartment in the Castro. I didn't understand if it was an actual place people paid to go or just some guy's apartment. But we were there. Somehow I ended up at a glass table, always a glass table, with three stripper girls. They were young and wore glittery makeup and the highest heels imaginable. They wanted to talk to me but I'd passed talking hours ago. The girls left and were, one at a time, replaced by three fifty-ish guys from the neighborhood, formerly beautiful men going to seed. Like me they were well past conversation. We kept doing more and more and no one pretended it was fun anymore. No one pretended this was anything like fun.

About that time I started to feel strange. Tabitha saw me and said, "You don't look so good. I'm taking you out for some air."

When I stood up I fell down. I forgot my name and I didn't know where I was. Had I ever known? Someone said "Claire." I thought I knew her but no, maybe not.

Someone took me to a bed in a room in a secret wing of the apartment and laid me down and everything went black. I felt my nerves shake and people were asking for Claire again, whoever that was.

"She's having a seizure," I heard someone say. "Call an ambulance, she's—"

"Uh-uh, no ambulances. You get that crazy bitch out of here, now. I swear to God if you call an ambulance I'll kill—"

Someone helped me up. Tabitha took me outside. The sun had gone back down. It was almost night again. What I heard from her later was that my eyes had started to roll back in my head and I opened my mouth and clenched my throat as if to make a sound and didn't. I started to fall and Tabitha sat me down and leaned me against a wall. She stayed with me until the seizure passed and then ran into a deli and got an orange juice and poured it down my throat. I swallowed it and came back to.

"Wait here," Tabitha said. "Just wait one second, baby, I'm gonna go get you help. Okay? Don't move, okay?"

I sat on Castro Street. No one noticed me. I remembered my name again. I drank some more orange juice and the sugar brought me back to earth.

I stood up. I was standing okay. I looked around. I didn't see Tabitha.

I walked away and found my car.

The brake and the gas were not particularly well-defined, but I got the car started and going. The city was cool and dark. I spun through the streets. The sugar high faded off and I was back to the high of drugs and not eating or sleeping for days, weeks, months. For 115 days.

I was on the highway. Almost no one else was on the road. The sky was dark violet and unforgiving. To my left the bay glittered, looking deep and endless. I knew it was neither. I rolled down my window and the outside world roared to life. I rolled it back up. One hand on the wheel, I rummaged through my bag for my last envelope from Adam. I found it—"The Last Galapagos Chameleon"—and did another big bump on each side. Blood ran down my face.

I felt a cold rush and then an ugly feeling in the back of my head and smelled smoke. I heard a long honk and a series of metallic crunches. Flashes of color and then everything went dark. I tried to open my eyes but I couldn't find them. Nothing was moving or seemed to want to move.

It was dark. It was as dark as it had ever been.

"Shit, man. Shit shit shit. Call nine-one-one."

"I got warrants and no license. I ain't callin' nine-one-one."

"We can't just leave her."

"Fuck, look at her, hold her tongue or somethin'."

"Oh shit. She hurt bad. We got to call—"

"Help me pick her up. I know a place."

"She need a hospital."

I had another small seizure. My nerves shook as the electrical storm passed through my brain.

I felt arms on me and I realized I was on the ground. I remembered I'd been in a car.

"Put her in the back. Careful—"

I felt arms, cool air on my back.

"—I know a place."

A car. Long lights pulling on the walls and red monsters ahead. Hands on me again and the smell of redwoods.

"They gonna take care of her?"

"Yeah, they gonna let her stay. They ain't kick no one out." Someone laughed. "Not even me."

"She gonna be okay?"

"We all gonna be okay someday," the voice said. "But I don't know about today."

58

WHICH WAS HOW JENNY came to open the gates of the Dorje Temple in the morning and find me curled up in a semi-fetal ball under a redwood tree with my jacket pulled over my head, wet and shivering, blood on my face and in my hair, glass cuts from the accident up and down my left arm, somewhere in between unconsciousness and death.

They took me in and brought me to bed in a cot next to the lama's room. The lama called a doctor he knew who came over and said I was basically fine, just wasted and bruised and malnourished and dying. But easily curable.

"Just keep her off drugs and feed her," the doctor said. The lama told me later he said it like it was the easiest thing in the world. Like I hadn't been trying to do that all my life.

I slept in the cot for a few days. When I woke up everything ached from the accident. I felt exhausted. I didn't really want to be saved again. The lama was sitting next to my bed with a pot of green tea with herbs mixed in.

I drank some tea. He asked if I could eat a little something and I said no. I stared at the wall.

"We don't go through these trials just for the hell of it, you know," the lama said. "We go through them for wisdom. For purification. So we don't make the same mistakes next time."

I didn't want a next time. I didn't want to learn any more fucking lessons. I wanted to be with Tracy again. With Constance. With Paul. With people who loved me. I wanted to start over with them, to be someone else. Let someone else figure out who bludg-eoned the professor in the library with a candlestick. I didn't give a shit. I wanted out.

I curled up in a ball and pulled the blankets over my head.

"Go fuck yourself," I said.

"You know, I've seen you try so hard to end it," the lama said. "So many times. And I feel like it's kind of bullshit."

"Thanks," I said. "And you can take your fucking pearls of wis-dom and shove them—"

"No," he said. "Honestly, Claire. I've never seen anything like it. You know there are people who would give anything to be you."

It was the stupidest thing I'd ever heard. If anyone wanted to be me they could have it.

"I mean, you so clearly have something to do," he said. "Most people, they try to kill themselves and, you know, it just happens. Most people, they kind of float through life with no direction and no signs and never even know why they're here. I don't think you really get that. You, you're fucking indestructible. Look at you. You're covered in scars, you've ruined yourself with drugs, and you've put yourself in more danger than anyone I've ever known. Or heard of. Did it ever even cross your mind"—he sounded pissed off at me now—"that things happen for a reason? That you're here because people need you?"

"Your fucking platitudes—"

"Without Constance," he went on, ignoring me, "we'd both be dead by now. No question. And somewhere there's someone at least who wouldn't have made it without you. I know it. I mean, you're not giving me much evidence here of being a useful person, but I trust her. Apparently you're being kept around for *some-thing*. I mean, it could have been you. When she was killed, when your friend was killed, that guy—I mean it *should* have been you, a thousand times over, and it never is. I wish I were that fucking important. I wish the world gave that much of a shit about me. I really do."

I didn't answer. He made a pissed-off noise at my awfulness and left, shutting the door sharply behind him.

• • •

The next morning I started eating again. The day after that I got out of bed and walked around the grounds a little. The next afternoon I helped some of the kids with a gazebo they were building.

After a few days I ran into Jenny in the kitchen. She was making tea and she ignored me.

"Hey," I said. "Thanks. For letting me stay. I know—I mean, I'm sure you didn't want . . ."

She looked at me.

"You fall down," she said. "We all fall down. You going to get back up?"

"I think so," I said after a minute.

"I think so too," she said. "I think some people, we always get back up. Always."

That night the lama came into my room, where I was reading a Donald Goines novel for the second time. The monastery was a nice place but their library sucked. I made a note to buy them some books when I got back to City Lights.

"So," the lama said. "You haven't heard from Andray, have you?"

"No," I said. Of course, I wouldn't know if I had—I'd lost my phone the night of the crash, and also hadn't checked my email since then.

The lama looked worried. I'd never seen him look worried before. He sat down on my bed. I felt like we were kids at summer camp, sharing secrets. I'd never been to camp but it looked like this on TV.

"Trey called me," he said. "First a few weeks ago and then again last night. Andray took off with some girl he met in Kansas City. They were supposed to meet up in Las Vegas but Andray didn't show. Hasn't answered his phone, hasn't called Terrell either."

I helped the kids finish the gazebo, and helped them start a new yurt. After ten days the lama drove me into town, where I rented a car and drove back to my place in the city. There was a stack of mail in the slot. I had a few hundred emails. A lot of client inquiries. A few looked promising. A woman whose son was being accused of a murder she knew he didn't commit. A man who wanted to find some missing paintings, stolen from his family in 1942. Sounded kind of fun. But everything still felt heavy and dull, dirty and old.

Nothing from Andray.

I called Claude. The lama had called him, so he knew I was alive at least.

"I'm sorry," I said. "You were really cool and I treated you like shit."

"I didn't see," Claude said. "The whole time we were working on the case, I didn't get it, what was going on with you."

"It's okay," I said. "No reason you should have."

"Yeah, well," he said. "I am trying to be a detective."

We both laughed.

"Do you still want to work for me?" I asked. "It's cool if you don't. I'll give you a recommendation, your last few weeks' pay, whatever."

Claude paused for a second. "Do you still want me to?" he said.

"Of course," I said. "You're the best."

"Then I do," he said firmly. "Working for you is the best thing that ever happened to me, Claire. I'd be lost without you."

I stopped and didn't say anything for a minute. Then I got him started working on the murder case I'd picked up at the Fan Club. The woman had sent me a few emails with all the information she had about her brother's case. I believed her that he was innocent. Maybe we could save him. Or at least get him out of jail.

59

SOMEHOW ME AND DELIA became friends. I told her all about Lydia in her big loft in SoMa.

We sipped hot tea and looked out her giant windows at the gray foggy street outside. Delia seemed sad. I knew she missed Paul, missed Lydia, missed everything and everyone, like I did.

"Hey," I said. "Want to see something cool?"

We drove for nearly two hours and by the time we got to the Double J Ranch it was night. Before we turned up the drive I made a few adjustments to the security system. No one would know we'd been here at all.

I cut the lights and turned up the drive and stopped at the gate. I opened up and let us in. Most of the little horses were sleeping, except a few who snacked on grass and dew. We got out of the car and looked at them.

"Oh, Claire," Delia said. "They're beautiful."

"I know," I said. "I kind of love them."

The little black guy was sleeping when we got there. But after he heard my voice he woke up, shook himself awake, and stood up and came toward me.

"Oh, Claire," she said again. "He likes you so much."

I scratched the little guy just where he liked, on the hard top of his head, and Delia fed him some carrots she'd brought from her fridge.

Then we opened the gate and we let them out. We let them out the back door, not the one that led to the highway, but the one that led to the Bohemian Club's woods. To Paul's woods.

It turned out a neighbor was poisoning them. He was putting tiny amounts of poison in very small apples and tossing them over the fence. No one knew why. Did he hate all horses? Did he especially hate tiny horses? Mysteries never end. A guy from the Spot of Mystery saw one of the horses wandering off to the woods to die. He was a smart man, an ex-detective from Houston, Texas, who'd gotten into trouble with liquor and bad women. But he was still smart, and when he saw the horse lie down he took a hair sample from the dying little thing. Jake paid to get it tested and they came up with arsenic. Now the neighbor was facing charges and the horses were safe and the man from Houston was becoming a detective again. I gave him a good chunk of the fee I'd gotten for the case and he'd gotten his own place in Santa Rosa and had been dry for two months.

Delia and I opened the gate, but no one left. We stood there with the gate open and some of the horses came and sniffed at it and eyeballed it, but no one left.

Except the little black guy. He came to the door and stepped halfway through and looked at me. Then he went all the way through and stopped and looked at me again.

"You're welcome," I said. "But you know it's gonna be rough out there? No one's gonna feed you or comb your hair. You're gonna be on your own. You'll tell the other animals where you're from and no one will believe you. They're gonna think you're a fucking lunatic. You know that, right?"

Delia crouched down and looked into his eyes.

"He knows," she said. "He'd rather be real."

He ran. He galloped away like a fucking stallion. We locked up the gate behind us and left.

And that was the Case of the Missing Miniature Horses.

That night I drove to Oakland in my rented car and sat around the fire with the Red Detective.

"Solved your case?" he said.

"Kind of," I said. "She did it. The wife in the living room with the gun."

271

"How's it feel?" he asked.

"Like it's still not done," I said. "Like I've still got a case to solve."

"Like a missing girl case?" he asked smugly.

"Maybe," I said.

"Told you," he said, and it was the first time I'd seen him smile, which he tried his hardest to conceal.

"What is left behind when a mystery is solved? Is there a nothingness, a vacuum, a hole?" Silette wrote. "Is it possible that some mysteries are better left unsolved, that we are sometimes better off with nothing than something?"

The next day I went to go solve my case. My missing girl case.

Lydia met me in an interview room, ugly and institutional. She was in her orange jumpsuit, handcuffed, dirty, and humiliated, just as she should have been. If we had been anywhere else I would have killed her with my bare hands.

She was already crying when I came in.

I told everyone that I went to Peru for the Case of the Golden Pearl and just lost touch with Paul, but that wasn't what happened. What happened was that he asked me to call him.

"You never call me," he said. "And then you do that thing where you leave."

He didn't say it as an accusation; he presented it as a fact. We were on the phone. It was late at night. That was when we had all our real talks, late at night on the phone.

It was true: I never called him, and I did this strange thing where I would leave, in the middle of the night after sex or the next morning or sometimes just while we were hanging out, having dinner or watching a movie or walking around the city.

It was always a case. But it was never a case. I left because every time we spoke we were getting closer. Because every time, something seemed to be revealed between us. *Oh I always* and *That's my favorite too* and *I know just what you mean* and *I can't believe you also* and the unspoken but always present *How have I not known you forever? How is it I was here without you, and now you are so close to being everything?* Something that seemed like it had been there all along.

"I'll call you," I said. "It's, you know, it's hard for me. But I'll call you."

"Because you know," he said, and he said it without accusation, without anger, "I can't keep doing this. This isn't fair."

He was also bruised, scarred by life. Who wasn't? I had no monopoly on pain, I knew that.

"I know," I said. "I'm sorry. I'm so sorry, I'm just—"

"Don't be sorry," he said, and I thought I heard him smile. "Just call me sometimes, okay?"

I promised I would. And then a few days later I got on a plane to Peru without telling him and I never called him again.

I couldn't imagine any circumstance, in any lifetime, where I would be able to tell Paul how I felt about him. That I loved him.

We didn't speak for a while, when I got back. I heard he was dating someone else and I pretended I didn't care and everyone believed me. I took a case finding out what had happened to a missing girl and it turned out she'd drowned in the bay. I stopped eating and stopped sleeping and ended up in the Chinese Hospital, Nick Chang by my side. Then I went to New Orleans on the Case of the Green Parrot and when I came back I ran into Paul and Nita in the vegan place in Chinatown and he told Nita he'd been in love with me.

We'd spoken occasionally after that, friends, and when we'd run into each other that night at the Shanghai Low I felt that undertow again, that thick black current pulling me back toward him. And I thought maybe, just maybe . . .

And then Lydia walked in.

Lydia sat in her prisoner's chair in her prisoner's outfit. I sat down in the chair across from her.

"I loved him so much," she said, still crying. "I couldn't stand it. It made me crazy, loving him so much. He always loved you more," she said. "I knew. I pretended I didn't but I did. I was his fucking substitute, his second-best. It should have been you together, not us. None of this would have happened if you'd just loved him back."

"Is that why you killed him?" I asked. "Because you were jealous?"

"Of course not," she said. "I didn't mean—I never wanted to. It's not like I planned it. You think I wanted this to happen?"

"I don't know what you wanted," I said.

"I thought—" she began. "I don't know what I thought. I really don't. But I guess in some way. With the gun. Like, I could make him love me. Like, I never knew—I never knew how to make anyone love me, and I knew no one ever did. I mean, I know why. I know that. But I thought, not consciously, I mean, of course I know you can't force someone to love you. I just wanted him to love me so much and . . ."

She trailed off and started to cry harder.

"I'm so scared," Lydia said. "I'm going crazy."

I didn't say anything.

"I keep thinking he's here," she said. "I keep thinking, *Well, I'll call Paul and* . . . Or I keep thinking he's really with me, in the room, and he knows what I did and—"

"Maybe you're not crazy," I said. "Maybe he is with you."

That made her cry harder.

"I want to die," she howled. "Please, just kill me, Claire. I know you want to."

I thought about it. It wouldn't be hard. I figured she meant it, and she wouldn't fight back.

I could take her neck and just *snap* it.

I did want to kill her, kind of.

I reached across and put my hand on her arm, right above the elbow.

"Oh, Claire," Lydia said. "I'm so scared. Please don't forget about me," she said. "Please don't forget about me in here. I'm so scared."

"I won't," I said. I squeezed her arm.

"I want to die," she sobbed. "Oh God. I don't want to live. Please. Please help me."

There are no coincidences. Only doors you didn't have the courage to walk through. Only blind spots you weren't brave enough to see. Only tones you refused to admit you could hear.

"I'll visit you," I said. "I won't leave you alone. I promise. I

274

won't forget about you. We're going to be okay," I said. I reached over and put both my hands on her arms and kissed her on the forehead. "We're going to be fine."

I didn't know if I believed it. Maybe not this time around. But someday.

I stayed with her until the guards made me leave.

The Case of the Kali Yuga was closed.

60

THAT NIGHT, AT HOME, I found the Cynthia Silverton comic I'd taken from Bix. I flipped through until I
found the ad I was looking for on page 108.

BE A DETECTIVE, the ad read, MONEY! EXCITEMENT! Women and
men admire detectives. Everyone looks up to someone with
knowledge and education. Our HOME STUDY course offers the
chance to earn your DETECTIVE'S BADGE from THE COMFORT OF YOUR
OWN HOME.

I took out a piece of paper and a pen and wrote:

To Whom It May Concern:

I am already a professional detective, but I would like to improve my skills. Do you offer a continuing education course? Or
may I enroll in the standard home study course despite my age
and experience? Please reply at this address . . .

I wrote in my address, signed it, and mailed it to the address in
the ad.

61

A FEW DAYS LATER I called the lama. Still no word from Andray. He'd called Trey, who'd likewise heard no news.

I was on Stockton Street, in front of the vegan Chinese place. Through the plate-glass window I saw the TV inside.

Enlightened Mistress is one and all, the TV streamed. *Everyone is an Enlightened Mistress. Service is happiness, happiness is your birthright, and nirvana is a bird in your hand. Even in the darkest night, one star will always shine.*

When I hung up with the lama I called Claude.

"Start a file," I said. "We're starting a new case."

"What should I call it?" Claude asked.

"I don't know yet," I said. "But I'm going to find Andray. That's our next case. We're finding Andray."

62

A FEW DAYS LATER I set out early to Las Vegas in my rented Kia. I'd agreed to keep it for the month. No sign so far of my Mercedes, which I figured was for the best. At least it wasn't a homicide scene.

I was in Oakland before I was sure I was being followed. It was a 1982 Lincoln Continental, one of my favorite cars. White exterior, blood-red interior.

I began to think he was following me on the Bay Bridge. Since just about the spot where Paul's car died. He'd been with me since Chinatown but I thought I was being paranoid—it wasn't so strange that someone else would be driving from Chinatown to the East Bay on this oddly sunny day. Then halfway across the bridge he didn't pass me when I braked a little, taken strangely by surprise to be reminded of Paul again, Paul again and again. I decided to find out for sure: I hopped off the highway in Oakland and drove to an obscure spot I knew, a little marina and landing where a few Victorian buildings had somehow lasted through Oakland's many renovations.

The Lincoln kept pace. I wasn't being paranoid.

The Lincoln lagged a little behind but then when I stopped at a red light it put on speed to keep up with me. Not many people were around. A few women who were maybe prostitutes, a few workers from the factories nearby, looking for lunch.

And didn't stop.

The first time the Lincoln hit me from behind I didn't think; I just ran through the red light I'd been stopped at—there was no cross traffic—and put on speed as fast as I could. But the Lincoln was faster than I would have guessed and soon it cracked my rear bumper again, sending a sickening, shuddering thump through the car.

I got my ass in gear and tried to outrun it. I didn't. The third time, the Lincoln hit me from the side, ramming its massive front bumper nearly through my passenger door.

The Lincoln sent me sideways into a parked van and I was going to die.

It backed up. I realized I wasn't dead. My door was crammed shut against the van. I undid my seatbelt and made a dash for the passenger-side door.

It was stuck.

I dropped to my back and pulled my legs into my chest, planning to kick out the window. But before I could I heard screaming and a screech and a terrible, grating metallic crash. I felt like I'd been tossed about by waves at the beach and lost my footing; underwater, kind of fun, and then you remember: Oh, wait, I'm drowning.

"Holy shit!" I heard someone scream. "You killed her! You fucking crazy? You killed her!"

My head cleared and the sound of metal on metal stopped and I resurfaced.

I think maybe he has, I thought. I looked and saw a flash of red and white where I thought my legs should have been. *I really think maybe he has.*

"Motherfucker!" I heard someone else scream. "That lady's gonna die!"

The irony that I may now be dying in a car crash was not lost on me.

I felt my eyes close. The waves pulled me back under. When I swam up Tracy was waiting for me at the shore. Tracy was an adult, my age, and she wore a black dress and a big, ratty black fur coat, her white hair in a ponytail. Behind her I saw the Cyclone cycle and the Wonder Wheel spin.

When I came out of the water, soaking wet, she laughed, a little smirk playing around the corners of her mouth.

"You're in for it this time," she said. "And I am *really* going to enjoy watching you get out of this one."

"I don't understand," I said. "What did I do?"

"You started looking for the truth," she said. "And now, you're gonna finish."

Seagulls squawked overhead, circling us, hoping for food. It was winter. The beach was empty except for a few Polar Bears in the ocean, the old men who come and swim in the icy water every winter.

"Is this it?" I asked. "Are we at the end?"

"Not yet," Tracy said. "But don't worry. We'll get there soon enough, Claire DeWitt."